PRAISE FOR K. V. JOHANSEN

Praise for *Breath and Bone*

A joy to read. *Breath and Bone* is a wonderful tale of rescue and redemption, family and friendship - all told in a gentle and lyrical voice that harks back to the great fantasy of the past.

– Tom Lloyd

KV Johansen employs a classic fairy tale trope as a starting point for a dark fable of witches and demigods. Lyrical and finely honed, *Breath and Bone* mixes conflict, magic, and intrigue to great effect

— Anthony Ryan

This fairytale-like story has both teeth and heart. KV has created something very special here.

— K.D. Edwards

PRAISE FOR K. V. JOHANSEN

Praise for *Gods of the Caravan Roads*

Fans of C.J. Cherryh, Elizabeth Bear, and George R.R. Martin will find the same intelligence, wit, and mastery of language.

— *ForeWord Reviews*

Johansen has found a winning combination: the modern epic fantasy penchant for a cast of thousands and the golden age feeling of a tale of Conan or Fafhrd and the Gray Mouser dueling with gods gone mad.

—*Publishers Weekly*

[A] fantastic series which deserves to be read far and wide, as it's simply one of the finest epic fantasies I've ever read – rich and lyrical, timeless and unique, powerful and poignant, wondrous yet real, full of characters that will stay with me forever, and a world I feel privileged to have visited...

— James Latimer, *The Fantasy Hive*

BREATH AND BONE

K. V. JOHANSEN

First edition published 2026

For information, address
Candlemark & Gleam LLC
2523 Solstice Trail
Chapel Hill, NC 27516
mes@candlemarkandgleam.com

Library of Congress Cataloguing-in-Publication Data: In Progress

ISBNs: print 978-1-952456-33-6
ebook 978-1-952456-34-3

Cover art by Laura Galli
Editor: Melissa Scott
Proofreader: Ellis Duspiva

www.candlemarkandgleam.com

PLACES OF INTEREST IN THE TRAVELS OF HEDGE & PONY TO THE VILLAGE OF UNDER-ICE
N
W
E
S
ICE
NORTHWESTERN FELLS
EASTERN HIGHLANDS
R. RHUNATAM & MARSH-LANDS
SMITHSFORD AT DAHRES HEAD
KING'S DUN LAKEFOOT & AVONDON
E.H. INN
RHUNABURG
LAKE OF BIRDS
DAHRES WATER
GREATER DAHRES R.
THURBRIDGE
THE LOWLANDS
UPPER BRIDGE
R. MOSSADON
R. RHUNAVON
GARRAN-IASH LANDS
JELAGEN'S STRONGHOLD
RAMSLEAP
UNDER-ICE
LAMMERGEIER'S PASS
WHITE MTS.
GHEDHAYNOR
APPROXIMATE ROUTE FOLLOWED, ON IMPERIAL HIGHWAYS, TRIBAL BYWAYS, AND THROUGH WILDERNESS
200 MILES
MMXXV

CONTENTS

1

IN WHICH ARRANY STEALS A HORSE

Young Arrany did not like the way the bears were looking at her. They were altogether too knowing, and, she considered, malevolent. All very well to tell herself that cave bears generally confined themselves to eating plants. Claws, though. Big claws. And teeth. The previous autumn she'd seen a pair of the boars, the great he-bears, fight—roaring, snarling, grappling, savagely biting—and been glad she was much lower down the valley on her errand to round up the witch's goats. These were sows, she thought. Smaller. They stood only as tall as the top of her head at the shoulder, which was not so tall as all that.

Quite tall enough.

She tried an innocent smile, not for the bears, but for the half dozen humanfolk with them. Armed, armoured in a motley of leather and scraps of mail, and with the self-satisfied swagger that said, whether robber band or ill-governed chief's guard, they figured they owned this road, or at least the bridge. She should have followed her first instinct and turned aside, gone down into the thick-wooded ravine and tried to find her own way across. They had come swarming out onto the old stone bridge, three behind and three before, when she was halfway over. Two of the robbers—definitely robbers—were mounted on skinny horses. Three, including the boy on the yellow horse, had bows, and though the boy had his unstrung and stuck carelessly through a strap, the other two were strung, and if they were held casually down at the side, there were nonetheless arrows swift to hand. And then there were the bears, blocking the way ahead.

"Blessings of the day, friends," she offered. "Is it much farther to Thurbridge?" That was the largest town she knew of on this old imperial highway, which she'd been following northerly along the valley of the Rhunavon since turning to put the great ice-shrouded heights at her back, and knowing, every step, that she'd been a fool. Setting out on the road in the year's waning, as if the one she sought might vanish away like dew in the sun for her delaying. As if she hadn't been in service to the witch, hiding her thoughts, hiding everything, behind a meekly downcast gaze and quiet obedience, since she and her brother had come to that high meadow in the height of green summer, a year and more gone. A sensible lass—well she knew it—would have bided her time and waited for spring and the greening of the world, but no. She told the story over in her head to herself every morning, how she'd panicked, stolen what little she could lay her hands on—a loaf, a cheese, a few apples—and slipped away in the night. Shameful. Cowardly.

Wild godlings are chancy beings, maybe, but she ought to have thought things through. Her dying on the winter roads or starving as a beggar in some town wasn't going to find the one she sought any quicker, or be much use to anyone, least of all her unfortunate brother. It might be that summer was just ripening into autumn; the second cut of the hay all in, the grain swelling golden, the earliest apples yellow and red, falling soft and squashing into the road from the hedgerow trees to the delight of the wasps, but she had half the old empire to cross, on her hunt for the little northwestern lake called Dahres Water, and the wild godling said to live in the hills above its shore. She'd have done better to wait, bide her time, and set out in the spring.

Not that it was actually me she was looking for.

"Thurbridge, is it? Far enough," the big man on the brown horse said, and the lot of them grinned, a couple of women nudging one another. Thurbridge, of course, lies where the Rhunavon is joined by its more easterly sister, the Mossadon, growing great and broad and flowing unbridged from there north to the Lake of Birds, which some say is merely a vast broadening of its channel, a pool in the river, and that the Rhunatam, which flows from the eastern end of the lake north to the sea, is no more than the continuation of the Rhunavon. But those are arguments best left to the scholars in their universities in Thurbridge and the towered town on the eastern hill overlooking the ruins of the imperial city of Ghedhaynor. "We might see you safe on your way to Thurbridge."

"Very kind of you."

"There's a fee to consider, of course."

Of course there was. Everything she had, down to her boots, likely, and lucky if they stopped short of taking the shirt off her back. She leaned on her staff, picture of shabby weariness, her cloak, patched and darned, hiding the sax she wore fastened to her double-wrapped belt along the small of her back. She hoped. Not that she could fight so many, but it might protect her another time, if she didn't lose it now.

"I'll have to thank you and find my own way, then, good friends. I've not a farthing to my name. Looking for hire, in fact." Brightening up. "Might your lord or lady be looking for a herd? Goats, sheep, cattle, swine?"

Not altogether a fool, only young and impulsive, as the young are, and she knew what she was about, now. She had a lifetime, a short one, admittedly, of not-getting-hit being a well-practised art, and to be charming, to be funny, was a strong shield.

One of the bears shuffled closer, big broad head lowered to snuffle her face, reminding her of the old mastiff that had guarded the porch of her mother's hall when she was a child.

"Bears?" she asked. Make them laugh and maybe she'd get out of this unscathed. Arrany didn't quite dare reach out to scratch the beast's ear. She'd never heard of anyone but the travelling folk out of the east taming bears, and these men and women had the tongue of the northern range of the mountains.

"Bearherd," the younger woman snorted, and elbowed her companion again. "Go on, little sister, try. Get them moving, we'll watch."

The bridge was a high double span, humping up and down and up again, two gentle waves, with a low parapet. The water far below, a tributary rushing to join the Rhunavon, ran swift and shallow, braiding white around rocks. Beyond it, the road ran through more open woodland, grazed by wild beasts or maybe pastured herds. Not much cover, though the sun was slipping down into the west, shadows gathering. Make a run for it, get off the bridge and down into the ravine, all vines and thorns and tall lush green, and hope they didn't find her worth the sweat and mosquitoes to harry out. Might be her best chance, she considered. But the two with horses could ride her down before she got off the bridge, and there were the bows to consider. And the bears.

Tame bears. She raised her staff towards a bear's rump, meaning nothing more than the tap she'd give a cow or goat to start it moving, yelped as the man on the brown horse seized and wrenched it from her grasp, swinging his horse in close, just about knocking her over and raising the staff over her head.

"Don't touch the bears."

"Here, leave her," the boy said, and crowded his yellow horse in. The bears didn't like that, grumbling a warning and for a moment Arrany was caught there, ground between the horse and the boy's knee and a bear's shaggy flank. "You're the ones told her to try it." He flashed a grin down at her. "Let her go, Wolcha. She's got nothing worth taking."

The younger woman moved in even as the bear shuffled away. Arrany struck her reaching arm aside.

"None of that," the woman said, and slapped her, while the other plucked at the thin red cord about her neck, dragging out the little sparrow carved from antler. A charm against notice. Protection on the road. "That's pretty."

"I saw it first." The younger woman, one of the archers, snatched and the older shrugged and let her have it.

"Take it if you want, Tia. It's hardly worth fighting over. The boots might fit Tiny. I'll take them back for him."

"Come on," the boy said. He had vhalbairn eyes like her brother, a metallic sheen to the brown of them, vertical pupils like a cat. Human enough, otherwise. Maybe it had been he who'd seen through the protection, Arrany thought. Almost two weeks she'd been travelling, doing odd labour for a bowl of pottage and a bed in the haymow, with the mountains marching ever on her left shoulder and now at her back, sometimes nearer, sometimes farther, but slowly dwindling overall. And no trouble from humanfolk or wild beasts or tame, till now. "She's not worth it. Bigger fish'll be along."

"No reason to throw this one back."

"Bet she's got something Jaslyn wants."

The boy scowled at that. "Grandma'll have your ears if you're suggesting what I think."

"Just a kiss. Go on, take a kiss off her."

"I can find my own kisses, thanks, unlike some. Though I won't say no if she offers." The boy, Jaslyn, winked at her. "Maybe some time when you're not hassling her off the road? Go on, little bearherd. We'll throw you back till you're grown and your purse is fat."

"You don't give the orders," the big man said.

Jaslyn's eyes narrowed. "Someone's getting above himself," he observed. "If grandma—"

"Grandma, grandma—when your grandmother names *you* her lieutenant, then you can tell me to stand aside. Till then, you jump when you're told."

The boy wasn't going to win, not from the way the others were jostling and grinning. "Some brat's looking for a thick ear," one of the men growled.

Confusion then. Shoving, horses upset, heads tossing, a bear snarling, rearing up on its hind legs, a threat that had a horse squealing and shying away and the humans yelling and scattering, not so easy with their pets as they pretended. Arrany wrenched herself free of a gripping hand, felt the fiery pain of the amulet cord about her neck slicing skin before it broke, and took off at a run, the satchel that held all she still owned in the world thumping at her hip. Off the bridge, down into the ravine, hide. She was small, her cloak was a drab brown, her hat a faded green...maybe she would have had a chance.

A yell, and hoofbeats. Quick glance back; Jaslyn riding after her. Couldn't run faster, couldn't survive a leap from the parapet, the river was not so deep as all that. Hooves, the horse nearly on her, alongside, matching her. Arrany sprang away but he had grabbed her, he was saying something, laughing, up, come up, he said, dragging, come up and I'll take you on to Thurbridge, and she was falling and she grabbed at saddle skirt and almost she was under the hooves but the horse was trotting by then, and between her and the boy she was still upright, running alongside. He wanted her to put a foot on his and come up and—

Yell. "You fool!" she would realize it was, later, the big man shrieking. "Tia, you damned fool!"

And Jaslyn's tug on her hand that should have helped her up behind had brought him down, his eyes wide, confused, mouth open on a grunt, a word broken, the horse circling around, equally puzzled. "What?" Jaslyn said, and she was lying on the road with him heavy atop her, no cuddling, no kissing; he had fallen. There had been a horrible crack like axe hitting log; he was atop her but his head had struck the road.

He was still. Arrany wriggled free and laid him gently down. There was an arrow standing out from his back, which didn't make sense, they'd shot Jaslyn and he was the robber-queen's grandson. They were yelling, they were running. The brown horse, the bears—racing ahead.

There was blood on her hand. There was blood soaking his back. There was blood pooling around his head.

They were going to kill her, then and there. They meant to. One of them did. They had missed.

Shouts, cries, a roar and the bears rushing towards her.

Arrany snatched for the reins, got a foot in the stirrup, heaved herself up. A while since she'd been on a horse and some might say the ponies of the Marshlands didn't count, there not being so far to fall, but she had her balance, knew the shift of muscle and living will under her, dropped low and dug her heels in and the yellow mare took off a gallop, another arrow hissing over her head.

Behind her...the bears, for a little, but she had too great a start and they turned or were called back. Galloping, galloping, till she must let the mare slow and still she kept her at the trot, on and on, walking to breathe her, trotting again. Shadows stretching into night. Nothing behind her. Nothing on the road at all, only her and the robber-prince's stolen horse.

A long, long road lay ahead. The lowlands, the uplands, the bare sheep-downs and the hills. The high country. Old imperial highways, eaten by turf and the leaf-mould of a hundred autumns. Village lanes and drovers' paths and the pack-pony tracks. Bridges, fords, villages, rare towns. Chiefs' halls and the halls of queens and kings, though she avoided all the latter. She had a horse; she had a bow and was a better shot than the robbers had proven. The marshfolk are fowlers, after all. Errand-rider, merchant's escort. There was work to be had and she avoided travelling alone when she could. Winter caught her, though, and she scraped a bare living in a walled town of five chiefs, serving in the kitchen of a chief's hall and hiring herself and the yellow mare out to carry burdens about the town, to earn her stabling. They were both of them lean and weary when spring came, overworked and underfed.

Sometimes she dreamed of Jaslyn. Robber on the highway, handsome, bronze-eyed vhalbairn lad reaching for her hand in a dance, and the arrow thunks into his back and he falls against her...and she would wake cold and sweating and blinking tears for a fool young man she never even knew.

Long road ahead. The lowlands, the uplands, the bare sheep-downs and the hills. Into the high country of the northwest, and the hills rose, and rose. Stony fells, low mountains beyond. Up the Greater Dahrun, through the king's dun, on to the town at the lakefoot, the east of the lake where the Great Dahrun flows out to curve away south and curve again to seek the western sea. The shore road south of the Dahres Water. The road she'd set out to follow, desperate road, not understanding how far it was she had to go, in the golden days of harvest.

She was chasing a song, a rumour, a name, was young Arrany.

A legend, was what she was chasing. Now she let herself think the name, now she was so close and the witch of Under-Ice, who held her brother in thrall, so far behind. Not the godling, not Thallyn, the little god of the land who turned minstrel, they say, after the fall of the thrice-damned emperor and wandered the world alone till the wounds of her heart healed and she went again into the northwestern lands which had given her birth. Not her. But Naskanna, that name was Arrany's seeking. Naskanna Deathdealer: vhalgod warrior, traitor, among the greatest of the vhalgod emperor's captains, his daughter. Emperor's bane. The hero who'd taken the emperor's head. Naskanna, who went wandering in the world, they said, and loved a wild godling, and had gone with her into the hills of the north-west.

Naskanna, who might, if she could be found, save Arrany's brother.

Me, I was just a means to that end.

Shows what humans know.

2

IN WHICH A STRANGER COMES TO SMITHSFORD

It was shaping up to be one of Hedge's bad days, rare though those had become over our long years. Yet still, come they did, for all you'd think the past well-left behind us. But nightmares had ridden her hard, that night, so that she had twitched and whimpered and leaked tears she would have hotly denied, if she'd been woken to know them, but I hadn't risked it. A temper, the vhalgod had, caught in weakness, and besides, half waking into grief and fear she could forget where she was, and when, and lash out with a hand that forgot its claws. Better to hold her gentle, to wrap her in arms and legs and tuck close and whisper soothing nothings till the dreaming ebbed. Lost brother, lost honour—Hedge would deny she saw it that way but she did—loss of all she'd been born and raised and shaped to be, just and right though her rejection of it had been. The nightmare was maybe her sire's voice, his poison words telling her of all that. Or maybe she dreamed some battle lost, maybe her brother's dying, or a certain grim fastness in the south that in a weak moment I might admit came crawling like worms and rot into my own dreams too. Though there was a cure for that, for me, at least, and it was remembering fire and sword and the blue sky opening up above and Hedge, Hedge, Hedge, who was fire and sword and glory in her rage... And now the arrogant wretch hadn't spoken a word but to grunt at the breakfast I had roused early to so painstakingly prepare, hot oatmeal bannock, dew-wet wild strawberries piled on a dock leaf, duck eggs beaten up with the last of the butter and only a bit of ash fallen in; the vhalgod had taken staff in hand and gone striding off into the dawn, scattering ducks.

Hard to stride off all grim and menacing with a dozen speckledy ducks squawking indignant outrage around your feet, but Hedge managed it, veering to the left at the offering-stone, the grey boulder crusty with lichen, feathery with ferns and big as a small cabin, to plunge down the steep twisting way to the lakeshore.

I sat—broodingly—on the warm stone of the doorstep for a time, eating the strawberries and watching the white mist rising from the lake below, filling the hollow of the hills, hiding the little pine-dark islands. The ducks were foraging for slugs in the wattle-fenced vegetable patch, murmuring cheerfully among themselves and trampling the new-sprouting beans. Forgiving souls, ducks. If ducks have souls. I have my doubts. Though soul and wit don't necessarily go together, witness not some few humans of my acquaintance. I went down to shoo them out and prop the wooden hurdle that served as gate back in place. Eventually, when it seemed Hedge was off to roam for the day and had not gone down merely to dunk her head in the lake, I ate a good chunk of the bannock (burnt on the outside and sodden in the middle, because cooking is something best left to less distractible mortals), and a precise half of the pan of cooling eggs. Set the rest indoors on the table with a cloth over against flies. Splashed my own face with icy water in the stone-carved basin, strictly forbidden to ducks, filled where the spring came trickling ledge to ledge down the cliff-face, flowing out to wind its way to the brook, and eventually, to find the lake. I shook myself, abandoning human seeming, and went trotting down the path, leaping the stepping-stones where it crossed the channel from the spring, hooves a hollow drumbeat beneath the oaks. I took the right-hand fork, which ran away along the hillside above the lake for a good couple of miles, beaten earth track turning to soft-tramped old pine needles, before circling down through hillside pastures and the stone-fenced croplands of the village for a few miles more, joining the broader road that the pack-pony trains followed away through the fells. The dew was burning off and the day was promising bright and warm, by then. A good gallop there on the flat, into Smithsford, and I wanted a run to shake my temper out.

A rider was just crossing at the ford as I came charging down on it. Bony yellow mare, a hand or so taller than me at the withers, and her rider a slight figure, slumped and sagging for all it was fresh morning, and the horse, too, came up from the water trudging, as if she had a long road behind her and was already wearied at the sight of the high hills ahead. A young woman, it was, riding the yellow mare, and hair as yellow as her horse tied back in a long braid. Broad-brimmed hat, a leather jerkin over a faded red tunic, wide-legged russet trousers tucked into tall boots. She had a quiver at her shoulder and a bow under her knee, the hilt of a sax sheathed along the small of her back, just showing if you knew where to look, and a cloak rolled up and tied behind her cantle. Saddlebags didn't bulge with much; she was no pedlar, no minstrel or bard, either, by the look of her. Some chief's or merchant's armed retainer, or a mercenary looking for hire. Trouble, maybe. Though young, for any of those things. Save trouble.

The land that gave me birth, that western headland over the sea, was burnt and dead, defiled by slaughter of all its folk, a place of mounds and mourning, and I was a living god. I didn't go back there. I'd settled in the cave under the cliff above the Dahres Water a generation and some years since, I and Hedge with me, when our years of wandering grew weary. Whatever wild godling had lived there once had been lost and gone, another victim of Emperor Eksandron of cursed memory, and Smithsford had grown at the ford of the Little Dahrun under my protection, the grandfather of the current smith being the first, building his forge and then his house, with his wife and son and son's wife who kept bees, and the son's eldest daughter was the first babe born in Smithsford. She was Marsin Smith by the time of these happenings, with children of her own, and her sister

Ashill had brought in two lads from the king's dun of the Hrastnor on Great Dahrun; they farmed together and she brewed heather beer and made chokecherry wine and kept the tavern. A dozen households now in Smithsford, and we even had our own witch, Goodbrother Bessamy. It was become a stopping place for the pack-trains that wound up through the pass to the wild highlands beyond, carrying trade-goods from south and east and returning with grey fleeces and worked antlers of the giant deer and copper ingots and lead. My folk, they were and are, wild godling though I am and no town-god to live at a chief's elbow. We look out for each other, Smithsford and I.

A single rider Smithsford could have dealt with. That they'd let her ride through unchallenged seemed to say that if she meant trouble, it wasn't to them. Or to me. Still, I always liked to know who and what was passing on the road thereabouts. Besides, she looked like she had a story, and though I'll never make a bard—that takes *study*, years and years of it—I'm minstrel enough not to let the chance of a good tale pass me by.

The rider raised her head as I came down the road, which had been beaten wide and bare there between the stone walls by the cattle of the village going up to pasture and the traders' ponies climbing to the westerly route through the fells. Young, she was, surely not even twenty winters behind her yet, and her eyes pale blue in a tanned face. She reined her mare a little aside, but made no move to threaten me. Wild or stray, she figured rightly that a galloping horse was none of her concern. So I slowed, not to set the yellow mare jigging about, and came on at a neighbourly trot, circling around to get a good look at her. Fluttered up onto the twisty branch of an apple tree leaning over the drystone wall, just to see what she would do. The crow, like the mouse-dun wild horse of the open woodland, comes easy to me. The wolf, not so happily, though I've been wolf long days at need.

"Godling Thallyn," the mercenary lass says, and that I was not expecting. She took off her hat and bowed in the saddle. "Thallyn of the Dahres Head, my name is Arrany, of the Esrineyn in the Marshlands. I've been seeking you."

I had half a mind to fly off and leave her, or fly off over the ford and into the smithy, to ask Marsin Smith what she thought she was about, letting yellow-haired Marshlander infant hireswords loose on me without warning. It was a quiet life we'd come here for, built our cabin—Hedge had done the building—dug our garden—aye, that was Hedge, too—planted our orchard—that work had been mine, trees I understand, if not a vhalgod's urge to turn cottager. But the look of this lass was that of someone who'd been too long on the road, worn dry and weathered and weary, with a weight of trouble on her shoulders, and I'd seen that look on my vhalgod too long, aye, and worn it myself. How could I not have some fellow-feeling? So I didn't tease her more, but dropped down into the road with a caw, furling my wings and landing on my feet—human-like, bare and dusty as my hooves had been. I was decently dressed, at least, which isn't always the case, a deerskin tunic I'd pulled on that morning, all cut in fringes along the knee and a bit of shell-beading around the neck. Hedge is a restless sort, always needing something to be doing with her hands, and there's only so many knives to sharpen. She'll take up spinning one of these days and be after me to turn shepherd.

Human, I am as you see me, neither short nor over-tall, lean and some—that'd be Hedge—say graceful, darker brown of skin than is common in the north, my eyes blue as winter sky—Hedge's words—and my hair light acorn-brown and curling. Mostly Hedge cuts it short, because she says otherwise I look like I'm trying to turn myself into a bird's nest, all twigs and leaves. And no, I can't change my shape, be man instead of woman, be taller, paler, darker, red-haired, a child, be a black wolf instead of tawny, a bay mare or a piebald. Why not? It doesn't work that way, and you've listened to too many minstrel's tales if you believe otherwise. Hark to the true bards; they know better.

Anyhow, "Good morning to you, Arrany of the Esrineyn," I say. "And what brings you to Smithsford seeking the godling Thallyn?"

"Godling Thallyn," she says, "To tell the truth, it's your handfast companion I'm seeking, the vhalgod captain Naskanna."

That, I was not expecting. Hedge is just Hedge, and I'd have been surprised if any in Smithsford remembered she ever had another name. Not that the name of Captain Naskanna, Naskanna Deathdealer, is forgotten; there's songs enough about her, but they generally don't mention me, not even—especially not—the ones I made myself.

"Are you indeed," I say then, mostly to give myself time to think, and what I think is, well, whoever or whatever sent her here looking for Naskanna, captain of the second company of the Emperor's Golden Guard, must have been very certain, and very persuasive, for she's come a long road and no mistake. So she's not going to be put off by my telling her I've never heard of any such person. And she's been the night in Smithsford, probably supping and sleeping on a bench in Ashill's tavern, and that's plenty of time for all the village to have come to look her over and tell her that whatever the name, there's definitely a vhalgod woman living up under the cliff with the wild godling, and has been since first the god and their grandparents came to this place.

"You'd better come up the hill, then," I say, "and tell us all about it."

I gave a leap up into the air and flew off ahead of her, circling back to be sure she took the right way where our path branches off from the track north through the fells. Once I saw her turning up the long climb under the pines, I climbed the air myself, up into the open sky, and rode the winds down over the lakeshore...up again, towering elms along the brook that comes down our cliff in a waterfall east of us, the oakwoods, the little clearings of our garden and orchard, the pines that climbed and climbed again above...Nothing moving but some deer, and a fox that knew better than to come near Hedge's ducks, and away up where there was more stone than tree, some shaggy wild goats. The pack of wolves that hunted farther east was moving up higher, a great cave bear and her cubs were trundling down to the sweet lush water meadow of another nameless brook where moose, too, were browsing...no, it wasn't with my eyes I saw all this. I rode the wind, and I swam the currents of the life of this fell-side that I had made my own, and finally, having powers of her own and knowing I was searching and with better reason than to complain she'd let her breakfast grow cold, Hedge let me find her, and what was shadow became light and I spiralled down to see her, picking her way rock to rock across the rushing torrent that was our brook a half-mile above the waterfall.

I came down onto a stone mid-stream, landing light on my toes, flinging my arms wide for balance because maybe I'd misjudged a little and the stone was not so stable as I thought, rocking in the churning water. "We have company," I called, as Hedge took another leap past me, using her stout staff to thrust herself flying, landing dryfoot on the far bank. I sprang after her and she turned to reach a hand to steady my landing.

Beautiful, she is, my Hedge, as the wild wolf is beautiful, and the heights of the fells against the sky, and the eagle on the wing. Taller than is human wont, as are all the vhalgodkind, and ashy of complexion, whitish shading into grey, dark about the eyes and lips, and blunt black claws to her fingers and toes, fanged foreteeth, harsh-boned and craggy-featured, maybe not the common human run of beauty, you might say, but an elegance in lines and the planes of her face to catch and hold the eye, her hair black as my crow's feathers, and her eyes copper, warm as fire.

"Company, I know," she said, and if she wasn't in so grim a mood as what had taken her off without a word in her nightmare-raddled waking, she was not yet smiling. "Trouble, Pony. Jinn warned me."

You see, it wasn't only the captain of the Second Company of the Emperor's Golden Guard I'd brought with me, when I settled into the cave in the cliffs of Dahres Head. There was Jinn, prince of the empire and son of the emperor by one of his human wives, doubly a prince, for she was queen of an eastern tribe in her own right. And Jinn was half-brother to my Hedge, and with her he had slain their father the emperor in the taking of the city of Ghedhaynor in the great uprising of the human tribes and lands, and there Jinn had died, torn asunder and burned by his own father, and his soul cursed by the emperor in his dying to wander lost forever in the Beyond rather than finding any rest in this world or the next.

And maybe that was so, that Jinn's soul wandered outcast and lost and unresting, but a piece of it Hedge had caught as he died, there even in the midst of the fighting and the horror, and she had bound him by that into a bone of his own wing— you'll be thinking, rightly, that few enough even among the vhalgods themselves were winged vhaldrachen and it was even rarer among the vhalbairn, but he was one of the blessed—and so her brother had anchor and a thread to follow in his lost wanderings. How it was, I don't fully understand, it being a thing of the vhalgods and nothing of the gods of the earth and such magic as we might claim, and nothing like a human witch's working either; maybe it was that he dreamed, and what he dreamed was his haunting of Hedge, and the flute she made of his wingbone.

However it was, sometimes Jinn came to Hedge unbidden, uncalled, into her dreams where she alone might speak to him, or sometimes in the dancing flames of our fires, and the mist off the lake and the deep dark of the pool beneath the falls, and if I was by, I might see him too, so you needn't make that doubting face that says you think my Hedge mad and I little better for humouring her. The vows we had made between us, she and I, bound us close; she felt, a little, the ebb and flow of the tides of the earth, as godlings do and vhalgods do not, and I had come to share a little in the bond with her brother, which I do not think entirely pleased him, at least at the start.

Sometimes, she might call him, by the flute to which he was bound.

And sometimes, rarely, so rarely, she might call him into a semblance of life in the world by other means, at great and dire need. But dire indeed, they both knew well, that need should be.

What I thought of it, well, it's not always comfortable, to know your beloved's brother can wander in on you unbidden and unexpected. I'd never suggest to Hedge, though, that it might be more respectful and seemly to bury that last relic of her brother or give it to the pyre, rather than to carry a piece of him around with her. What do I know of such things? I'm a wild godling born of the earth's dreaming; I have no sibling, and vhalgod ways are not human ones, either.

"Well," I told her, "Jinn may be meaning our guest is the trouble, and he may not. It might be that the trouble follows on her tail. Either way, we may as well go down and meet it."

3

IN WHICH ARRANY TELLS OF HER BROTHER'S PLIGHT

We went back down to our house together, Hedge and I. A stony path, steep and twisting, past bird-singing thorn, beneath pine, now following the course of the brook and now climbing above it where it churned black in a narrow gulley or plunged frothing white down an abrupt defile, till we came where it sprang step to step down shelving stone by the waterfall, and so along under the cliff, past the little drystone barn Hedge had built back when she kept a cow, and the duck-house raised on stubby posts under the pear trees. We wild godlings don't generally go in much for building: a cave, an ancient hollow tree or a den under the roots, a cabin of woven willow in a grove—those will do us quite comfortably. But I had Hedge to think of, and what I'd begun as just a bit of a lean-to at the mouth of the cave where we'd finally settled, she'd turned mason and finished as a snug stone cottage built against the cliff, with a roof of green turf over birchbark sweeping from a high ridgepole down to low eaves, a window with a wooden shutter against the winter, a door with proper iron hinges from the smithy, fireplace and chimney, a plank floor planed smooth—small, aye, only the one room within, but there was nothing finer down in Smithsford, then or now.

Arrany had dismounted at the offering-stone to pour out a little of the ale in her flask, properly courteous, and come on up afoot. There she was sitting on the doorstep while the yellow mare cropped the sweet grass and shuddered her skin at errant flies. She jumped up when she saw us coming—the lass, not the horse. The horse merely lifted her head, gave me a long look and a friendly nod, and ducked her head to grazing again.

"Godling Thallyn," Arrany said, and bowed low. "Lady Naskanna." Another deep bow, which won a snort from Hedge.

"My mother was only a soldier of the Golden Guard and not the emperor's wife," she said. "I was never a lady. And I don't go by that name, thank you."

"Arrany, meet Hedge," I said. "Hedge, Arrany. She's come wandering to us out of the Marshlands, but I think maybe that's not the whole of it and her story wanders farther afield than that?"

Arrany bowed yet again, a little uncertainly.

"Pony," said Hedge, getting the full two syllables out of it. She meant, stop teasing the lass and pretend you have some manners. "And you, girl, don't keep bobbing up and down like a dipper-bird. Have you eaten?"

"I—yes, my—yes, Hedge, thank you. I broke my fast at the tavern." I knew Ashill and her menfolk wouldn't have let Arrany ride away without every corner filled, scrawny as she was. They're good folk, down in Smithsford.

"I haven't," Hedge said. "And it's nearly noon. Pony, eggs?"

Since the ducks were laying well, only the one setting, and we hadn't been down to Smithsford for a few days to trade them around for other things, there were plenty of eggs in the cool of the cave beyond the heavy aurochs-hide curtain—aye, it's a sanctuary, a holy place within the hill, but it's also cool and very handy as a cellar and storeroom. No butter or ham or bread to offer our guest, and I'd not put the peas to soak for supper's pottage. Such little homely matters slip my mind, more often than not.

"You eat up your breakfast first," I whispered, nudging Hedge, then, to Arrany, "And you, lass, go tend to your good mare. Put your gear in the barn and let her graze; she won't stray far and no wild beasts will take her while she's under my hand here."

Vhalgods take a lot of feeding. Hedge did wolf down the bit of breakfast I'd left her, while putting more wood on the fire and using a handful of horsetail to scour off the iron griddle I'd left with burnt crumbs and all, giving me orders to fetch this pan and that crock and be off to the garden for greens. By the time Arrany was standing hesitant at the threshold, the door open wide to let in the sun, there were eggs boiling and cakes from the big crock of buckwheat sourdough smoking on the griddle, a dish of vinegared lettuce and cress, a new round of waxed cheese cut open on the table, and the plates and cups set out all proper. I'd even stuck a spray of the first wild white hedge-rose and some blue flag irises in the chipped cup we never use, to make things nice. A guest, after all. True enough we had folk from Smithsford in and out all the time, but that was more like what I thought family would be, if either of us had any family.

I wasn't counting the ghost.

"Ashill sent you this, La—Hedge," Arrany said, and offered an earthenware jar, its stopper sealed with wax, which I knew would be the chokecherry wine Hedge is so fond of. The lass even managed not to bow, handing it over.

We took the bench along the wall and put Arrany in the chair that didn't wobble. Eat, I told her, when Arrany gave a nervous little nod that wasn't a bow and tried to begin, "L-Hedge, I've come to—"

She fell obediently silent. Ate, neat and polite, but not at all slowed by the large breakfast she'd certainly had. Someone who had grown used to not knowing where her next meal was coming from, and anyway, she needed fattening up. Hedge poured wine for our guest and herself, though I stuck to heather beer. Strong stuff, Ashill's chokecherry wine; it had little effect on Hedge, but could take the unwary by surprise. Arrany praised the food, her nerves easing, and lost a little of her heavy, beaten-down look, though she still wore the hardship of the road heavy on her.

"That's better," I said, when we'd all pushed back our plates. "Let's take a stoup out in the sunlight, lass, while you tell Hedge what you're wanting with her."

Hedge filled our cups again all round and out we went, sitting on the stone, stretching our legs in the sun. Plenty of room for three on the broad stone doorstep.

"So," I said, "what's brought you here to us, seeking a name so long put by?"

Hedge pulled out the flute from the stiff leather scabbard that hung most often from a braided cord over her shoulder. Long as my forearm, it was, though far more slender. Polished smooth and softly gleaming, bound with silver bands at intervals along its length, the bone was not ivory-white but stained russet, as if it had steeped in a bog. Which it had not. I leave it to you to consider what had coloured it, so long ago. She put it to her lips and played. Just a little wandering tune, like a breeze through the pines, and its voice was low and mellow. Calling Jinn, as if she wanted him, too, to hear what Arrany might say. I felt his coming, just a little chill, a little touch of the dark night beyond the world. Maybe there was a swirl in the air that moved over the thymey lawn; maybe there was a place the bees went around. Arrany didn't notice. No witch, she, nor one with any talent in that regard, no other touch of magic, human or otherwise, in her blood. If I'd looked with meaning, I could have seen him, like reflection on water, there and not there, when you look just so. Sometimes it's easier not.

Arrany nodded gravely—not a bow—looking inward, took a sip of wine, took a breath.

"Captain Naskanna," she said. A sidelong look at Hedge, who'd left off her playing and sat now holding the flute lightly in her long pale black-clawed fingers, looking not at Arrany, nor at me leaning on her own shoulder, but at the chill place where the bees ignored the honey-rich thyme blossoms. Hedge nodded, once, as if to something her ghost had said. I hadn't heard, if so.

"Hedge," Arrany said. Another deep breath. "My brother is the prisoner of a vhalbairn witch. She calls herself—she calls herself Sikassyn, but I think her other name might be—might be Spider."

Oh, she had Hedge then, full burning attention turned to her, copper eyes glittering, pupils narrowed to fine slits, and the flute shoved home to its scabbard like she was afraid she'd crack it, rough handling in her clenching fingers.

"Spider," she said, and her voice dropped to a harsh growl. "Tell us."

Jinn—I saw him then, like a reflection in shadowed water—snarled and flared his wings, darkening the lawn where he stood as if some little cloud had scudded over the sun, and all the bees fled his chill.

This is the story Arrany told, maybe not as she told it then, but we found out much of the rest of it along the way, or thought we did, so you might as well have it now, to be going on with.

THEY WERE TWINS, Arrany and Penryl, born late to their parents, the eldest and only other living child nearly grown when they came along, and their father dying when they'd seen not but six summers. He'd been a vhalbairn man, with a touch of the vhalgod still to be seen in the metallic sheen to his eyes and the vertical pupils. A good man; their mother, Esmilly, had mourned his loss deeply, and doted on the son who carried his looks, which neither of their daughters did. Penryl had a knack for getting into trouble, Arrany said, though more often than not it was she who had to do the apologizing and the atoning. Penryl led and she followed, and if sometimes she admired and adored him and ran eager at his heels, sometimes it was that she followed because she could not hold him back and their mother would demand to know why, while Missal their sister stood virtuous at their mother's right hand, learning the ways—she hesitated there, Arrany did, then finished her thought—learning what the eldestborn should know.

Not only did he have the vhalbairn looks—well, the eyes, at any rate—her brother Penryl, but as he grew from child to young man it was clear he had the witch's gift. Their mother Esmilly was pleased with that; he'd be a valuable counsellor to his sister Missal in years to come.

And what, I did wonder, would her sister be wanting with counsellors? But I let her go on with her tale.

"He had teachers," she said. "Eminent witches of the Marshlands, of our own tribe and others. But—I don't know the way of it—somewhere, from one of those witches, maybe, or some traveller's tale, he decided he needed more."

Penryl, it seems, picked up the notion that a vhalbairn's magic ought to be a different thing, a deeper thing—that he ought to be learning more than mere human ways, and have more than mere human witchery at his command. And he heard that away off in the mountains above the springs of the Rhunavon, there was a vhalbairn witch, old, old, old and wise, a vhalbairn of the first generation, practically a vhalgod herself. And sometimes, he heard, she would take an apprentice, a vhalbairn lad or lass, for the sake of their kinship with her, and teach them the secrets that human witches did not know.

Now, Arrany didn't think that more than chance and tales, at the time, but later she came to believe, and Hedge and I had reason to think likewise, that it was Spider's art had fed out that rumour, threads spun to seek and lure just such young folk as Penryl was, and bring them to the witch of Under-Ice. To Spider.

However it was, one spring morning with the water still high in the ditches and channels and the Marshlands ringing loud with the calls of waterfowl, the songbirds singing and the mosquitoes whining and the mist lying over all, Penryl slipped away in the dawn, and his sister Arrany, since she could not prevent and would not betray, went with him.

"He wouldn't be stayed," she said. "He wouldn't—there was a girl, Tairna, a—a companion of our sister's, and he was—there was no formal understanding between them yet, he was too young, but there was a great liking, I thought, and our mother would have approved. Tairna was of a good family and not close kin. They were—well, Penryl was putting me off to spend time with Tairna and of course that would happen, but I'd been his, his right hand, his shoulder-companion, all my life, and he'd leaned on me so—I was jealous, like a child, that he'd so easily put me aside as he'd been doing, that last month or two. Missal said I was being a fool and so did my mother, and I suppose they were right. But then there was this tale of the vhalbairn witch, come from somewhere, the witch and her high valley of Under-Ice in the north slopes of the White Mountains, and he said he would go. There was no turning him. But—even at the time, I thought it was strange, he didn't say a thing to Tairna. I'd been afraid he'd ask her to go with him. But he didn't leave her so much as a word. And I—I was stupid, and glad of it. That it was me who mattered, me he'd told, not her."

They took what they thought needful for a long journey, and set out in one of those low slender channel-boats of sewn reed-bundles that the Marshlanders make, the ones like in size to a birchbark canoe of the forests. No word to their mother, or to their sister Missal, or to any living soul at all on the queen's ait of the Esrineyn. Ait, if you don't know, is their name for one of the countless islands made by the streams and channels that chop up all the Marshlands, and an ait might be half an acre or hold the better part of a village. So by the web of Marshlands waterways and the channels of the braided River Rhunatam they found their way to the Lake of the Birds, and hugging its shore went around easterly, before they abandoned their boat and went afoot into the Lowlands, till they came into the valley of the Rhunavon, broad and slow there, and went south upriver, working their passage on the river barges as guards or unskilled hands, doing what they could find to do, to keep themselves fed. Finally, they saw the mountains, distant blue rising into ice.

Into the mountains they went, wandering this road and that track, village to village, young Penryl asking, asking, for the vhalbairn witch.

And so to Under-Ice, a remote high valley. The village there was a ruin, the hollows of cellars open to the sky, the timbers from which the folk of that land built their houses rotting, hidden by raspberry and rose, by currants and grape gone wild, the pastures and hay-meadows and ploughlands all growing up in young spruce and pine.

But towards the head of the valley where the ice rose in a great towering, creaking, ragged wall of white, burning blue when the sun struck it, there was one house remaining, high-peaked and low-eaved, its shutters carved with stars, and there they found the vhalbairn witch of Under-Ice.

To Arrany's eyes, she looked like a vhalgod, the ashy skin, the dark nails, though they were not claws, the hint of a point to her teeth and ears, and the metallic glitter of her pale gold eyes with their cat-slit pupils. Her hair was white, a long braid falling to her waist, and for all her face and hands were lined with the fine wrinkles of middle life, when she smiled in welcome, young Penryl gazing on her was lost.

Arrany was jealous, of course she was. All that way she had struggled and suffered and laboured, her brother's companion, his good right hand, the one who had to mind the purse-strings and remind him, ever and often, they were nothing but just two more poor wanderers scraping a living how they might, husbanding scraps against the day when scraps would be all they had, and there they were, come to the end of his quest, and the witch, who gave her name as Sikassyn, was saying, "Welcome, Penryl, of course I can teach you, I see your great gifts, of course you could learn no more from the witches of your homeland, talented though I am certain they were, in their human way...And your sister may stay as well, if she will help out around the cottage for her bed and board."

So that was how Arrany began to labour for the witch Sikassyn. Reasonable enough, you might think. Arrany did. But more and more was laid on her; it quickly went from helping with this and that, whatever needed doing, to a time when all was on her shoulders, cooking and cleaning, tending the garden and the witch's pigeons and her herd of white goats. When it came to the cooking and the cleaning and especially the mending of her brother's clothes and the witch's own, her work was never up to the high standards that a vhalbairn who remembered the glories of Imperial Ghedhaynor expected as her due. *Is it too much to ask for some respect? I would think you might have some care for your brother's appearance and dignity, at the very least*...You know the sort of thing such folk say, with a smile they know full well does not hide their intent to wound. Only to mow the hay, swinging scythes in the hot sun, to rake and toss it and carry it cartload by cartload to stack for the winter, did Sikassyn and Penryl turn out to help, because good haying weather waits for no man, nor woman, nor vhalbairn neither.

Penryl, by the time that Arrany had threshed the beans and peas and winnowed them, and dug the yellow winter-turnips and carried the summer's cheeses down to the nearest market town in a cart drawn by a pair of goats, and back piled high with flour and salt, hauling along with the goats till her shoulders ached and her calloused hands open and bled, was sharing the witch's bed by night —no thought of Tairna of the russet curls and sea-green eyes left behind—and hard at his studies all day in the back workroom that was forbidden to such mundane persons as his sister. He hardly seemed to see her at all when he emerged for his supper, dazed and dazzled by all the wonders of the arts he was learning. Though never would he display any of them for her, not even to light a candle with a snapping spark of his fingers as the witch did.

"Not yet," he would say. "I'm not ready yet."

And his eyes fever-bright.

That's a spell of the magi, I wanted to say then, not an art of witches. But Hedge gave me a look, so I did not interrupt.

Arrany passed the winter tending goats and feeding pigeons, baking bread and culling the birds for the pot, and the rest of the time spinning the past spring's harvest of silky fleeces, though the witch found much to fault in her skill with distaff and spindle. She slept in the hay in the goat-shed wrapped in every cloak and blanket she could scrounge, to be away from the sounds of the lovemaking of her brother and the witch in Sikassyn's big carved cupboard-bed, and woke in the cold dawn to the same labours again, as the winter winds howled and the ice stretched closer and closer down the valley and the snow piled higher and higher.

Spring, and the goats kidded, and were plucked of their grubby winter coats. Arrany milked the she-goats and cleaned and washed and carded the fleeces, and the witch made cheese while Arrany dug the garden and tried to persuade her brother that they should move on, as he was so clearly learning little of the magic he had come seeking. He snapped and snarled at any such suggestion, called her selfish, called her jealous, said she betrayed him, turning herself into an echo of their mother, wanting him trammelled in a small space, never to grow to what he could be, never to fly.

Hardly any vhalbairn of the first generation had that rare blessing, the winged vhaldrach form; the children of that generation and their descendents, never, not that I had ever heard. And it was hardly something you could grow into as you aged, sprouting wings like a stag his antlers; only the very desperate or deluded would think it some transformation they might effect by magic. When Penryl had been infected with this dream of flight, Arrany did not know, nor if he even meant it literally, or only to say in poet's terms that she trapped him, held him back. But he said it, and he went away into the workroom, and sulked in silence, turning his eyes from her, for days. And the witch sighed and said how regrettable it was when siblings quarrelled, and could not Arrany try to be kinder to her brother, who had made so many sacrifices to fulfil the calling of his talent and blood, could she not think less of herself and more of him.

He was so distracted, so deep-lost in his studies, Penryl was, that often Arrany or Sikassyn herself had to prompt him to eat, remind him to bathe once Arrany had drawn and heated the water, coax and cajole him to leave the workroom and walk about outside in the sun. And Sikassyn would walk with him, the pair of them holding hands, and the sun would glint on the silver streaks through the rich dark brown of her hair and warm the yellow gold of his, and they would whisper together, and laugh like young lovers courting.

You caught that, did you? Arrany did not, had not, even when she told the story to us, which might have been some lingering beguilement set on her as well as her brother. But then, we had the advantage of knowing Spider and her ways.

Came a hot noon on the edge between summer and another autumn when a desperate boy arrived from the village of Ramsleap half a day's journey down and along the mountainside east, the place where a weekly market was held in the shadow of an abandoned imperial tower. The miller's boy, he was, riding the miller's white horse, and the miller's wife was in a bad, bad way with a babe coming wrong, and the midwives and witches of the village despaired of saving either of them. So Sikassyn, who was highly esteemed as goodsister and midwife, if yet eyed a little askance for her aloof and solitary ways, and was called on in all the worst cases for two days' journeying all about, was fetched by Arrany from the workroom where Penryl sat hunched and inky over a sheaf of loose parchment pages. She made haste to pack up a bag with various bottles and jars and leather-wrapped instruments of steel and bronze and an apron of heavy canvas. Ordering, "See you get those last beans picked and spread to dry, and leave your brother to his studies," she went riding away with the miller's boy up behind her.

That was when Arrany went for the first time all the way into the witch's workroom, not merely peeking from the threshold, and looked over her brother's shoulder.

"Just scribbles," she said. "Like a child might draw. Scratches and scribbles. Birds, and stars, and—like someone testing a pen. Words written and crossed out. Some of it I couldn't read, it was the vhalgod script, but nothing—nothing that looked like anything, you know? What I could read, that was just—just broken bits, random fragments. Parts of old songs, the lines that mention vhaldrachen, but those were about the only things that made any kind of sense at all. Numbers, like ciphering but not keeping any kind of accounts that I could see. Mostly it was just pointless little sketches, and unfinished sentences. Just *scribbles.* Sometimes a drawing of a wing, bones, feathers, tendons. That was all that looked like real study, and what could he learn from that, but that birds don't fly once they're pinned out dead? There were pages and pages like that. The table—it was all over this and that, the bones of a pigeon wing laid out, feathers scattered everywhere, a dead bat stretched to dry, dishes of herbs and ashes and ochre and chalk, bits of knotted thread, little knives—blood crusted on them, some of them—candle stubs, dried toadstools and herbs. There was one book open, written in a language I couldn't read—real writing, that was, not nonsense, the vhalgod language and script again, I recognized that much—with notes in the margins in red ink in the same hand and scraps of parchment and broken quills and any old thing stuck in to mark this page and that."

So, "What are you doing?" Arrany asks him, and Penryl looks up, frowning.

"I can see it," he says. "Almost, I can see the way. I'm so close, Arrany."

"Close to what?" she would have asked, but her tongue is silent and her mouth gone breathless, the shock of what she sees, for his face is gaunt, eyes sunken, his hands like claws, hair dull and draggled, beard patchy-shaved, his shirt hanging loose over his shoulders. He had not looked so when she served him his porridge at breakfast.

Had not seemed so.

Only bright thing about him, not his steel-blue eyes, which are dull and bloodshot and rheumy as an old dog's, is a glitter of gold at his throat. He wears a thin golden band about his neck, like the torc a lord might wear, she thinks at first, but then sees it is not; it is a closed band, with an engraved inscription flowing around it, something she again cannot read, and that, that she has never seen before. What jewels they carried away with them they traded for food and lodging along the road long since, and those were trinkets of rings and pins, nothing so fine and costly as this.

Hedge has hissed, is sitting up straight, jarring me off where I was propped on her shoulder, but I've sat up too, and if I'm not hissing like an angry cat, maybe it's because of the shivering, the shudders running under my skin, as if a cold north wind has sucked all the heat from this summer's day.

See Hedge, looking at me, putting a hand on my shoulder. Gripping, black claws pricking into the thin leather of the tunic I wear. Not to hurt. To hold. To anchor. To tell me, you are here and I am here and that is long, long in the past.

See me, rubbing at my neck with the back of my hand, hardly knowing I'm doing so. See Hedge catch at my hand, but I'm a crow,

I'm away, up into the clean wind, and rising, circling, frantic, as if I can shed something behind me, if only I fly high enough, fast enough, and never find it coming to me again.

See Hedge put a hand, gentle, heavy, not letting her claws prick, on the lass's alarmed shoulder and Jinn, still there, come to stand by Hedge, and reach, as if he might touch her for some comfort herself, but he cannot.

"It's all right," Hedge says to Arrany, and her voice is soft, kind. "Your tale distresses her. She'll be back."

So I circled in the clean air, as if I bathed myself, mind and soul and body, and I came back, and shook my feathers ruffling as if I had had a comforting wallow in the dust, and settled by Hedge again, shooing Jinn aside—Arrany must have thought I chased bees, though there were none—and Hedge put her arm around me.

"Go on," she said. "Your brother had a god-collar about his neck."

"A—what?" Arrany asked, looking up from her hands, clasped together and fidgeting, unhappy, but we were all awash with our distress then, and hers was only a little thing compared to mine.

"God-collar," I said, and I heard my voice break and rasp, my throat gone dry. Took up the cup and swallowed the last of my beer to ease it. "The emperor made them, with his own hands, the greatest of the vhalgod magi. He made them, and he sent his god-hunters to take wild godlings, and they put them on us, and they made us slaves. The emperor—fed on us."

"He what?"

"Fed—on—us. Aye, the stories you know say, he grew so arrogant in his might that he wanted none but godlings, the spirits of the earth itself, as his palace servants, to prove his great power over all this world he had conquered, but that was not the truth of it. The god-collars let him...drink the power of us, the strength, the bond to the earth. Stronger, he grew. Stronger and stronger, more fearsome, more terrible, and his madness grew with it. How do you think it was he was not put down sooner, when his tyranny and his evil grew so great for all to see?"

"He was always mad," Hedge said dispassionately. "Ever since the crossing of the Way Between, he was mad, if not before."

That was an old debate—was Eksandron mad before he and his followers were exiled from the world of the vhalgods, or was it the dangerous passage Between, was it the crossing of the Rift, that made him so.

That wasn't the time to become lost in that old discussion, and neither is this.

"Penryl isn't a godling," Arrany said. "He's only vhalbairn, and barely that."

"And a witch," Hedge said. "Though I've never heard of using a god-collar on vhalbairns or witches, either. Or even on another vhalgod."

"What would it do?" I asked. "To a mortal, a human, a vhalbairn? Even to an undying vhalgod, what would it do?"

"I don't know," Hedge said simply. "Nothing good." She added, "Trust Spider to make the experiment."

"I'd expect it to burn him to ash!" But clearly it had not. I shook my head, forced my mind back to the matter at hand. "How do you know to give this Sikassyn the name Spider?" I demanded.

"And why did you leave your brother in such a state, in such a place?" Rumbling edge of anger in Hedge's voice then, and I put a hand over hers where it lay on my shoulder.

"He wouldn't listen!" Arrany cried. "I tried, I tried to tell him, I tried to show him his own wasted face in the witch's silver mirror, and he would not see, or he could not. He called me selfish, jealous—other things, and in the end he—he struck me. He's never hit me, ever, not even when we were little children, not in his worst tantrums."

It was their mother was heavy with her hands, as we would deduce along the way, from the lass's casual remarks. A swat here, a slap there. *Silly child, I expected better of you, I make allowances for a boy without a father to look up to, but a girl should be wiser at your age...*

He hit her, and when she stood stupidly staring, she said, he pushed her away, so that she struck her head on the doorframe, and he went back into the workroom.

"Get out," he told her, when she had had her bit of a cry, and who can blame her, and had followed in again after him. "The learning here isn't for the likes of you. It isn't for human understanding."

And the sneer in his voice. That wasn't Penryl, not her brother, she didn't want to believe it. That was the teaching of the witch of Under-Ice, speaking through him.

There was no helping Penryl, she understood that much. Not by herself alone. The witch Sikassyn had not returned by nightfall, and by dawn, Arrany was gone, setting out on her long road to find Hedge.

"Her name," Hedge said. "Mine. Thallyn's. Where did you have them?" And again she asked, "Who gave you that name, Spider?"

"I—I don't remember. Maybe Penryl used it, once or twice? Her nickname, learned in their whispering together in the night? Why does it matter? He did use it," Arrany said, big-eyed and earnest. "That one book on his worktable, the one he was studying, he said, when I was arguing with him again, a last try before I left—"

"After he hit you?"

"Yes. But he didn't mean to hurt me even then. I don't think he ever remembered doing it, the moment past. That book—he said, he would have all the knowledge that was written in it, the secrets of the vhalgod magic, it was all in her book, Spider's book, that she'd written herself. He did say Spider, I remember. Spider was helping him to understand. I thought it was—a strange sort of pet name, really."

Hedge was looking away, looking at Jinn. "Aye," she said. "It was a name we gave her, in the Emperor's court. For...reasons." Jinn made a wry face and shook his head, reflecting on the follies of a certain imperial princeling, among others. "That she took the name Spider to herself as if it were a compliment says much about her."

"And why did you come looking for the name Naskanna, and seeking her with me?" I asked.

"I met strangers," she said simply. "Out of the east. The wandering folk. You know they have the Seeing? Three days I was on the road through the foothills, with no thought in my mind but to go home to my mother and lay it all at her feet, and I fell in with a band of the wanderers, and the great-father of the family, an old, old man, had me spill a drop of blood into a cup of water and ashes, and he saw my way clear in it. He gave me the name Naskanna. I recognized it, from songs, and he told me, I should find her with the godling Thallyn, in the northwestern hills. And so I began seeking my way to you, rather than returning to the Marshlands. And it took so long, it took so long, there were the robbers..." Well, we heard about that later, how the robber-queen's winsome grandson had been slain by his own fellows shooting at Arrany, and how they'd hunted her for days before she lost them and fell in with a cloth-merchant needing an extra guard to a big autumn fair. "...But the winter came and the snows, so I couldn't travel, and then the spring floods..." She'd lodged in the household of a town chief and his man, just folk who'd not treated her too badly, though she'd had to work plenty hard, she and her yellow mare both. "And it was so very far to come, and Penryl was so ill and wasted, he was wasting away and I didn't see it till the day I left him, I shouldn't have left him, no matter what, I shouldn't have—my father said, I had to look after him, always, I had to look after him, for the witch's blessing was a difficult gift to carry, and I promised I would. What if he's dead now, what if he's dead...?"

She was shivering, then, and starting to cry. You know how it can be, how when you've been doing a great, hard labour, and it's finally done, and you just fall down near broken because it's over at last? That was what swept over her, then.

I took her hands in mine.

"There now, Arrany-lass, hush and be easy. You've come to where you were going, you're safe here."

She was embarrassed by the way her voice quavered and the tears that welled, brushing it off with a joke, scrubbing over her eyes with a dusty sleeve. Too tired, she said. Too much of the cherry wine.

Too artful, that descent into frail tears, Hedge said aside, when I'd sent the lass off to wash her face, but I thought I might weep a bit too, if I were a young mortal with a fool brother fallen into such a snare, and I alone in the world to save him.

"Hm," says Hedge, and, "That's as may be."

She's lying, says Jinn, for the two of us to hear. Soft as wind in grass, his voice, though it wasn't speech heard by the ear. *Somewhere in that, a lie.*

"Is it all a false tale, then?" I asked, harsh, because I'd judged her honest enough, if maybe evading a few things she'd rather not admit to.

She's true enough in her pain for her brother, Jinn said. *But she weaves lies through her truth. You question her close, Thallyn, with the aspect of your godhead on you. You'll hear it then and awe of you will have the truth out of her.*

Well, I might have done so, if it hadn't been Jinn telling me I ought, I suppose. Maybe I should have done. But I didn't. You go pushing at a human that way, they never after get easy around you again, not quite the same way they used to be. Hedge used to say things about my wanting to shed what I am and pretend even to myself to be no more than some human minstrel, despite being no more human than I am horse or crow, and no more likely to give up racing the wind, on earth or in sky, than to take a vow of silence, and I suppose for a time that was true.

So, "Let her keep her sidestepping a while, then," I say, and Hedge shrugs to that, agreeing to let it be. "She's given us the core of it honestly enough, the matter of the lad and Spider."

Jinn allowed that.

"There's truth and then there's truth," I said, foolish-wise, like some annoying old village elder.

Truth and truth. You can judge for yourself, when the time comes, whether we ought to have pushed the lass a bit more on that.

Well, Jinn went, in that way he does, like the sun's gone in and the surface of the water's no longer reflecting, and Hedge, saying there were matters needed sorting and she'd promised eggs to Marsin Smith, filled a big basket—disregarding all proverbial wisdom—strode whistling off down the lane.

Arrany, seeing we weren't about to set off into the east at once, begged the use of a washtub and made shift to launder her clothes, and I pottered about tending to this and the other that needed doing before the summer was well on us, and remembered to feed our guest some supper, even if it was only leftover buckwheat cakes and cheese. I took her with me up the hillside with a couple of hatchets to cut springy juniper boughs, and we made up a bed of those with some hay and blankets to cover them in a corner of the cottage. The sun was setting by the time Hedge returned, having supped on a fish pie with the young witch in Smithsford, so we wished Arrany good night, settled cosy into her sweet-smelling bed, and retired to sleep ourselves.

"You don't have to come with me," was what Hedge said, soft in my ear.

"Don't be a fool," I said.

"Really, Pony. I'll be all right. I'll take care. I know you don't want to leave this place, this peace. You've earned it."

"And you haven't?"

A long silence, before she said on a breath, "No."

"Idiot," I said, and thumped her in the ribs, maybe harder than I meant to, because the breath went out of her in a cough and the lass in the corner under her blankets made some little disturbed muttering. We were silent, till she was.

"We'll leave as soon as we can make ready," I said.

"Aye," Hedge agreed, no more arguing. Then, "Pony," she says, and I think, all right, maybe a bit more arguing, and I draw breath ready to explain just why my fool vhalgod captain should not be going off to face down the likes of Spider alone, but she says, "The lass *is* lying about something."

I sigh. "Of course she is, my sweet dear fool. Of course she is, and I didn't really need a poor curse-bound ghost to see it. But there's truth enough, and pain enough, in what she says of her brother and Spider, to be going on with, and I expect the rest of it will be made plain in due time. Give her space. Would you trust us, really, if all you had of us were tales?"

"You always gamble on things turning out for the best."

"Why not?" says I. "You did."

See Hedge laugh, a quiet huff of breath, not to wake our sleeping guest. "Bessamy says he'll take the ducks while we're gone."

"Idiot," I said again.

See her sigh into my hair, her arms going around me, pulling me close against her. We'll leave things there for now.

4

IN WHICH WE SET OUT ON OUR TRAVELS AND HEDGE HAS HER OWN ADVENTURE

Arrany had come to us by the southeast, through the Lowlands below the Lake of Birds and across the downs, but Hedge was for setting out due east, along the edge of the fells till the land dipped down to the green hills and then rose over what we called the eastern highlands, though they were the western mountains to Arrany's folk. That would avoid the good folk of Lakefoot and the king's dun on Greater Dahrun making it the gossip of every market trader and wandering singer all summer long, how the wild godling Thallyn from up by the lakehead was setting off on her minstrelsy again, with her tame vhalgod at her side. A good argument, for all it would prove a harder route for Dandelion, the yellow mare, and one through lands where humanfolk were scarce and the great beasts of the wilds more common. I wouldn't have sent the lass that way alone, nor Hedge. The vhalgods are not exactly immortal for all they're called so—only very, very, very long-lived. And they're certainly not inedible.

The better part of a week passed before we were ready to set out. Hedge likes to make her preparations all proper, rather than trusting to the luck of the road, as I tend to do. That meant her sending me up and down to Smithsford to barter for this and that, and once with a purse of coin all the way to the market town of Avondon, while she was making twice-baked journey-cakes on the hearth and packing dried fruits and split peas and oatmeal and strips of jerky in waxed linen, and beans and oats for the horse. There's little forage on the heights. Good walking boots for Arrany, too, I had of a cobbler in the town, because her heeled riding boots, wherever she'd come by them, were not going to be her friends on the road we would take. I did wonder if we'd have a fight over that, if the lass, having gotten herself a horse, would protest going afoot again, but she'd only looked worried and said she had little coin to repay us.

"Add it to the reward you say your mother will give when we bring your brother safely home," Hedge said dryly. They'd spoken of that, Arrany and Hedge. Payment for this venture hadn't crossed my mind. A human child had come to me for help, that was how I saw it. What was I, if I did not take that reaching hand? But Hedge needed to eat. Not that I think either of us put great faith in any eventual payment from Arrany's mother, who seemed to have spoilt the one twin while neglecting the other, and made no great effort to find her darling once he bolted, for all her spoiling. If Arrany were to be believed, which was, of course, a question.

The evening before we planned to set out Hedge slipped away behind the aurochs-hide curtain while Arrany was packing the waxed canvas and leather bags that Dandelion would carry. I went after her. It's a deep, cool, dry space, my cave, the mouth of it narrow and low, but the roof rising high, then dropping towards the back close and jagged. In the forepart the floor is all sand and gravel washed out in the distant past, and old ashes, too, where once fires were kindled against the dark at the death of the year. In the wet seasons, when water seeps down from above, the smell of ancient smoke wakes out of the stone. Further back...well, this had been the sanctuary of another wild godling, fallen to the emperor, and away beyond, that's not for human ken; let it keep those secrets. We don't have need to go further down, deeper under the fells, very often,

Hedge and I. The outer cave is holy enough for silence, and for dreaming.

Hedge didn't need to pace out the distance to find what she sought. It called to her. She just dropped to her knees, scraping away the sand like a child at play on the shore, and brought up the long leather-wrapped bundle, shaking it clean. Gave me a crooked smile, because she'd been all for throwing it into Dahres Water and I'd said no, you never could tell when a time might come again she'd have need of it. I won't say that wasn't vision, nor prophecy, though this little adventure, off to pluck a fool boy from Spider's clutches, was far from the need I was moved to speak of. That time, if it be to come as I saw, lies yet before us.

Handy, though, travelling as a human on the road, to have a well-armed guard at one's side. Saves trouble in the long run. Scares off the small fry.

Out through the house, into the golden dusk, Arrany following, curious. Hedge unwrapped the sword, a plain-enough thing, a little gilding to the hilt was all, no fancy ornamentation, no jewels nor mystic words of threat and protection. She drew it from its scabbard, held it up to the sky. Dull dark grey with an oily iridescence to it, not the pale clean glint you'd expect of a blade. Vhalmetal, they call it, and whether it's mined as an ore in the lands beyond the Rift, or an alloy of iron and who knows what, none in this world can tell. Takes an edge that will cut a tuft of wool drifting on the stream or a chain of iron heavy enough to hold a bull aurochs, as they say, and strong, aye. Doesn't rust, either. More precious than gold, vhalmetal weapons; even the surviving vhalgods have lost the art of forging them.

Not her own blade; that was broken. This, for all it seemed a plain warrior's weapon, unless you knew how to look, was the emperor's own, till she took it from his dead hand.

Hedge said nothing, only looked the blade over and gave a satisfied nod, before she went inside again.

Arrany didn't say a thing, but her eyes widened, and her mouth set grim. Realizing, I thought, what it might mean, to go seeking aid from a captain of the Golden Guard.

And so come the morning, with the promise of a hot noon in the mist rising over the lake, we set out. I'd dressed myself as a human traveller might, linen shirt and wool trousers and tunic. Shoes, I never bother with, till the snow comes. Oh, and my old faded blue hat, which I was very fond of, though Hedge did say it looked like a squashed foxglove blossom. Hedge wore a leather jerkin over her tunic, filed her toe-claws to put on her tall boots, and braided her hair. You know she means business, when she braids her hair and puts her boots on. The ducks we had taken in the handcart to deliver down to Goodbrother Bessamy's keeping, the setting one with her clutch and all, brooding in her little wicker coop. And the hearth cold and the house shuttered. Lonely, it looked, the garden already desolate.

"We'll be back," I told Hedge, and she squinted at me as if I'd said something foolish but then, "Of course we will," she answered, because she understood I needed to hear it said.

Not much to tell of the first long days of our journey. Up, and up, through the fells and east, the three of us marching light with Dandelion to carry the better part of our burdens, though Hedge had her sword belt slung over her shoulder like a baldric, Arrany her sax and bow and all, and I took my willow-wood harp in its waxed leather sack on my own back. Wolves came about our fire one night, just to sing with us, which set Arrany and the yellow mare both shivering and huddling close in, though wolves are wise and mean no harm to those who travel with the gods.

Saw what might have been a dragon soaring, high and distant; lammergeier, Hedge said, but my eyes are sharper and I know what I saw. It rained only a few days, so the weather could have been worse. Down through the green hills where we came as strangers, the minstrel Pony and her companions, and if folk looked askance at the vhalgod that was the worst they did. The tale of the wandering hero Elaranor, vhalbairn daughter of Scholar Ashmorin, who was acclaimed king of the Truscana during the wars for his great wisdom as much as his winning of battles, did much to make the world a safer place for vhalbairns and even those vhalgods who renounced the emperor, cursed be his memory, and were willing to live peaceably with humanfolk. They're good tales, the deeds of Elaranor, and many of them are even true. Ask Hedge; she's in a few.

A quiet journey, all in all.

Well, except for the wild godling of the lions, but Hedge only told me about that later.

SEE THE MOON. Full, it is, and summer-golden, rising over the grey stone crests of the fells, and its little dog along with it, circling round and around—yapping, no doubt, as small dogs do—small bright spark, small dark shadow on the gold. See the trees, the long-reaching forest stretching up to these barren heights along the streams, the gullies, the fissures in the rock, dark shadowed deep, silver light shining. Hear the sounds of the night. Water chiming, thin bright notes falling like the song of a harp. The rasping call of the long-whiskered moth-hawk overhead. Bats, chittering to themselves, swooping and soaring, graceful night-swallows. Shifting stone, faint click and rattle.

Soft breaths rise and fall. They sleep, wild godling, mortal lass, close in against the shelter of a crumbling low cliff. Pony, shifted to a wolf in her sleep, memory of the wolves who came to sing the night before, or maybe it's only that she finds the rough ground less lumpy that way. Arrany, curled up as if she feels the night's chill, her blanket pulled up over her head, only her nose poking out. The fire burns low, nearly out.

See Hedge waking. Tall, dark flowing shadow, she is. See her feed the fire, the broken sticks laid near.

What you don't see is, she has her eyes slitted nearly closed, her face turned half away. What you don't see, as we lie there sleeping deep, yellow Dandelion standing hipshot and ear-drooped dozing close in by the cliffside, is the tension in the warrior, the wakeful power, on one knee there to the side of the fire, the sword laid under her hand. What you did not see, was the ghost, the presence pulling himself into the world, how he had come to the one who had bound him, how he had pressed cold against her, whispering, into her ear or maybe only into her mind, *Naskanna, danger, wake!*

Thus she woke, at her brother's warning. And now she looks out into the dark, away from the fire that has not ruined her night eyes, and she hears the soft click and slither of pebbles along the slope to the left, and she breathes deep and sniffs the wind, as a wild godling might have done, if a wild godling had woken, when Hedge, woken by Jinn, had heard the soft padding of paws and reached to squeeze her wolfish paw. But the wild godling had not woken.

She won't, whispered Jinn. *She can't. There's a sleep laid on her and the girl.*

But not on Hedge.

Whatever it was came stealthily, so Hedge was stealthy in turn. She yawned, and stretched, sat up, and made show of tending to the dying fire, never looking at it, as she brought the hilt of her sword under her hand.

Whiff of animal, warm and musty. Shadow on shadow, in the dark where crooked spruces cling against the slope. Shadow on shadow, flowing, breaking free, moving amid the scatter of broken rock below the cliff. Shadow amid the broken trees where winter icefall had come down. Shadow drifting—

Hedge moves. Leaps, like the wolf on the fawn, like the salmon up the falls, like the falcon to the air. She leaps, and her arm goes around a throat, and her naked sword rests its hungry edge against a heart wild-beating.

He is tall, tall as she, and his head is a beast's head, the head of a lion, and his body has the shape of a man's, rough-pelted like a winter lion down to his hips. He has a long tail, lashing slow and angry, human feet, human hands heavily furred like his arms, fingers tipped with lion's claws, but his legs are no more hairy than any human's, and he wears the shaggy hide of a wild goat as a wrap about his waist. He carries a staff, as most wanderers in the fells do, but the head of it is worked iron, a ridged shape like some overgrown seedpod. Mace, walking stick, quarterstaff; it could do duty as all.

"Call them off," she says. "Call your beasts off, or you die, and they swift after."

She'll deny her words were anything so fine. I say she's welcome to tell the story herself, in that case.

Voice low, hissing, growling, hardly to be understood. "You bear no weapon that can slay me. There are no god-collars here."

Bravado, that, and Hedge could have pointed out that a vhalmetal blade might take a godling's head as hungrily as it sought any mortal's, and a godling be a long time gathering themself together a body in the world again, but it was a thing they both knew, and both knew, too, that a wild godling had many defences, and perhaps the slaying might not come so easily after all, vhalmetal blade or not. And there were the lions.

They came padding, slinking close then, the she-lions, five of them in all, great shaggy beasts pale under the moon, the faint water-striping of their flanks making them seem to ripple and flow like a swift calm river's surface, passing shade to silver and back again.

As long as a horse, though they stood not so high at the shoulder, and their great tails nearly that length again twitching, as a cat crouched at the mousehole.

A rare thing even in that time, so far north as we were, rare even in the most remote and deeply forested valleys. You will not see the great tawny-pale striped lions anywhere now in these times, unless some few still haunt the furthest depths of the eastern forests, the far Darkwood.

That's now, though. This was then. Five she-lions and two close enough the swipe of a paw could have torn the flesh from her back, close enough a lunge might take her by the shoulder, the throat, and Hedge stood unflinching.

"We are travellers," Hedge said. "We bring no harm to you and yours."

"The pride does not hunt your godling, debased and fallen

though she may be, nor the young mortal. They sleep. My business is with you, vhalgod."

"What business might that be?"

"My sister," the lion-man said, "my sister, born with me of one dreaming, my sister is dead. And so no vhalgod shall pass through these hills of mine."

Something stirred, a breath of breeze, a chill that was not the night, a darkness that was no shadow. It drew moonlight into itself, took on form. Jinn, making himself more apparent, to Hedge, at least; that much cost him little effort, bound as they were.

Hedge's brother, in life, had favoured his human mother. Black hair with more curl to it than was common among vhalgods, brown skin with a grey cast to it that suited neither vhalgod nor human ideas of how a healthy young person should look, gentler features than his sister, though still craggy and sharp-boned to the human eye, and tall as Hedge, though lean and light in build, as vhaldrachen always are. Sharp front teeth and black finger-claws favoured his vhalgod father, and his eyes had been the colour of molten silver.

He was paler now, as if the colour were leaching out of him, and the soft silvering moonlight he drew into himself made him paler yet. Only his eyes burned with the full brightness of life.

Let me speak, Jinn said to her. *I know this godling. I knew the she-lion godling his sister.*

"No," Hedge said. Flat denial. Do you think it wrong of her? But there is a price to be paid for a ghost to take on substance in the world.

Oh, you might say you know ghosts, some of you. Faint pale forms, easier seen by night. Maybe you've heard them, the whisper of a familiar voice, or perhaps it was only some stranger whose path you've crossed. I won't deny it. But Jinn had been cursed, Jinn had been damned, cast out between worlds, and it was only the binding Hedge had made that let him find his way back to her at all. Even those ghosts you may have seen, whether memory and echo or true lingering soul, have only the most tenuous presence in the world, and you've heard the songs, the tales that tell how they may be given greater strength and a seeming of life. You've heard the songs, you've listened to the tales, of how such an act corrupts, how it draws, swift or slow, the lingering dead away from their true nature, how in time it may wake in them a hunger for life, one that, if fed, a little, a little more, may grow, despite all their understanding of their danger, despite all their will to resist, to deny it.

What's told is true. You may offer breath, to summon a ghost, if it be that a soul drifts still in this world, not gone beyond or into new life. You may by this offering give it, for a time, a little substance, make it visible, give it voice. That is a small thing, though even in that, little by little, as a ghost is summoned again and again, there is risk. For you. For the dead. Or you may offer blood, to lend a ghost not mere shape and voice, but strength in the world. Feed it on breath or blood, you feed it on life. It is only a matter of degree. But do so too often, and its need for life, its hunger for the warmth and colour of the living world, will begin to grow, to become to that soul a torment of desire. When their strength to resist fails, it can be a terrible thing.

"No," Hedge said. "Let me speak for you."

The lion-man growled. He heard only Hedge's words.

"My brother," Hedge said, "is with me. He says that he knew you in life. He says he knew your sister."

"I have sworn it, in *my* sister's memory. The life of any vhalgod who comes within my reach is forfeit."

"That," said Hedge, "is a wicked oath to have sworn, and it does your sister no honour."

Father of Lions, Jinn said, for all that the godling could not hear him. *No. This is* my *sister. Take my word, if you will not take hers: she means no harm to you or any in these hills of yours.*

Those hills were not the lion-man's hills to claim as he had, anyhow. But that's neither here nor there.

"My brother Jinn assures you that we mean you and yours no harm, we only seek to cross these hills to the east."

"Jinn," the lion-man said. He shook his shaggy head. "Prince Jinn? The vhalbairn, the human-born vhaldrach? You think that name will buy your way? The Prince of the East led all those who followed him to their deaths, human and godling alike."

"Human and godling, vhalgod and vhalbairn followed him, and if they did so it was of their own will," said Hedge. "And you cannot say, all went to their deaths. Far from all. Many died, it is true. And that they fought and fell was a better deed than standing aside, in that time. But many lived. They took the city. It was by their deeds, and those of the many others who rose, that the empire is no more."

"My sister died," the lion-man howled. "My sister, born with me of one thought, one breath, one dream of the world. We came into being together. We should have lived together, roaming the valleys, the hills, hunting the wild goat and the bison. Together we should have wandered, all the years of the world, and she is dead, destroyed by the emperor, gone beyond any returning."

No, Jinn said. *Lavinor. Her name was Lavinor, and she was with me in the taking of the city, but—I do not know that she died. If she did, there was nothing that would have prevented her finding her way back into the world. She was free of her god-collar. Tell him, Kanna.*

"My brother says—"

"No!" the lion-man said, and he swatted her sword aside—tried to, anyway, but it and she were gone, springing away over the back of a she-lion, to perch on an upthrust fang of stone. Reluctant to harm him, or the lions, when she still had hope he might listen.

"My brother says, she was free of her god-collar. Do you think once he took arms against our father he would have left any godling he came upon enslaved, whether they joined him or not? If Lavinor hasn't drawn herself together into a body in the world again, perhaps she isn't yet ready to do so. Have you called her? Have you waited, and listened, to hear what the wind and the stone might tell you of her?"

Or had he been too bereft and too angry to listen in patience to the tides of the earth, the great dream of which we are all part? Hedge did not ask that, but she thought it.

"She is slain and gone!" the lion-man roared. "You lie, you abuse the name of the Prince of the East to claim him for your own, vhalgod. I followed Prince Jinn myself, I came from the east following him, seeking my sister. You dirty his name when you hide behind it." And as if they were weapons in his hand—which it seemed they were —the she-lions flung themselves at Hedge.

She did not want to kill them, innocent beasts who only strove without understanding to do their godling's will. She did not want to shed blood and give wounds that might not heal. She did not much want to be torn apart and eaten by lions, either. Who would? So she fended them off with the flat of her sword, struck at tender noses, kicked and spun and leapt away to another jutting stone, crouched, ready to leap again. Teeth, lashing tails. They were wary, they had flinched from her blows, but a sore nose or two was not going to hold them off long. And the blood trickled down her sleeve, over her hand, dripped on the stone. Ripped sleeve. Ripped arm.

Jinn knelt by her, cold quick presence, put his mouth to it.

"Don't!" She pushed, as if that might move him away, rolled through him all silver and insubstantial as he was and came to her feet downslope as a lion pounced.

Pounced, and twisted away yowling in outrage, or maybe it was fear, as another vhalgod reared up between the beast and its prey. Vhalbairn, rather. Vhaldrach. Jinn snarled, flaring out his wings, leathery black. He wore a long, full-skirted coat of dragonscale in the style of the vhaldrachen, wrapped in front, slashed down from the shoulders behind to allow for the wings, with a broad sash of vhal-metal mail binding it about the waist below to close it. He bore a lance, or the ghost of one, and swung it, striking the lion with the shaft. The lion-man godling cried out as if he'd felt the blow himself and leapt towards Jinn, raising his mace, but he spared a hand to make a sweeping gesture that sent the lions circling behind him, growling but out of reach.

"Ah, *Jinn,*" Hedge said, and rose to her feet within the shadow of her brother's wing. Whole, he was, unwounded, the terrible damage of their father's wrath, the horrors of his death, not to be seen.

He spun the spear, leaned to bump her shoulder with his, as material, almost, as she, though that shivered and changed as if he were filled with swirling smoke, now thicker, blocking all light, solid as flesh and bone might be, now thinner, dissolving in moonlight. "It's all right, Kanna."

"It isn't. You shouldn't—"

The lion-man snarled, wailed. "No! I've sworn it! The vhalgod must die!" He swung his mace at Hedge's head. They blocked it almost absently, sister and brother, sword and spear together.

"Listen to me," Jinn said, furling his wings, but the she-lions were slinking around up the steep slope to get above them. "Vinya, godling of lions—don't do this. You do your sister's memory no honour when you make her death an excuse to kill those who offer you no threat, even vhalgods..."

"*Even* vhalgods, thank you, little brother," Hedge muttered. She turned to watch behind them and above, where the lions climbed, two to either side, two up onto the spur of stone. Not that Jinn needed someone to watch his back, but he could watch hers.

She wished Pony would wake up. Pony could manage the lions, Hedge thought. She had no doubt she herself and Jinn could kill the beasts, enough of them to drive the others off, pack-hunting animals not being utter fools, but she'd rather not have to.

"...and such an oath is not one you should keep."

A grunt of effort, a scrape of stone. She spared a glance from the lions to see that Jinn was forcing the godling back.

"Have you tried to find her?" Jinn asked.

"I waited," the lion-man said. "In our golden hills below the White Mountains, I waited, though all was waste, the land plundered, the valleys barren, the springs dry and the herds driven away. The land was dead. I waited, and she did not come home. So we went, the lions and I, following the bison, into the east we went, and back across the north of the world, hunting the caribou, and she did not come to us, and the winters were cold and the wolves were many, and she did not come. So I swore my oath, that I would make the vhalgods, who had destroyed our world and my sister, my prey."

"How many vhalgods have you slain since you swore this oath?" Hedge asked grimly. "And how many of them were innocent travellers who meant you no more harm than I and my companions did?" She was becoming less inclined to use the flat of her blade on this overwrought godling, if he swung that mace at her again.

At least, though, he had not thought to kill her sleeping. He had meant her to wake. In his own mind, at least, it had not been murder he intended, but some duel of justice.

Hedge says I make excuses for him that he does not deserve.

"Shut up, Kanna," said Jinn, and he struck and twisted with the shaft of his lance as if he fought staff to staff, and the godling's mace was wrenched loose from his grip and fell clattering on the stones. A swipe of his foot, a buffet of his wing; he knocked the lion-man to his knees, and the spear's vhalmetal point he pressed to the godling's breast was very physical indeed, and very sharp. "Vinya, this is not a land for lions."

"This is not a world for vhalgods."

"What other place do we know, those of us here now, those of us born to this world? There is no way back. How do you say, this is not my world, this is not my sister's world, when it is the only one we have ever known? We are earth of its earth, water of its water, breath of its breath, as your lions are. Dream of its dreaming. Soul of its soul. We can no more be sundered from it than can you. Vinya, let my sister try to call yours to us. Even fallen into the dreaming between, a godling may answer. Let her speak herself. I knew her, I tell you. She would not want you to take such a vengeance on wandering folk merely for being of this kind or that. Never."

The godling's answer was to sweep up his mace from the ground again and, shivering into a place between, a form godly, ghostly half-dreaming, to strike at Jinn's head. Almost, the vhaldrach was too late to twist himself from the blow. Almost, and flames flared around the both of them, ghost and godling, the cold pale green of the northern lights, became a burn like ice, eating at the seeming of matter Jinn had drawn to himself by the power of his sister's blood. The lions, loosed by the godling's command, sprang on Hedge.

Poor beasts. The flat of her sword would not save her then. She drove her blade deep into the chest of the first to reach her, dragged it free even as she fell under the second, striking and drawing across the back of the big cat's neck as it bore her down, a killing blow. The remaining three backed away, hissing. Hedge dragged herself out from beneath the dead she-lions, their blood hot and wet, soaking through to her skin. She yelled Jinn's name, leapt down to him even as he broke his contact with the lion-man, flung himself backward almost at Hedge's feet. He sprang up again in the shelter of her sword, swept a hand, not the spear, through the blood that soaked her tunic, and put himself within the lion-man's arms, close as a dancing partner, trusting to Hedge to block the downwards swing of the mace or avoid it.

Openhanded, Jinn struck, palm spread on the lion-man's pale-furred chest. Blood of the godling's cats, of his kin, the bond he had made with them. Maybe it would be enough. And Jinn spoke a word in the tongue of the vhalgods, a word of their maguscraft, and all the draining life of Hedge's wound that he had taken into himself he put into it, vhalgod blood. And the godling folded to the ground, knees first, staring, blinking, only puzzled, a little, swaying, and then crumpling forward. Hedge caught him before his muzzle hit the ground, laid him over on his side. Touched his throat, where no pulse of life fluttered.

"You killed him," she said. "By magery, oh, Jinn—"

Jinn shook his head. Held out a hand for her to help him sit up, for he had fallen flat, but he was the shadow of stone and the light of the moon and the cold of a winter wind again, and all her hand met was a chill in the air.

"Sleep," he said. "A long, long sleep." And Hedge, kneeling with her other hand still on the lion-man, did feel that, not a breath, but within, the spark of life, such as it is in a godling.

"How long?" she asked, and looked to where the three living she-lions had sunk down, two curling, one sprawled, as kittens drop into sleep from play. No breath stirred the dust before their nostrils, but they did not seem, when she went over to lay a hand on one, quite dead.

Jinn shook his head. "Till his sister Lavinor comes again to wake him, I think. I hope. That was in my intention." Which, as you know from the tales, is the true power of a vhalgod magus, their words only a form to hold what their will would shape. "A sleep untouched by cold and heat," said Jinn, half chanting, as if he went over in his mind some teaching—he had had great scholars and magi, human and vhalgod both, to tutor him as a boy, which his bastard-born sister never did. "Untouched by thirst and hunger, by pain, undreaming, out of time. I hope." He shrugged. "I couldn't let him kill you, Kanna. I didn't want you to have to kill him."

"We can't leave them out on the mountainside," said Hedge, getting to her feet again, looking around, as if she hoped to see some cabin they had overlooked.

"You're hurt."

"Scratched. It will mend." Which her shirt and tunic wouldn't, not without needle and thread, and by what means was she to keep Pony from wondering how she'd come by not only the rips in her clothing, even if she did manage to sew them up before anyone else woke, but the four bloody gashes in her arm?

Scratches, hah. She still has the scars, though among all the others, who's to notice, she says.

Jinn made a helpless motion of his hands, as if he would help. Looked over to the dead she-lions, but all life was fled them, their pooling blood no use now to feed a ghost. Had he fed on their life's blood spilled in the moment of their death, rather than using it to bind the godling, he might have made himself strong in the world for a much, much longer time. If he had been willing to risk the desire that might have waked, made the horror of the dark empty Beyond pulling him back that much harder to surrender himself to again.

"I can't help. Do you want me to wake Pony? The lion-man's bespelling of them will be fading."

"Let her sleep." Hedge sighed. "I don't want to thrash all this over, how it would have gone differently if only I'd woken her to talk him around, and you know she'll want to. And the child doesn't need to see this slaughter. Poor creatures."

Jinn shivered, drifted to mist and was gone. But he was back almost at once, not in any clear form, even to her eyes, only a shadow, a voice in her mind.

There's a cave. Narrow, but deep. They've made that their lair. Down around behind that farther spur of stone.

So alone—foolish of her, I wouldn't have said she'd done ill, I'm sure I wouldn't have said we should wake the lion-man to try to argue him into a changed mind, even if I could have woken him, which I could—well, be that as it may, Hedge alone lifted and carried the lion-man, heaved over her back, into the deep recesses of his lair, where there was a nest of bracken. She laid him carefully there, lying on his side. Carried the smallest she-lion to curl beside him. Dragged, careful as she could, the other two, left them close as if they had warmth to share.

She did not try to raise a cairn over the two dead she-lions, only straightened out their limbs, closed their eyes. The birds of the fell would give them the burial of their kind; she was swaying with weariness, and her arm throbbed. Jinn was at her shoulder, aware, but unspeaking, hardly to be felt at all.

Then she trudged back down to where we slept, Arrany and I. On the way, she turned aside to a trickling stream, stripped off tunic and shirt and breast-band, scrubbed them in the cold water that is best for removing blood, cleaned her arm, and went to hang the wet clothing over sticks near the dying fire, which she built up high again with the last of the wood we had gathered.

"What have you been doing to yourself?" I asked sleepily, as she rolled herself and her blankets up against my back. Even through the blankets, she was cold as ice.

"Walking," she said. "Bad dreams. It's nothing. I snagged myself on the branch of a dead thorn-tree and cut myself. It'll mend. Go back to sleep," she added, as I started to stir into more coherent wakefulness. "It's nothing, Pony. Sleep."

It wasn't nothing, but she didn't want to talk about it, so I let her not talk about it. I turned over and pulled her closer, wriggled and dragged at blankets till there were none between us and twice as many over her, and held her while she shivered herself to sleep. In the morning, I very carefully did not ask about the gashes on her arm, which she smeared with a salve from the pot given to her by Goodbrother Bessamy—a very claw-laden dead tree, it had been that she met. Nor did I ask about the shirt and the tunic, which needed a great deal of stitching.

Nor, for that matter, her insistence that we take a different route than we had planned, the other side of the high crest we had been approaching.

She would tell me in her own good time, I knew. She always does.

5

IN WHICH ARRANY IS MISPLACED

Heading up over the high pass we fell in with company, other travellers who were as glad to have us join them for my songs as for my armed companions, and from there we turned southerly, to go along with the high land on our right shoulder. The solstice was past by then and summer rich, the land all lushly green and golden, honey-rich and berry-ripe and the milk flowing plentiful, the folk well-provisioned and welcoming. Never a better time for journeying. We meant to come to where we could cross east below the Lake of Birds through the Lowlands, to come to the valley of the Rhunavon and retrace Arrany's route up into the White Mountains.

Meant to, I say, for that's when they snatched Arrany right from under our noses.

An evening of rain, it was, and strong wind and thunder cracking over the lake, whose shore we were following. Pink-white sheets of lightning splashed the clouds, and we'd been glad enough to see the looming bulk of an old imperial inn sitting between lake and highway. Another road branched off inland there, and a bit of a village had grown up around the inn and the meeting of ways, as so often happened. Sometimes those old inns were ruinous, and sometimes they'd become a covered market or a chieftain's hall, but often, like this one, they still offered shelter, though for weary travellers rather than imperial functionaries. The Emperor's Head was its name, and Hedge strode under the swinging bright-painted sign over the arched passage and through to the open yard without a second glance, though Arrany looked up at it, the ugly grimacing severed head and fallen crown—he was handsome enough in real life, Eksandron was, may his soul flee outcast and howling forever—and looked at me, and to Hedge, and back at me again. I shrugged. He might have been her father, but there'd been little love between them even when she was still a loyal soldier.

Hedge spoke to the innkeeper and saw Dandelion stabled. We bespoke a small room to ourselves on the gallery towards the back, and joined the throng in the common parlour for a dish of what was hot and a mug or two of the hopped Lowland ale. Warm and dry and nicely full, for whoever did the cooking at the Emperor's Head was a rare hand with a pie, I took a chair with my back to the fire and tuned my harp, but I didn't begin to play, only set it down by my feet and waited to be invited.

There was another harper seated by the fire already. And there is, of course, a due politeness to be observed. He was a proper bard. Burnett, his name. Grey hair, grey beard, fingers gnarled and knobby with age, when we came in he had nevertheless been drawing from his harp a slow tune of such sweetness and beauty, like a thrush singing to greet the dawn, that I could happily have sat and listened all evening. He had a girl with him, his granddaughter Henza, his apprentice, and she played a wooden flute that danced over and under and through his tune. Then he passed the harp to her and rubbed his painful hands when he thought no one was looking, and she played and sang herself, with a little smile at me that was friendly enough, but a challenge as well. When she was done she gestured to me with an open hand, so I gave them my name, which was Pony, and a song I'd made for the smith of Smithsford when she was courting, a light little thing of lovers in spring, and then I bowed my head to the old bard and packed my harp away again, to show the evening was his—he and young Henza looking a bit tattered and down at heel and like they might be in greater need of whatever coin the company chose to share. It's a hard life, that of the road.

A story, the company called for, and the old bard said, well, there we all were on the shore of the Lake of Birds, and they were on their way to Rhunaburg, he and Henza, and did we know the tale of Prince Tavris and the King of the Marshlanders. They did, of course, though you may not. It's one of the old stories that has fallen by the wayside these days, though the bards still learn it, and the scholars have it written down, the better to argue over what's truth and what's fancy. It's not so often told by the fireside as it used to be, for Tavris stayed true to his blighted father Eksandron in the civil wars, and died at his own brother's hands as they fought in the air over the harbour at Ghedhaynor. That loyalty to his father and the empire gets him tallied among the wicked vhalgods in the end. In his own lifetime, though, Tavris was a prince beloved in tales of adventure: generous, valiant, honourable, and just—all that a prince, vhalgod or human, should be—and even after Ghedhaynor ceased to be anything more than town and a university sitting amid the ruins of a once-great and terrible city, he was regarded by the folk of Rhunaburg as their own particular hero, till they forgot, I think, that he was anything to do with the empire at all.

If I saw that Hedge was frowning, I thought it was because she didn't like to hear of herself in songs, for she comes into that story. It must hurt, to remember a time when your brothers were living and by your side, and to hear of their doings made nothing but a story on another's tongue, knowing what would come.

And if I saw that Arrany had gone off to talk with a table of assorted folk, at least one of whom looked to be a Marshlander boatsman, by his short jacket and his broad-brimmed hat of tight-woven reeds, I thought nothing of that either, beyond that she'd be wanting a bit of news from her home. Besides, the Marshlanders did not come off well in this story of Tavris and the great serpent, and likely enough she knew it.

I won't give you the whole of the story here, and not as Burnett told it, chanting the traditional way with the harp his granddaughter played running a soft murmur beneath. The meat of the matter was that long before the empire tore itself apart in blood and fire, when great Rhunaburg was only a town on the point overlooking the mouth of the Rhunavon, not the stone-walled city it is now, that town was sore beset, for the Marshlanders who dwelt on the swampy isles between the mouths of the Rhunatam that drained the lake were united as they never had been before and never have been since, under a single king who had brought the kings and queens of all the tribes of the Marsh under his sway and held the banks of the Rhunatam in fear of him so far south as the Lake of Birds itself. For some years they had been preying on the shipping of the lake as the wolf preys upon the lambs in spring, seizing goods, seizing captives, selling those not swiftly ransomed into captivity, and generally making no small nuisance of themselves. But in a dark autumn of storms the trouble went from bad to worse, for that was the season there first began to be tales of the great serpent.

Boats set out and were never heard from again. Wreckage was found, floating, broken boards and spars, but little other flotsam, for somehow the crates and barrels and baskets of the goods they carried were never found, till they came to other ports of the Lake of Birds as cargo of the Marshlanders' reed-bundle boats. And there were bodies washed ashore or found floating, arms and legs and even heads torn away, or arms and legs without bodies, and it seemed as if some great beast had been at them, flinging its supper about, as maybe you've seen a puppy play with a rag doll, tossing and shaking and ripping. Ships of hunters were sent out to protect the cargoes and the trade of the tribe of Rhunaburg. The ones that never met the serpent were the lucky ones, for their spears and arrows were little use against the thing that rose against them, dark beneath the waves, a vast bulk armoured and armed with jagged fangs and spear-spiked fins and a tail that lashed and twined and beat and crushed the keels of the little ships of the Lake of Birds like eggshells in the hand.

What the bard didn't say was that bones-rotted Eksandron was even then turning his mind to the north; he had already sent his god-hunters up the valley of the Rhunavon, and the godlings of the valley were taken or destroyed, and the godlings of the coast around Rhunaburg, and that was why, it may be, that the King of the Marshlands and his great serpent wife came to seize the town in the first place.

Aye, the serpent was none other than the wife of the King of the Marshlanders, and whether she was some creature of the Marshlands or a thing born of the depths of the Lake, or a human witch who'd learnt an ancient magic to change her shape I never heard, but a time came when the attacks were no longer confined to shipping, for the serpent came slithering by night up the lanes and alleys of the town, and carried off young and old alike from their beds, leaving broken doorways and smashed walls behind. The King of the Marshlands sent a messenger to say he could give Rhunaburg protection against the curse of the great serpent, but the chieftains of the town must not only pay tribute to him, but give over all shipping on the Lake of Birds to the reed boats of the Marshlanders.

The council of chieftains gave the king soft words meant to put him off while they worked, they said, to gather together the treasure he demanded.

In those days, having brought all the lands of the east under their dominion, the legions of bloody Eksandron's Ghedhaynor had crossed the Lammergeier's Pass and defeated the tribes of the upper reaches of the Rhunavon. Their fortresses and their stone highways were spreading through the northern foothills of the White Mountains, and their scouts and their spies (and the accursed emperor's god-hunters) ran northward down the valleys, in forest's shadow or on the wings of the wind—the wings of the vhaldrachen, rather.

The chieftains of Rhunaburg sent a messenger themselves to the imperial fortress near to where the Rhunavon, flowing westward, swings round to the north, a fastness that was not so much the frontier of empire as a beachhead soon to be overleapt, and offered to put themselves under the protection of Ghedhaynor, if only the vhalgods would come and free them from the terror of the serpent.

Out of the frying pan, as they say.

But they called for help, and the empire, in the person of Prince Tavris, answered. He'd been sent to make some assessment of the doings of the commanders of the legions in the north, to be the emperor's trusted eyes and ears, but the human story would have him simply a wandering hero waiting for adventure to find him, as either way it did, and he set off down the river valley to the north. In some versions of the tale he comes a lone hero flying swift in answer, for he was winged vhaldrach, but as Bard Burnett told it he sailed down the river with companions: Naskanna, not yet named the Deathdealer, who guarded his back; Atana his foster father, who was a Duke of the Crossing, as they called the nobles and officers who'd followed cursed Eksandron on the dangerous journey through the Rift from the land of the vhalgods and who stood at the prince's side to offer counsel; and his brother Jinn, a young magus fresh from his studies, not yet the great commander of the Emperor's scouts and spies he later became, and just recovering from a long illness. I'm surprised memory of that had lingered into the bard's tale.

When they came to Rhunaburg matters had gone from bad to worse, for the serpent had come in the night and carried off the daughter of one of the chieftains, her life to be the payment for the town's surrender.

It's a story of fear and terror, of brave warriors of Rhunaburg slain on the threshold of the hall, of a daughter lost, a father distraught, a council divided against itself—for some there were who knew full well that it was the empire had deprived them of the godlings who might have protected them and would not at any price have had the the vhalgods there, thinking it better to give themselves over to human Marshlander rule. The prince, grant him his due, ignored the advice of Atana, who put little value on human lives and saw only an opportunity for Eksandron to add Rhunaburg to his empire without the expense of conquering it, and of Naskanna, who did not think she could do much as his bodyguard once he went flying off without her. They would have had him wait and lay cunning traps, which might have lost more human lives, but which would not have put Tavris's imperial person at risk. But Tavris ignored all their arguments, flying off with only his still-fragile brother at his side to track the serpent to her lair. The two princes, vhaldrachen both, ventured alone across the lake and all the way into the wild Marshlands to rescue the kidnapped maiden.

There's no denying the bravery of Tavris and Jinn, and the danger they put themselves in to bring the child back to her parents, and true enough that Tavris fought the great serpent and for all his strength and skill with his vhalmetal halberd had a hard fight of it, and there was the king and his Marshlander warriors to reckon with, too. The princes did not escape unscathed, either of them, but the lass was saved and those chieftains of Rhunaburg that would give over their town to the protection of the empire had their way. And whether in the long run Rhunaburg came out of that with honour, well...

I suppose it's all water under the bridge, as they say.

As the bard was telling his tale, there was coming and going, night falling and candles lit, and more folks come in off the road out of the storm. Locals from the village, too, as word went out there were storytellers come. So, picture the folk coming in, hanging hats and shawls and cloaks to drip, shaking water from their hair, other folk going off home or to find their lodging places, and then, as the bard was just finishing his tale, there came a great crash of thunder and someone calling, the horses are out, and we all—all who had beasts stabled, along with those who thought a little excitement worth a wetting—went rushing through into the yard, where true enough there were rain-wet horses and ponies and a few donkeys milling about, confused and peevish, and a small terrier yapping angrily at the lot of them, for what good that did. Of course, the rush of folk to sort out their own set the dog yapping worse, the horses spooking at all the flapping hats and wraps and waving arms, and with the dark and someone swinging a lantern, it was a while before sensible heads prevailed and Hedge was able to shoo the bystanders inside. Meanwhile the wife of the innkeeper couple and I, and those who did have beasts stabled, got our own quietened and back to their stalls. Only then did the stabler come woozily in search of her masters with a great lumpen bruise blackening on her temple and a tale of strangers, their faces hidden by scarves, turning the horses loose and thumping her when she tried to stop them.

So there was an outcry renewed, and I don't know if in all the confusion the poor old bard and his granddaughter were able to collect the coin that should have been their due for such a well-told tale. I hope they at least got their supper and their night in the warm and dry. The innkeepers took the poor stabler away to tend her head and set her lad to tallying the beasts. His memory wasn't of the best, but everyone found their own with none missing, and it seemed maybe that whoever had raised the alarm had scared the thieves off before they could make away with any animals. We were all inside again, wet and angry, wet and laughing, wet and puzzling as our nature took us, when Hedge loomed out of the shadows and plucked my sleeve.

"Where's Arrany?" she asked.

I looked around. I didn't see her.

"Out to make sure Dandelion's taken no harm?" I suggested, though, come to think of it, I hadn't seen her in the yard, nor in the stables after.

"No. Not in our room, either. I've checked."

"She must be here somewhere." I shook my head at someone calling for me to take my turn at the entertainment and give them the song of the great cattle theft of the Hirran-Rasi, casting around, looking through all the shadows. No Arrany.

Her hat, though, was fallen down under a bench in the corner where she'd sat talking to her fellow Marshlander and his cronies, and I ducked in amongst the folk chattering there now, with apologies, to pick it up. Did they see where the Marshlanders had got to, I asked, and they knew nothing of any Marshlanders, they'd seen the empty corner and taken it, after the excitement of the straying horses.

You might be thinking, we should have asked Jinn, but the ghost comes and goes, in accordance with his own will or maybe some unchartable tide of the outer darkness, and the presence of a great crowd of the living makes it not so easy as at other times, for all that Hedge herself, and the flute she carries, is a beacon to draw him, an anchor to hold him, the heart and centre and root of his presence in the world. Which is to say, he hadn't been there with us in the inn, not that I'd noticed, and Arrany's peril, comrade of the road though she'd become to Hedge and me, wasn't enough to draw his notice through that connection binding him to his sister.

Hedge was already striding through the entry hall and bursting into the kitchens beyond. I went trotting after her, to catch up before she broke something. Or someone.

"The Marshlanders," she demanded, and be sure it was a demand. "The Marshlander boatman in the common room and the crew with him, when did they leave and where did they go?"

A busy kitchen, with a great brick stove, and young folk washing dishes and chattering loud, pots still bubbling, cooks still stirring, someone coming up wide stairs from a cellar with a tray of mugs, and the stabler sat in a chair by the fire with a poultice of some sort bound to her forehead and the old innkeeper-man putting a steaming cup into her hand. They all looked up staring, as well they might. But a bit of talk convinced even Hedge that they knew nothing of any Marshlanders, beyond that aye, a party with a Marshlander captain had come in off the lake just as the rain started that evening, and they'd not taken any rooms, but meant to sleep in their boat. Aye, goodfriend, Marshlanders did that often enough, came down along the coast from where the Rhunatam flowed out from the lake, that river that spread itself in uncounted braided channels through the Marshlands, seeking its way north to the sea. Traders, fishers or eelers with a catch to sell...

Not that this lot were all Marshlanders, by their tongue, the woman who'd brought them their soup and pie said, some of them having the speech of Rhunaburg, that sounded all slow and mooing, which is why in the fireside stories they say the folk of the Lowlands have cows' tails. What had they talked of, goodfriend? She hadn't listened, you didn't listen, when you were serving guests, you only heard this and that, goodfriend, you know how it is. Though true enough, they'd been talking with that yellow-haired lass we'd come in with… And then remembering just what had occurred, Well, she'd thought they all looked respectable enough or she'd have told the masters right off, she'd never taken them for horse thieves.

"Our friend is no horse thief and nothing to do with your pranksome traders, beyond having speech to catch up on news from her homeland, as any traveller might," I said. "And what does a boat crew want with horses? It seems to me it wasn't horses they were after stealing, but our own lass, and what kind of an inn is this, that it lets those who steal away young lads and lasses go about their foul trade in its very parlour—?"

Hedge tugged my sleeve to shut me up before I outright accused the landlords of abetting slavers. For all that the overthrow of the emperor, rot his bones, put an end to such practices in law there were always rumours of young folk bought and sold and apprenticeships that were no such thing.

"Boat," Hedge said to me, and drew me away. We went out and an inn servant came running after us, to show us that we could get to the pebbled hardstanding and the docks of the inn through another arched gateway out of the yard by the rear stable wing. Sent to soothe our tempers and show they were no friends to whoever had done this, I supposed, and once my temper cooled I could admit, sent because they were decent folk and outraged as we were. Not that the gate had been left open, he assured us, and not that they'd gone that way, because he'd seen them go out the front while everyone was rushing out to see about the horses. But it would be faster for us—

He squeaked as Hedge grabbed him and lifted him up against the wall. He was a young lad, and small. She only needed one hand. "You saw them leave. Was our friend with them? The pretty girl with the yellow hair?"

Perhaps our tempers were not so soothed as all that.

"Maybe?" he said. "I don't know, goodfriends, I only keep up the fires and sweep the floors, I don't serve at the tables, to be getting a good look at girls, pretty or otherwise. More's the pity."

Cheeky little imp, he was.

"But there were a dozen of them, a mixed party, two or three Marshlanders and the others folk of the Lowlands, and they all left together in such a rush. And the thing is, I thought it was one of them cried the alarm about the horses, coming in from the privy."

"Put him down, sweetheart," I said, because Hedge was about to try shaking more out of him, and it didn't seem to me there was more to be had. "She's..." Aye, we had travelled long enough together, grown close enough in caring, I had the sense of Arrany by then. I reached, and I felt, and I found what I reached for. "She's on the water, out on the lake."

Hedge snarled, not at the lad, though he flinched from it, set him on his feet and patted his head by way of apology, as if he'd been a dog unfairly scolded. And he lifted the bar of the water gate and let us through, so we could go down to the hardstanding where the Marshlanders' long reed-bundle boat—lake-runner, he called it, ones they made for use not in their own marshes but for lake-trading, with a short mast and lateen sail slung below a long yard—was manifestly *not* waiting.

Waves crashing up, curling down in white froth. Clouds breaking, wind-torn; ragged rents letting a night sky bright with stars show through. The storm was ending. It would be a while before the waters calmed, though, and I feared for anyone out on the water in a small boat this night. The Lake of Birds in a temper can be more sea than lake, for all its waters are sweet.

Those reed boats, coated with the black tar that rises to form pools in some of the sandy ridgelands of the Marshes, bend and flex with the swells, ride them up and slide and twist, and stay afloat, so long as they're not rotting and waterlogged, and surely the Marshlanders knew what they were about.

Well, the innkeepers had talked themselves back around to thinking we and Arrany and her abductors were all in some mischief together by then, so we went quiet to our room and made no more fuss about our missing companion, whose cloak was slung forlorn on the wide bed along with the rest of our gear.

"Off you go, Pony," says Hedge. "I'll meet you on the road."

And I ruffle up my feathers and perch on the windowsill. A crow's no good for the night, so I take the shape of a grey owl instead. A bit awkward at first, as when you try to do something delicate with your wrong hand. But off, as she says, I go.

Finding the boat wasn't so difficult, for there wasn't much out on the lake at all by night. They had the sail raised and were scooting along at a fair clip, not keeping near inshore, either, nor running to the north. Bound easterly, they were, the boat rushing up and leaping down the waves, the man with the broad straw hat—he had a scarf over it, tied tightly under his chin—leaning hard on the steering-oar and another keeping hold of the sheets, as shipfolk call the ropes that work the sail. Some of the others looked as if they'd rather have been elsewhere, gripping tight amid the barrels and bundles lashed to the deck, crouching low as if they feared to be flung over into the deeps by the boat's salmonlike leaping, though a couple were making themselves useful by bailing with hide buckets as the water came flying over. And there at the foot of the mast was a sort of bundle, worryingly limp, a sack half-wrapped in tarpaulin, you might think, but I knew the boots sticking out of it. Bought them myself in Avondon.

I circled the boat, landed to cling to the yard, twisting to peer down at Arrany. Alive, and as I swayed there she moaned and moved a little. One of the crouching people prodded her and said something about getting more of the same if she didn't mind her manners better. By which I understood they'd thumped her as they bustled her out in the confusion of the horses, and almost I dropped down among them, to set them between the terror of wolf and wave. But common sense said I hadn't the strength of the earth under me here, to put the fear and awe of a godling on them, and they were a dozen, armed with knives and spears, and if they did for me I might be a long time drawing myself back together in any bodily form again.

I let go the yard and floated down, soft in the dark. Nothing but the broken starlight in scraps between the clouds, not a single candle-lantern lit. They didn't notice me. I called out then, a soft *whoo-hoo, whoo-hoo,* and went flapping up again as they yelped and flailed about in startlement. If Arrany had begun to get her wits back, she would hear that owl close by her ear and know herself not abandoned. Or so I hoped. It was all I could do, till they came again to land.

6

IN WHICH ARRANY IMITATES THE ACTION OF AN OTTER

Arrany heard the owl calling, close by her head. In her muddled dreaming it was trying to tell her something, but she couldn't understand what, and that distressed her, so she muttered and moaned and tried to thrash herself free, which got her a kick in the ribs and another warning to lie quiet or they'd throw her overboard and have done with. It didn't occur to her then that, since they'd gone to such lengths to carry her away, they must want her alive; she groaned and lay still, trying to sort out what had happened. That Marshlander—he'd said his name was Cornan, of the Sharbeleyn in the southeastern channels—had caught her eye and beckoned across the wide room, and she'd gone over to see what he wanted, uncertain but that he might have recognized her and be carrying some message from her home, uncertain, if that were the case, that she wanted to be either recognized or given messages, which were likely only to be demanding that Penryl bring himself back to their mother at once. But the man, a nosy sort, had only been wondering what a daughter of the Marshlands was doing wandering the roads got up like a merchant's guard—as if she couldn't possibly be that in truth, and then, sensing he'd offended, he'd turned to gossip of the Marshlands. Had she heard that the firstborn daughter of the queen of the Esrineyn, her heir, had caught herself the second son of the king of the Centamineyn to wed that spring, and not a month after the wedding wasn't the old queen Esmilly dead of fever, having gone out with some of her household after the spring run of smelt and taken a chill in the sleet of a late spring gale instead? And the king of the Wesgelteyn, Wesgarfel, he was, well, he was dead the winter past. Fever, that was, too, set in his lungs, as was the way of death on the Marshes for the old, as she'd know as well as him, and King Wesgarfel had named no heir so his son and daughter were dividing the land between them in the old way. That was only going to cause strife and misery in the long run, Cornan was thinking, and what tribe was Arrany herself from? Somewhere in the west, by her accent...?

Arrany thought she remembered she had said Centamineyn, which wasn't the truth. Had used her own name, which wasn't wisdom. Remembered, later, how he'd looked, then, dragging the woman next to him close, arm around her shoulders, whispering against her ear, but catching at Arrany's sleeve when she pushed back from the table and would have risen to leave. She hadn't wanted to make a fuss, had not wanted to be there at all, her stomach gone sick and heavy with the good food and ale sitting like wet sand and her mouth dry and her mind gone to a strange buzzing, like bees swarming, taking all her thought.

Dead.

So she had sat, perched on the edge of the stool, putting his hand off her. He was drunk, some small bit of her still living thought, and looked around, but Pony was in the midst of the crowd intent on the old bard telling his story by the fire, her face alive with her delight in the tale, and Hedge was watching the godling with a look...well, someday, maybe, it might be she'd find one who would watch her the way Hedge watched Pony, that was all.

Was she looking for hire, Cornan wanted to know? His crewwoman had pushed away and gone out to the yard, seeking the privy, she supposed. After, Arrany would remember how she'd stopped to mutter quiet with two and three others of the crew on the way.

"I could use a good hand with the boat, my crew's mostly outlanders and not a webbed foot among them..." which was a Marshlander joke. No, she told him, and made no excuses, lost all need to make those polite excuses, only pushed away, gone clumsy, gone sweating and angry and if he'd laid hand on her arm yet again she'd have struck it off with hot words, but suddenly all the room was in an uproar, people on their feet crying out the horses were loose, thieves, fire, who knew what all. Someone had grabbed her and swung her around; her head had slammed one of the posts that were scattered through the broad room holding up the floor above and she'd fallen, stunned. They'd pulled her up—she wasn't sure who they were, only the Marshlander Cornan was among them—and rushed her out the front door in the midst of them. When she stumbled, they dragged her up and carried her. Through the dark and the rain, she writhing and thrashing like a landed fish, and down in the mud by the hardstanding as they ran their boat out. She yelled once, and they thumped her again as they hauled her all anyhow over the side and dumped her in. She'd thrown up then, she thought she remembered, sick with the knock on the head. Her mouth still tasted foul. They'd wrapped her up in something heavy, rain-wet, and dragged a sack that smelt of mouldy grain over her head; by then the boat had been alive, running the waves. She'd heard the creak and squeak of the yard being raised, the mast groaning as the sail caught the wind...Then nothing, only a hazy sort of miserable half-sleep in the bad dream that was no dream, till the owl called.

Pony, she thought.

Her mother was dead, and the owl was Pony. And her mother was dead, but Pony knew where she was, Pony would come, with Hedge, and she wasn't lost and abandoned. So she curled herself up small to keep warm under a fold of the tarpaulin—having, in some corner of her mind where none of this was real, a water-woman's grim thoughts about the slovenly sort of master who would leave his awning piled in a mouldering heap—and tried to work the sack off her face a little, so she might make a guess at where they were heading, but the few stars she could glimpse between the tattered clouds wove and blurred and smeared across her vision, threatening to make her throw up again, so she shut her eyes against them.

And her mother was dead.

They'd taken her sax and her knife at some point, but at least her hands weren't tied. Even armed, what could she have done against so many? Well, seized the captain and forced the crew to put her ashore at peril of his life, she thought, and kept that thought for later, when she was not so sick and dizzy, and might get her hands on a weapon again.

They sailed through the night. Arrany slept. In the dawn she woke, and though her head ached, a thud thud thud like the slap of the waves, and she had a tender swollen lump on her temple, she did not feel so queasy and feeble as she had. Mostly, she felt hollow. If her mother were behind this—if she had gone to such lengths, sending thugs like these to find her and Penryl and fetch them home—but her mother was dead and this would be the third summer of their absence from the aits of the Esrineyn and it was unlikely anyway that any agents of their mother's would adopt so violent an approach. Carry messages, argue, order her return, to face accusation and yelling and the mounting of an expedition to the far unknown White Mountains and Under-Ice, to fetch Penryl home, yes. Not this.

Third thoughts were, this travelling the coast of the Lake of Birds was the first she had come so near the Marshlands since they left, the first she'd come within reach. She'd been a fool. She should have argued for going south from Dahres Water, and crossing through the Lowlands as she'd come.

But how could she have known?

Missal—Esmissal she would be now, and married, hope the young lord she'd chosen either knew his own mind or had no objection to having his life run for him—had never had much patience with her younger siblings, never much tolerance for their mother's indulgence of Pen. To send word out to haul them home by force, that was Lady Missal. Queen Esmissal. Penryl was hers, her witch, an asset to her hall and thus it was her right to have him home, that was

Esmissal's thinking. And what was a not-particularly-useful younger sister's aching head and humiliation to that right?

"So," Cornan said, leaving his post at the steering oar to another and coming to squat down by her. "Where's the other one?"

"What?" she asked.

"The boy. Yellow-haired girl, Arrany by name. Yellow-haired boy. Pen-something."

"Penran," said one of the women, with the accent of Rhunaburg.

"Penryl," corrected the other Marshlander man.

"Whatever," said the captain. "Where's he got to? That young queen'll pay for even one, I have no doubt, but more for the full set."

"Never heard of him," Arrany said, with her heart pounding and her belly sick, in a way that was nothing to do with the rough waters.

"Hah," said the man, and chucked her under the chin, like she was some toddler acting cute. "A falling out among thieves, was it? Well, half's better than none at all."

"Thieves!" Arrany cried, and bit her tongue on *we* before it escaped her. "I'm no thief, and I've never heard of this Penryl. You've got the wrong woman."

"Yellow-haired girl, blue eyes, straight nose, small chin, dimples, not over-tall, name of Arrany. Yellow-haired boy, a handspan taller than the girl, vhalbairn eyes the colour of blued steel but human otherwise, straight nose with light freckles, weak chin, name of Penryl," Cornan said. "Nineteen years of age or thereabouts. Eight imperial taler for the pair of them, delivered alive and hale to the custody of the queen's hall on the Queen's ait of the Esrineyn or to the Esrineyn factor in Rhunaburg, and why's she paying such a price to get her hands on you, and alive, unless it's that you've something she wants?" He considered. Shrugged. "Spies, maybe? Assassins? Poisoned the old queen, maybe?"

"That's a lie!" she cried. "We're Missal's—the young queen's—own brother and sister."

He considered that. Snorted. Slapped her across the face. "That's as may be. I did hear there was a younger lord. But that's not the word going around, only that there's good coin to be paid for handing you over, so lady or not you may be, it doesn't much matter. Where's the other one, eh?"

"How should I know?" she asked, with her lip swelling and her cheek stinging, and angry tears starting in her eyes. "Left me and went off on his own spring before this, chasing some girl. Down to Ghedhaynor, she was bent on going. The university there. What would I do among the scholars? So I took service with a merchant of Thurbridge and went my way, and he went his." Anger in the words. Contempt, for stupid brothers who turned their backs on loyal sisters to chase new-met girls. Truth, enough to stop them trying to beat some other answer out of her, which she feared. Not that she had secrets to spill, none they didn't already know, her name and kin, only she feared the beating as any sensible being would. "And we're not thieves, nor spies, nor assassins, the river and sea stand my witness, it's only that she's desperate to have word of us, this bounty she's offering, of course she is, we're her only near kin save a few cousins. Penryl's her heir, till she has a child of her own. She won't thank you for this treatment of me, you can be certain of that."

Cornan snorted. "Doesn't sound any loving sister to me, setting a bounty on you. Wouldn't be the first time a queen had good reason to want brothers or sisters dragged home and kept close under her eye, would it?" He grinned.

True enough, her grandfather had come to wear the crown of the Esrineyn after he returned from service in some eastern war, he and a handful of close friends, fellow mercenaries, one of whom lived long enough to be remembered by Arrany as a dreadfully scary old woman indeed, and grandfather's elder sister had died not long after, and there were whispers...but there were always such whispers, when a queen or a king died unexpectedly.

No, she didn't, she wouldn't believe Missal wanted them dragged home to keep close under her eye for fear of them. Only that she'd grown up thinking Penryl and his witch-gift a resource of her own to command, and now that she was queen, she was going to have him back, if it took drastic measures even a possessive mother hadn't ventured. Their mother Esmilly would have been hurt, and angry, and hidden it behind a cold face. They'll come home when they're good and ready, her anger would have said, when they're cold and tired and hungry and finding the world beyond the Marshlands isn't at all houses tiled with gold. And she'd have sent her hunters out, that was certain, they'd been dodging them all the way to the Lake of Birds, till they lost the last of them in Rhunaburg. But Missal—aye, Arrany thought, that was Missal, the angry impatience, the reckless act without thought of what it might cost, how the sort of folk to go laying hands on strangers for hope of a reward might treat a body, when it was no longer a feeling being but only a weight of silver in their mind.

She feared, once she fell into Esmissal's hands, she would not easily get free again, to run back to Hedge and Pony. And no more than their mother did Esmissal have any power to bring against a vhalbairn witch, a magus, maybe, to have Penryl away out of her toils safe and sane.

Eight taler. That was twenty-four silver marks. At least her sister didn't value her siblings cheap.

"Well, thief or assassin or long-lost sister, makes no difference to me. Eight taler for the pair; that's four for you, anyway. So you be a good girl and make no trouble, and you can try your stories on the factor once we've got our twelve marks out of him."

None tried to prevent it, when she got her arms out of the heavy swaddling tarpaulin, freed herself of the sack and settled it over her shoulders for a bit of warmth, rain-wet as she and it both were in the dawn chill. An open boat, all the frames exposed, and the big block of the mast-foot. The cargo looked to be mostly barrels covered in tarpaulin. Salt eels, by the smell. The light grew, golden bright, the rainstorms past; they were sailing east. If they had been carrying her to the Marshlands it would have been north. She could hope the factor was some respectable citizen of Rhunaburg, someone who would know why the new queen had put a price on her head and treat her accordingly. Which ought to leave opportunity to escape, to rejoin Hedge and Pony. You couldn't lock Lady Arrany of the Esrineyn in your cellar, not if you wanted her sister's goodwill and continued patronage, no matter how aggravating Missal found Penryl's, and by extension Arrany's, behaviour.

Could she risk it?

Dared she?

What if the factor thought like Cornan, that lady or not, she was thief, killer, rival for the crown? And Penryl wasting away in the bed of the witch. What could Hedge and Pony do against a boat?

The sun brought little warmth to Arrany, damp and chilled to the bone as she was. A dozen of them, she counted. Too many to fight, and they weren't going to be charmed; it took no pretence to wrap her arms about herself, shivering, shoulders hunched, small and draggled and afraid. Studying her captors, squinting against the rising sun. They were a grubby, unpleasant lot, not folk you'd want to ship with, given a choice. Three of them Marshlanders, small light-haired folk like herself, and the rest of them of other kindreds, mostly bigger, stocky in build. She remembered an accent of the upper Rhunavon last night, rolling around the clipped, slurred version of the imperial vhalgod language that formed the one speech all the different human lands held in common, the trade tongue, it was beginning already to be called, rather than its own right name.

"Better tie her, captain," one of the Rhunaburger women said, and Arrany glared, narrow-eyed.

"Where's she going to go?" Cornan the captain asked. "She's not going to sprout wings and fly like a vhaldrach." He chortled at his own wit. Arrany, you may well imagine, flinched. And glared again. Cornan had Arrany's sax, and her knife and her purse, all still on her long belt, which the man had fastened loose about his own waist.

They left her down at the mast's foot out of the way, atop the heap of tarpaulin. At least, when they got their own breakfast, hard barley biscuit and chunks of greasy smoked eel with small beer to wash it down, one of the Marshlander crew brought Arrany her share. She made herself eat it, for all her aching head and sore mouth, and her fear-quashed appetite. She'd need her strength. Thanked the boatwoman who brought it nicely, too, meek and mild as new milk. Kept her ears open.

It seemed the boat was one that plied the Lake of Birds, doing a bit of this and that. Carrying cargo for others, doing a bit of trading of their own... Not, Arrany deduced, above a bit of plundering and theft, and none too fussy where their cargoes came from, either.

One of the men came over, nudged her with his toe. "Got any coin hidden in your boots?"

"No," Arrany said gloomily. Not that she expected the man to believe her, and sure enough, a little later they had the boots off her and were slitting the seams of them, looking for hidden pockets. Ruining good footwear to no point, that was.

About mid-morning a crow came slanting down the wind and circled the boat, cawing.

"Ill-omened vermin," one of the Rhunaburgers said, and a woman nocked an arrow to the string. I rose and slipped away side-long towards the shore again, trusting that Arrany, who seemed in better shape than last night, had seen. If they'd been less noticing and the boat larger, I'd have risked landing and hidden myself away, otter or wildcat, but as it was, it had been hard flying to chase them down and I couldn't keep following out of sight. They left me behind as I angled in to the distant shore, and aye, had to drive off my fellow crows and revive myself with the head of a dead fish washed up on the shingle, and I still wasn't fit for flying far. I hunkered down in the dense silver-greenery of a poplar tree shading the road and drowsed, waiting for the sound of boots marching a long swift stride and dainty hooves trotting after.

"They're making for Rhunaburg," I was able to report to Hedge, about noon of that first day of our pursuit.

"Rhunaburg, or any little lakeside village between here and there," countered Hedge, ever one to plan for the worst. She calls that being a realist.

"Well, at least they're not carrying her off into the Marshlands."

"Why are they carrying her off at all, that's what I want to know."

"We can ask them once we catch up."

"Oh, Pony, my dear, I am not planning on doing any asking of anything, when we catch up."

"Then there's no point your wondering why, is there?"

Hedge shrugged, conceding the point.

I didn't go flying out again, to exhaust myself over open water, but kept that sense of Arrany's whereabout in my mind, so that I could near as not point to where the boat was, drawing farther and farther away, but always following the lake's southern shore. Walking, Dandelion and myself, at Hedge's heel, while her long strides ate up the miles and she fell grim and silent into the measured beat of her marching, as the legions of the emperor had eaten up the miles, carrying his standard of the falling star across the human world. We stopped only to let the horse have feed and once in a while a little sleep, and I think Hedge might have abandoned her, only we both knew that care of the horse, which was after all not ours, was as good an excuse as any for me to force Hedge to have care for herself, and besides, if the horse didn't carry her armour, she'd have to lug it on her own back. But the wind held true out of the west and I could feel that Arrany was being carried farther and farther away.

ALMOST A HUNDRED MILES, the Lake of Birds is from end to end. The wind blew clean out of the west and, no need for tacking, drove them on like a leaf scudding over the waves, swift, swift sliding, towards the free city of Rhunaburg. Maybe it was the blow to the head Arrany'd had in the inn; such a wound does funny things to the mind, sometimes. So, there's no denying it, does grief. Something made her reckless, foolish-reckless, anyway, and though I'd like to say it was the fault of her youth, there's no denying she'd done well on the road since fleeing the robbers on her stolen horse, what with finding shelter and work through the winter, finding her way to us alone... finding us at all.

However it might be, the way Arrany worked it out, Hedge and Pony afoot might take four or five days to travel so far. No, she had not much faith in our ability to cover the miles—but she reckoned that for her on the boat, by noon of the following day, or sooner if the wind held true and strong from the west, the red-tiled roofs of Rhunaburg would loom on the horizon, bright in the sun.

Night fell. She had been quiet through the afternoon, docile and defeated at the foot of the mast, nursing her bruised head and mouth. She ate what they gave her, didn't try to have speech with any of them, didn't meet anyone's eyes. Given up to her fate. Come sunset this night they took the bundled awning into which she had been huddled and left her shivering in the cool wind with only a sack for blanket while they rigged the awning up behind the mast. Most of the crew rolled themselves up in cloaks and coats and blankets under it, leaving just the captain again at the steering-oar and one of his Marshlanders in the bow as lookout, where this time they had hung a lantern. Perhaps they expected others to be out on the water, night fishing or the like. Given where it was hung, and where the lookout chose to perch, Arrany considered it was not likely to do much more than spoil the man's night vision. The moon had waned and waxed to the full and was waning again, since we had come down from the high fells, and it was not yet risen.

She waited, and watched the stars turn the hours of the night away. The Marshlander woman took the captain's place at the steering-oar; another of the crew replaced the watchman and did not relight the lantern when its candle guttered and went out.

The stars wheeled through the sky. The moon, an amber crescent, rose in the east with its little dog circling it. The chatter of the water under the bow, the rhythmic knocking of the waves, worked on her, urging sleep. Arrany fought to stay wakeful, pinching herself, but her body betrayed her and she would jerk suddenly from a doze she hadn't intended, heart pounding, searching the sky again, frantic to judge the time. Soon, soon, she told herself. But not too soon. She slept, an hour, maybe more. Woke with a jerk. The sliver of moon and its little dog climbed higher, grew silver-bright; the stars that ran before summer's early dawn were rising. Soon, if only—aye, she looked, craning her neck up, rising to her knees, to eye the southern horizon and the east. They were dark and ragged, blacker than night, blacker than the soft star-spattered dark of the sky. Trees. A shoreline curving northerly. The boat was running in towards the coast, or maybe it was that the curve of the lake came over to meet them, on their course for Rhunaburg. And was the east, maybe, showing a faint lightening, just the promise of the night's thinning?

No more time to waste.

Web-footed Marshlander or not, scrambled wits and the weariness of grief or not, youthful recklessness or not, what she did next was folly. Careful, careful, moving slow to make no betraying rustle, no sudden accidental rap or knock, Arrany unfastened the horn toggles of the leather jerkin she'd had from an old guild-guard in the town where she'd wintered. Worked it off, and slowly, slowly shucked her woollen tunic. Waited, listening. No alarm. The lookout watched ahead; the cargo and the awning hid her from the steersman; the crew slept. She undid the drawstring of her trousers, much patched but good heavy woollen cloth still, and worked them down over her hips, pulling her socks away with them. Shivering, shivering, in only her linen drawers and shirt. Then she crawled, stealthy as an otter in the night, and like an otter, she went slipping sleek and sudden over the side. The boat rocked a little. Holding her breath, headfirst into the water. Deep, she swam, as long as her breath held out, and then she surfaced, treading water, to get her bearings.

There, the boat, flying eastwards, no outcry, no alarm. Not yet. There, the shore, looking a good bit further than it had when she was dry and settled aboard the boat, wrapped in her musty old sack with the mast solid against her back. The water was not bitter sea-cold, but hardly a warm bath, and the strong wind drove the waves slanting along, where she wanted to come to land as shortly as she could. She knew better than to fight against them. Arrany stretched herself on her back in the water and with gentle movements of hand and foot began to swim for shore, not cutting directly across the waves but not letting them push her into the long angle, either. Softly, softly she went, till she judged the boat too distant to make her out amid the waves even if they did light their lantern again, whereupon she rolled and set out at a faster stroke, still careful of splashing, with the distant trees her aim.

A longer, harder struggle than she had imagined, and she had known it would be no easy thing. On. On. Only the gasping of her own breath, the soft splash of a clumsy kick. Then shallows, hardly understood; all was cold, was limbs heavy as if her bones were turned to lead, was aching shoulders, aching thighs, the burning of water unexpected in the throat. Grating touch of stone. Slow realization that she had done it, she had come ashore, and the sun was bright and low in the northeast, seeming to rise from the lake, its fires dripping down to run out over the waves, and the boat—she crawled, stumbling on stones, crept like an animal out of the water, up onto the boulder-strewn shore to the shelter of a leaning willow and only then dared look. More than one sail showed on the water now, white, brown, ox-blood red, but only one dark-tarred reed boat with the high curving prow and squared hen's-tail stern, the dirty-white sail spilling wind, hanging slack as they laboriously tilted the yard full upright and twisted it around the mast, to swing about on the other tack, working their way back along the shore as near against the wind as they could come. Searching.

Had she been seen, between water's edge and the trees? Pale skin, pale hair, all in white linen. Nothing she could do now, if she had been. Arrany turned and clambered through the willow, not knowing where she went, only inland.

Dense wilderness, no cattle pastured amidst the trees. She knew from our talk that the imperial highway we had been following left the western end of the lake and struck down to meet the Rhunavon at a great westerly curve of its snaking course, but lesser roads crossed all that land below the Lake of Birds and there was a well-travelled one branching from the highway up along the lake to Rhunaburg. These woods, she knew, would only be some rough woodland that the road skirted; coming through, she would find herself among forest pastures or village meadows, if not on the road itself and...well, she did not know, precisely, what she might do then. Beg help until her friends should come, she supposed, or simply hide herself in some hay-barn and hope to hear a crow.

Perhaps that woodland had once been cleared, or it may be a

wildfire had burned it off, a generation before. There were great stumps where once mighty elms and oaks had reached to the sky, but now it was all dense young trees, mostly birch, pine, and silver maple, fighting for the light, and vines tangling and strangling, wild grape and ivy and wild cucumber dangling its lacy white flowers, with thorny roses of a yellow-flowering kind that flung their canes high overhead, supported on the branches of other trees. No breeze stirred the air. Woodpeckers yelped and warblers sang, and something big came crashing her way, sending her scrambling up the nearest climbable maple, though whatever it was, moose or a family of wild boar, maybe, passed without her seeing. Raspberries and roses fought wherever any opening above let a shaft of sunlight slip through, and she was soon scratched and bleeding as if she'd been savaged by cats. Exhausted, hungry, sweaty in movement and shivering whenever she paused for rest.

The sound of tinkling water drew her. Arrany was desperately thirsty, for all she'd water enough in the night. A narrow, moss-banked stream. She knelt and drank from her cupped hands, ate wild strawberries that grew around the roots of the birches, and then followed the brook. It was easier going between its deep-cut banks; it ran eastward and plunged springing down a series of tiny falls into a broad brown creek. Easier going again; she might walk upstream in the shallows of the creek and so come to either the road or village lands. It was warmer, too, in the sun, and she turned with better heart to set out, telling herself soon there would be tended lands, soon some kindly householder, the heel of a loaf, a cup of milk, the gift of even of a cast-off tunic or threadbare blanket to wrap herself in.

A shout. "She's there!" A splash, as of someone leaping into shallow water. Swift glance around, to see the running figures of two big Lowlander men of Cornan's crew. She bolted up the bank, futile, hopeless hope to lose herself again in the green tangle, but she was exhausted and weak, and went down full length in a snarling thicket of wild grape.

They seized her, hands like claws, and shook her, and hit her for running from them, and bound her hands behind her and hit her again. Dragged her back along the course of the water, splashing in the shallows, clambering over roots and rocks, down to the creek-mouth where the reed boat waited. They left her bound, dumped among the roped-down barrels, and Cornan kicked her in the ribs for good measure. His four taler had nearly escaped him. They poled themselves out and hoisted the sail; the wind caught them and sent them skimming east again, for Rhunaburg.

LATER THAT DAY, Hedge and I clattered over a stone bridge above a broad creek and back down along the rutted road through a heavy green woodland, and never knew till much later how close Arrany had come to being there waiting for us.

I flew out scouting again, came back with good news, as I thought it. "They've lost time. We're nearly on them again. I don't think they'll put in to Rhunaburg so much before us."

We still had no idea who it was who had taken her, or why. Perhaps she and her twin had left some feud behind them in the Marshlands. And at the back of our minds, we wondered, naturally, if Spider had decided to send hired swords after her, to bring her back to the mountains, but that seemed unlikely in the extreme. Spider had what she wanted and if she'd thought she had any reason to fear Arrany, the lass would have been dead before Penryl had been a week under the witch's roof.

"You go ahead," Hedge told me. "Keep an eye on her. But don't go starting an affray in the middle of Rhunaburg. There's a city godling there, maybe more than one, and they won't be pleased at other powers coming in to stir up trouble."

I gave her a nod of my head and flick of my tail, breaking into a canter, then leaping up into crow. Black arrow, I was, rising up above the trees, skimming over them, green, green, shadowed; green, green, flickering bright. Down to the lakeshore I went, and flew there, with that dirty sail and the reed boat always in the corner of my eye. The wind still set westerly, but it had played out its strength and was only a gentle breeze now. No tacking for them, but no wild race, either. Not one they would win.

I was waiting on the coping of the guildhall bell tower over the harbour in the warm red light of evening, when the reed boat came slinking in among the wharves and warehouses.

No unloading of cargo. Only a half dozen or so of the crew, scruffy men and women going ashore with their one great bundle, rolled in grubby tarpaulin, slung between them. It didn't so much as twitch.

Greatly foreboding, I floated down on silent wings to follow it.

7

IN WHICH I FAIL TO BE AS POLITE AS I OUGHT

Her helmet is a vhalmetal cap rising recurved to a high spike like a slender spearhead, with hanging curtains of mail all about it to protect the neck, a long nasal bar to stop, perhaps, a sword slicing through one's face. When vhalmetal meets vhalmetal, though, who can say which will prevail? Her armour is a high-collared coat of scales—real scales, black-green mottled and shiny. Dragonscale, they call those coats, but like vhalmetal itself, who in this world knows the truth of it? Hedge was born after the crossing; she's heard the same stories we all have, and maybe has better reason than we to doubt them. Once the helmet was gilded, the uniform of the Golden Guard. Once it had wings, but they are wrenched away, their rivets broken. Long ago we scraped the gilding off and sold the golden flakes; only faint traces remain in the crevices of the relief of tiny savage creatures, fanged and winged and clawed, about the band.

Not often Hedge puts on her armour. Even if the helmet no longer shouts aloud that here is a warrior, and by the wings a commander, of the Golden Guard, the coat declares her a soldier of the emperor, not some clerk or cook or groom. Or, perhaps, someone who has slain a soldier, and taken it.

Hedge was wearing her coat of scales when she came in the western gate of Rhunaburg in the hot afternoon the next day, leading a very weary, dusty yellow horse. The watch at the gate eyed her warily. They didn't quite move to bar her way with their halberds; they wondered if they should. But her helmet bumped along slung at Dandelion's shoulder, and though she had belted on her sword properly, her hand did not come near the hilt; she bowed her head politely to the man and woman on guard and gave them good-day, like any respectable traveller. So they let her pass.

Where, she was thinking, was that troublesome wretch Pony, and what sort of mischief had she gotten herself into?

Well, let me tell you.

I didn't think that letting Arrany be carried off bundled up like baggage was the best idea. I—make no bones about it, I was afraid, a sudden, wrenching panic, that they carried a corpse, that my calm, cautious thinking that they wanted her alive and whole and thus better that we should follow and snatch her from them when we could do so with less risk, safely ashore, had gotten her killed. I was swooping down—about to drop among them, about to be wolf savage and deadly, to scatter them and claim Arrany, living or dead, for my own, when there came hurtling at me a sense of strength, an anger almost as great as what had burned up sudden in me. Outrage at trespass, it was, striking me like a blow, and then in the same moment it *was* a blow, a great buffet of wind and the dirt and grit of the street flying with it, tossing me up and away and into the side of a warehouse. Barely, I twisted, tucked wings in, so I only hit and bruised my back, dropped, snapped my wings out, wheeled about and struck in my anger, no longer crow but eagle, talons raking at her breast, the great heron that was, for a moment only, a real and solid being amid the whirling storm. She clapped her wings back and rose away, feathers flying, blood-flecked. I hurtled after her as if she, not the startled folk below, were my enemy.

We grappled, rolling in the air, and down in the street the people carrying Arrany yelled in alarm and scuttled away, stumbling in the wild disturbed wind, blinded by dust, dragging their burden along bumping over the stones, and I heard, through the yelling and the hiss of wind and the shriek of rage that was my own, Arrany's voice, "Pony! Pony! Hedge!"

I wheeled, flipping in the air, talons again raking the heron's breast as its long beak stabbed and ripped feathers away from a wing, so that I flew stumbling myself in the air, crashing down unbalanced atop the bundle that was Arrany, leaving a spatter of blood over the pale canvas as I rose again and ripped at a man's face, banked aside from the swing of a long knife, snatched with my vicious hook of a beak and tore a woman's ear away—

"*Pony!*" Her voice a deep roar, and Hedge is upon us, Hedge's sword singing as it parts the air, as it parts limb from body, the blade that is about to strike me down out of the air, and her raised arm, shieldless, blocks the diving spear of the heron and knocks it aside, and I am tumbling on the dirty cobbles, back on my feet, a tawny wolf snarling, flinging myself after a fleeing man, but, "Pony!" she calls again, and her mail-backed leather gauntlet is clenched in my ruff. She shakes me as if I'm an errant puppy. "See to Arrany," she says, and I remember that these are humanfolk, only stupid, ordinary, bad humanfolk, who are running away in terror, and Arrany is safe, the bundled canvas abandoned and thrashing as she tries to emerge from this cocoon, and I do not need to run them down and hurt and maim and kill, to do so now is no part of any rescue and can do nothing to change what is past—

It is an old wound, a scar that has flared into pain at a careless knock.

Hedge's hand is still on me, still holding me, sword in the other, watchful, but they are gone and I am crouched human and shivering. Jinn looms at Hedge's shoulder, half-seen to my eyes, mist and shadow. Watchful, silent. No part of this fight, which is ended, only he watches, and I'm ashamed, that he saw me in such a madness.

"All right," I say. "It's all right, Hedge. All right."

And she lets me go, and I fling myself to where Arrany struggles to her feet. I take her in my arms, hug her hard and tight. She hugs me back, confused, patting my hair. "It's all right," she tells me. "I'm all right, they didn't—" She tries to be reassuring but she can't speak that lie, dressed only in wet drawers and shirt, tattered, scratched, and blood-stained all over, as if they have beaten her with thorny switches, and her face telling the truth of how they have used their fists. But she thinks it is I who need comfort.

I had a daughter, once.

It was a long time ago.

~

THE MAN whose arm Hedge severed died quickly, life pouring away with his blood. I hardly noticed, to my shame. But then, I did not care, and now—I only remember what I felt then.

The godling of the city walked to us. Her breath still came hard, almost panting. Tall, she was, and thin, pale-skinned, yellow-eyed, with a crest of long black feathers amid her long white hair; feathers white and black sleeked down her throat; the backs of her long-fingered hands were grey blue. She wore a long gown, pale blue, sleeveless, belted with linked golden plaques worked in figures of fish and boats. Her long pale feet had long pale toes, with long pale horny nails like Hedge's claws. The gown was torn, stained red at the breast.

I sank down to my knees on the cobblestones.

She frowned. She brushed a hand over herself, slow, as if she wiped off something distasteful and must be thorough. Shook a dust of dried brown blood away, and the gown was mended, and changed as well, flushed the colour of lavender.

I said, with my head bowed, "Godling of the city, I beg your forgiveness. I was in pursuit of those who held my friend captive and were carrying her away."

I had come into her city without asking leave, which was discourtesy, and had angered her by that, because it might have been a threat. I had let loose my rage and she had reacted. Though I think to attack me as she had done without speech, without naming herself, without demanding an explanation as to why I was in such hot pursuit of humans within her city, was discourtesy as well. There was fault, it cannot be denied, on both sides. But I was the one who had first struck to draw blood.

"I am Tarsisia of Rhunaburg, of the Rhunavon," the godling said. Her voice was low, soft, like wind in reeds. "You did not come to the shrine of the willows. You did not ask my leave or my aid."

"No," I admitted. What is the shrine of the willows? It's the home of Tarsisia, the heron-godling of Rhunaburg, a walled garden on the shore of the Rhunavon, surrounded on three sides by the city, a place of peace where willows grow, and irises, and marsh-marigolds and forget-me-nots. White violets cover the lawns, and small birds sing in the silver-dappled shade. I did not know that then, but that was no excuse. I knew at least two godlings made their home in the city, the heron-woman and a godling whose usual shape in the world was that of an elderly human man. I knew what courtesy was due, when I came as a stranger to such a place.

I will not let humans wall me into a garden, no matter how domesticated Hedge becomes. Never. But that's neither here nor there.

"You have brought a vhalgod within my city," the godling Tarsisia said. "A soldier of the Golden Guard."

"Aye," I said. "But soldier no longer. She is with me. She is... mine." I drew a breath. "I am Thallyn of Dahres Head, of the fells at the head of Dahres Water, and the fault, the offence, is mine, my doing and none of hers." My hand throbbed, skin torn, nails broken and bleeding. I did not try to heal myself. Contrition, I felt, was called for. And Arrany, unsure of what was happening, shivered beside me, also on her knees, where she had no need to be. Hedge loomed behind us, sword lowered. Well, she could not sheathe it, fouled as it was with the blood of the kidnapper. I think she feared to move, to draw attention to herself, lest the heron-godling do something to which she must react. Jinn had faded and gone; maybe of his own will, maybe at Hedge's urging. The heron-godling had, I think, never been aware of him. I licked my lips, tasted human blood. "I do not think this dead man is of your city, but even if he were, he was chief among those who carried off our companion, those who have held her prisoner, to what end I don't know, and brought her captive the whole length of the lake, misusing her as you may see for yourself."

"No. Not of my folk, though some of his people are. He himself is a stranger here. As are you."

"We came to save our friend."

"He—the captain, Cornan—that one—" Arrany gestured at the man who lay in the pooled blood, his severed arm and fallen sax some few yards away. "He thought he could have a reward of the Esrineyn factor if he handed me over, he thought the queen would pay, to have me back. I haven't done anything—I'm not a thief or—or worse, whatever they thought. She's just high-handed, my sister, she doesn't like that we've gone off into the world on our own. I promise you, Godling Tarsisia, I'm no traitor, no thief, no assassin. I bear my sister no ill will and she must know it. Only—only I can't go back, my brother's in peril of his life and I need to bring help to him. To bring Hedge. Hedge and—and Thallyn came to rescue me. I knew they would."

Tarsisia stalked closer, menacing as Hedge herself could be, but it was only her abrupt way of moving, that she set one foot fully before she lifted the other. She laid a hand on Arrany's head.

A long, long moment. Arrany raised her face to meet the godling's eyes. I don't know what all passed between them, then, but I saw that Tarsisia accepted the truth of Arrany's words.

"Take what is yours and go," the heron-godling said then. "Take this daughter of the Marshlands, and tend to her hurts. And have a care for your manners, should you ever come again to Rhunaburg, Thallyn of Dahres Head."

And she was gone, a heron lifting into the air, great wings beating.

"That," said Hedge, letting out a great sigh, "could have gone better."

"Could have gone worse," I said, and took the hand she offered to pull me up. "Arrany, love, let's get you out of here."

I found her cloak rolled up and bundled into one of the packs on Dandelion, and her hat, which, aye, was maybe a silly thing to worry about having retrieved, but it made her give a choking little laugh as she hugged the cloak tight around her. Hedge was investigating the dead Marshlander man.

"Your blade?" she asked, and Arrany, looking at the weapon she lifted from where it lay by the dead hand, shuddered.

But, "Yes," she said, sensible-like. "I think he has my knives, too, and my purse. And that's even my belt!" Indignation, as if there were some insult in that. And she burst into tears.

Well, that's the way of it, when you're pushed and twisted and all is pain. It comes out, one way or another, and tears are a better relief than some. I rubbed her back and found soothing words while Hedge retrieved what she could, scrubbing all clean on the abandoned canvas. We could hardly strip the dead man to clothe Arrany, though, stained and soiled as the body was, lying in the welter of death.

We made Arrany peel to the skin there in the street and dressed her in her own change of linens and bits and pieces of spare clothing, her own and ours. Hedge's better green tunic came down past her knees and we had to roll the sleeves up to find her hands; the riding boots she'd packed away while we were going afoot weren't the best for long hiking, but better that than unseasoned bare feet, till we could find her new shoes. Carried the packs on our own backs and put the lass up on Dandelion, who blew wearily.

"Sister, is it?" Hedge asked. "The queen?"

"My mother's dead," Arrany said bleakly. Lady Arrany, she was, of course, but she never asked us to call her that. Well, godlings don't have much respect one way or another for human titles, and Hedge, bastard or not, was an emperor's daughter. "Early this spring. I didn't know. My sister's offered twenty-four silver marks to the one who brings us to her or to the factor here. Alive," she added, being fair. "I don't think—I don't believe she thought, what might happen, putting a price on us that way, just because she wants to get us home and have Pen back as the witch of her hall. She's just—impatient. Always."

We took ourselves out of the city by the southern gate with never a sign of those of the boat crew who'd fled, or the ones who'd remained with the vessel—no, I wasn't disappointed, I was done for now—following the river-road only a half a mile or so, before we came to a little long low white-plastered tavern that kept an odd room or two for travellers.

A heron passed us several times, making its slow flapping away along the river.

We passed a heron several times, standing on one leg in the shallows.

In the tavern, we ordered a hot bath for Arrany, and a thick pea soup with chunks of peppery dry-cured sausage hidden in it, and good rye bread and a creamy soft cheese with a musty white crust, a speciality of the area, we were told, and fine indeed it was. Hedge produced tweezers to pluck the thorns out of Arrany, smearing all her scratches and cuts and broken bruises with one of those mysterious ointments that she got from Goodbrother Bessamy. This one smelt of honey and pine resin and creeping wintergreen. Then, with Arrany tucked up snug in the feather bed, we sat on our own harder mattress, a straw tick and a quilt on the floor, and shared some more bread and cheese and a jug of the sharp-hopped north Rhunavon ale.

SHALL I TELL YOU A SECRET? When I was a slave in the imperial palace, kept to work the emperor's gardens (for he claimed to value godlings as slaves above all others, though the truth was, he drained our power through the god-collars, to feed his ever-growing own), I loved a lad. He was human, my Ilyu, a young warrior enslaved, a captive from the far unconquered north, and he cleaned the stables. And I and my wheelbarrow fetched manure from the stables, to make the emperor's cabbages grow. Tall, Ilyu was, pale-skinned and burnt red in the summer sun of Ghedhaynor, white-gold the long braid of his hair; sweet and shy and tender, a lad of twenty summers or maybe twenty-one. And we loved, as folk hurt and lost and angry and despairing love, in their stolen moments alone together. And I did not think, bound in my human form, the god-collar draining strength and life and my connection to the earth and my control of all that I was, that as I suffered the pain and indignity and mess of a human woman's body, that the rest would follow. Which it, naturally—by nature—did.

My northern lad was taken from me before he ever saw his daughter, struck down dead by the emperor's own hand, only for being the one holding the bridle of a horse when it shied from the swooping of a swallow, unseating not the emperor, but his dignity. I gave birth to her alone, in secret, among the tall rows of artichoke, and in secret from those who oversaw the gardens of the palace and the barracks of the garden slaves I nursed her—aye, there were others among the garden slaves, human and vhalbairn and godling, who helped me hide her, for those early months. Till one betrayed her.

They took her from me. I never saw her again. Her name was Iliya, in memory of Ilyu her father, and she had fine curling hair so blonde it was nearly white and pale brown skin and eyes blue as the northern sky.

They said she was thrown into the harbour to drown, to be rubbish washed up again by the tide, but whether that was truth or only another whip to my back to punish me I've never known.

Sometimes I think she lived, that I must have known, godling that I am, if she had died then, flesh so recently torn from my flesh. But sometimes I know that is a lie I tell myself, that I have no way of knowing whether she died then or lived, given to some other slave to raise elsewhere, discarded to die or live a foundling, whether she lived a span of human life, whether despite the god-collar some of what could have been her true nature leaked into her blood and bone as she grew within me and left her one of those long-lived, strange-gifted halfling godbairns one meets from time to time, more often in the old hero stories than in real life.

I do not know.

She is an old wound, my Iliya, and sometimes it catches me all unawares, as is the nature of scars, and it aches like thunder.

WE DID NOT TALK. But it was good, the warmth, the solid mass of Hedge, sitting side to side, hip to hip, and her arm over my shoulder.

8

IN WHICH WE RUN AFOUL OF OUTLAWS

Our journey up the Rhunavon valley was uneventful, after that little misunderstanding with the heron-godling of Rhunaburg. We stuck to the river-road, though we could have cut off a great eastward bend by going up into the hills. The yellow mare was tired, we were tired, Arrany was battered and grieving; the highway, that stretch of it, was well travelled and safe. We didn't have money for an inn every night and it did rain a lot that summer, but a minstrel was always welcome under someone's roof; if there was no inn proper, some village elder or chief would offer us a bed, or the tavernkeeper their front room.

Petty chiefs or village councils ruled much of that land along the course of the Rhunavon, though there was a king or queen or two in this side valley or that. Thurbridge, of course, was governed by the university and the guildmasters, an uneasily yoked team, then as now. No godlings there. I was keeping myself quiet and out of the way of all my kin, still feeling a little ashamed of my loss of control in Rhunaburg. At Thurbridge, where the Mossadon out of the east mingles its waters with the Rhunavon to seek the northern sea, we did for a time leave the river after crossing it just above the city on the grand towered bridge there, to follow the old imperial highway that cuts due south, till it finds the Rhunavon once more, crossing again to the western shore on a great bridge of stone arches (no towers, though). We travelled on again, still following the highway, between the terraced vineyards and orchards where green fruit swelled. And so on, travelling through the villages and little market towns as the racing of the river from the south grew swifter and the hills climbed rougher and higher, the land showing its rocky bones through the pelt of forest, and on the horizon, a faint pale smudge that was our first glimpse of the White Mountains. Over six weeks it was, since we had left Rhunaburg.

Folk were cooler to strangers there, especially those who looked as if they might be up for taking what they wanted, rather than asking, but my harp won us goodwill to counter Hedge's sword and the wariness humankind always had of a vhalgod. Arrany had begun to practise her bladework with Hedge every night, though the sax against a vhalmetal longsword is a foregone conclusion. Hedge cut herself a hazel stick to use instead, and bought a bundle of new arrows so Arrany could get in some practice with her bow, bringing down hare and pheasant for us on the nights we slept out. A new seriousness in her, a grim focus that hadn't been there before. We were coming up into the more lawless lands, and the danger of brigands was not far from anyone's mind.

Especially near in our thoughts, such matters were, the evening we came upon the smoking ruin of a farmstead. We were into the foothills by then, the land steep and twisting, all stony hillsides, the pines and birch clinging precarious, while in sudden valleys and ravines the shallow rushing streams and lesser rivers braided their way through rapids and around islets overgrown with willow-scrub and wild grape and brambles, all the waters rushing to seek the Rhunavon. Boar churned the earth beneath the trees; moose browsed in the intervale meadows along the river; giant deer and little roe, grazing the sweet grass and greens that grew between the stones of the road, bolted from us. There were signs of bear, too, in shredded tree trunks, torn-up anthills, and ravaged patches of wild berries. Wolves, as well, who drifted along our route, wary, curious, and came snuffling close to our camp at night, though they would not have done us any harm, not with me along, even had Hedge not taken the sensible precaution of keeping Dandelion in close by the fire and hanging our food sacks high above. The only signs of human settlement we had seen all the past two days of marching had been a loose village of roundhouses straggling along a valley side below the ruin of an imperial fort. Houses and outbuildings alike were built of stone robbed from the fortress walls, with deep-sweeping thatched roofs to shed the great winter snows. Folk were cutting the hay in the small steep meadows, seizing their chance in a few days of hot sun, and the little stone-fenced fields of rye and buckwheat were tall and green, the buckwheat, indeed, edging towards brown, and the first plums blushing with red and gold and dusky blue. For each family, one or two red cows, an ox, a handful of spotted goats, would be grazing amid the more open woodland or amidst the sprouting stumps of timber-felling. We spent an evening among them, pleasantly enough, and were seen on our way in the morning with warnings that the road grew dangerous as it climbed towards the mountains, out of reach of the patrols of the chiefs of the Garraniash, of which tribe this village was the last outpost.

The lonely farmstead we came upon that evening looked no different from the village houses of the previous night, save that it was of unworked fieldstone and stood solitary below a pinewood. And, of course, the burning. Though the stone walls of the ground floor still stood higher than Hedge's head, within there was only a heap of charred timbers and still-smouldering thatch.

No reek of roasting meat. That was a relief.

No sign of anything living at all, beyond a half dozen hens, black ones and buff, scratching around the trampled kitchen garden. They fled us, wary survivors of some larger flock, seeking shelter in a large and tangled raspberry patch. The outbuildings—neither a cattle-barn nor goat-shed, for in those parts such beasts commonly shared the human hall in winter, but woodshed, smokehouse, summer pigsty, privy, those stilt-raised granaries the mountainfolk build—even the new hay that had been stacked around tripods of posts scattered near about, had all burned. That seemed vindictive, not mere raiding.

Hedge and I split up to scout around the farmyard, met back where Arrany was standing in the empty doorway of the dwelling side of the house, using a salvaged pitchfork, its wooden tines already smoking, to try to shift some of the straw and poles of the roof aside. Hedge carried a black hen tucked under an arm, stroking the bird's back absently, as if she had been a cat.

"Leave it," I told Arrany. "There's no one under there, living or dead."

"They've gone up into the woods," Hedge said. "Not back downriver towards the Garraniash."

"The farmfolk or the raiders?"

"The folk of this place went up the hill. Their cattle were driven to the road south."

"It's maybe six miles, a couple hours walking from here to that bridge where the robbers caught me. I think. I'm not sure," said Arrany. "It was over a little river flowing into the Rhunavon, and this kind of countryside. What about the river?" she added, arms hugged tight across her chest, not realizing, I think, how she hunched, making herself smaller. "The Rhunavon itself, I mean. There's no road over there, but could we cross, go up the eastern shore till we're past this land? Cut along to the east, even, and come up to Under-Ice that way?"

"Maybe." All wilderness along the eastern shore here, wild and steep, and there were no bridges, if memory served me true. One or two had been thrown down in the war and never rebuilt. "If we could find someone to ferry us over. We won't make very good time, not travelling as we are." Hedge and I alone, with no packhorse, no young Marshlander unused to forests, would be different. "Better maybe to lie up here a few hours and travel on by night?"

Hedge nodded to that. "Have a good supper, rest the horse now."

"Are you going to eat—that?" Arrany nodded at the hen, settled tranquil now, eyes half-closed.

"Why not?"

Arrany shrugged uncomfortably. "It just seems—a bit like you've rescued her."

"From wandering off to feed the foxes?" But Hedge laughed, then, and tossed the hen, gentle, so she spread her wings and landed to ruffle her feathers back into order, disgruntled. "It would take too long, anyway, to pluck and clean and cook her. Maybe the folk of this place will come back seeking what they can salvage."

"Little enough left," I said. "If we're making camp till nightfall, best be on with it. Tend to Dandelion. I'll check if the well's fit to use."

It was fouled. I'd expected that. No bodies, at any rate, not even a dead hen, but filth pitched in from the pigsty. There was intent not only to rob the farmstead, but to ruin it. We found water clear enough for the horse (and it wouldn't have bothered me, either), running down from some source higher up the hillside, only a little stream, channelled away from the farmyard by a ditch with a field-stone dyke along it, maybe to stop meltwater running down to make the spring thaw even muckier than it had to be. It would do for cooking pancakes to wrap around the cheese curds and fresh greens the villagers had given us that morning to see us on our way. For drink ourselves, our flasks had been filled with buttermilk.

I did wonder why such a well-established farm had only now been attacked and despoiled, if it had existed for untroubled years, as looked to be the case, on the fringes of the territory Arrany's robbers claimed. A story there, I thought, and I might have gone up into the woods on a hunt to find out what it might be, if I hadn't known what Hedge would say about dragging Arrany into further troubles with lawless folk.

We didn't quite go so far as to cook on the ruins of the house, but raked a good bed of coals out of it, onto the muddy flagstones of the dooryard, and salvaged some unburnt hay, a treat for Dandelion. I won't say I didn't enjoy a little of that myself. You'd think, when the summer meadows grow lush, you'd have no appetite for hay, but there's something about it, new-dried and sweet, that's the smell of the warm sun itself, as much as blooming clover.

A good meal, a few hours rest. The sun had set and the hens gone to roost in the low branches of a plum tree; we took to the road again. The moon, waxing gibbous now, was high, and shed a bright silvery light, its little ruddy dog circling. Not so good for travelling unseen, but a gang of highway robbers were more likely to be active by daylight, when normal folk were travelling, especially if they'd been feasting on the spoils of a successful raid. I figured we could march through the better part of the night and, having put ourselves over that bridge crossing the tributary where Arrany had been attacked, and hopefully beyond the gang's likely patrol, camp once the moon set.

Arrany's bridge was not a couple of hours south, but little more than half a mile. Beyond, the feet of the mountains climbed steep and ragged against the stars.

"I'll scout," I told them, and became an owl, perching on Hedge's fist to ruffle my feathers into order, stretch my wings and find my balance. As I may have told you before, horse, crow, woman, any of those are just me. Other ways of being, even the wolf I so often lived as in the first years after the hyena-rejected emperor fell, never fit me quite as well. I flew high, then, back and forth over the bridge, circling above the ravine. Saw nothing but a family of foxes hunting water-voles and a weasel about the same business. A great stag, taller than a tall human at the shoulder and the span of his velvet-covered antlers that of two humans lying head-to-head, crossed the road before me. I flew on, watching with owl's sight, listening with owl's ears that could hear the mouse scurry beneath the snow, for any sign of people on the road or lying in wait along it. All clear to the north.

So of course, they came from behind, out of the woods between the burnt farm and the bridge Hedge and Arrany, following in my wake, had just crossed. Not hunting us, though we didn't know that then. Searching for the folk of the farm.

Our bad luck we had waited for nightfall after all. Our miscalculation, that we'd thought the swelling silver moon, throwing its light down along the road, our friend.

I heard the cry, a shout of warning, a command. "There he is!" Wheeled in the air, sped back, low, swift—saw—

Hedge, turned to face back the way we had come, sword in hand and Arrany thrust behind her. Arrany, sax drawn, trying to push Hedge, standing solid as an offering-stone, behind her in turn, as if her slight figure might be any shelter, and why was she thinking Hedge needed her protection? Figures flitting over the bridge, running with spear and axe—and bows, they had three archers—the whole pack of them, a dozen humans, rushing up, yelling threats, yelling confused instruction to themselves: *Get around behind—you missed, you fool—No, I didn't, I got him square in the back—Who's that boy?—Get the horse! Where'd they get the horse—*

Yelling generally, because sometimes humans are stupid and need to yammer like hounds.

And Hedge, my Hedge, sinking down to her knees. Arrow, I saw only now, standing out from her back. Another was deep harmless in a saddlebag, but I didn't note that then, only the dark stain spreading.

"It's not *them!*" Baffled outrage in that man's cry and he comes up unheeding of Arrany, his attention on the fallen vhalgod and all the others rushing up bravely then, as if they had feared whoever *them* might have been more even than the sight of a vhalgod they've shot from behind without warning. But Arrany swings and slashes and carves up his sword arm, so he drops his blade and follows it down to the road, his life flooding out of him, for in sheering his hand half away she's opened the great vein in his wrist.

They seize her, their bows useless in the crowd they've made, and it would have gone ill then, because I'm still too far back up the road, too far, but something rears up over, dark and cold and angry, sheltering them both beneath his wings, and the air turns cold, frost sparkling on the road for all it's high summer, breath smoking and twinkling into snow, and I come in, feathered wrath, claws extended, and if you think I was angry back in Rhunaburg—

They scream. They die, some of them, one and two. I'm wolf and they are only a tangled confusion, trying to flee and tripping one another in their own flight. And Jinn—more than blood enough, then, and he does not wait for any to offer it, but drinks, and his lance takes one and two and a third dies, neck snapped and flung aside, and it's Arrany who has the wit to get in close to Hedge, to shield her with her body and blade, and Hedge tries again to push her back to safety, shouting something at me, something—

I'm into the woods, bounding after a fleeing woman.

"Thallyn!" A roar, that, and how she finds the strength I don't know, but it brings me back.

"It's done, it's done. Thallyn, stay here, Naskanna needs you." That's Jinn, crouching, daring to put a hand on my hand. Solid hand, if cold, solid as living flesh might be, and blood stains his lips.

"Don't do that," I said, crouched there myself, a hand still braced on the road. And with the other, shaking, I saw it was, I wiped at his mouth. As if he were a little child who'd been untidy with his porridge.

"Seemed necessary," he said, and set a kiss, gentle and brotherly, cold as the touch of snow, on the backs of my knuckles. He was not normally so affectionate, sardonic being his more usual mode where I was concerned. "I'll go after them. You stay and look to Kanna."

"*No,*" said Hedge, and battle-mad though I'd been, even I didn't think loosing Jinn to kill again a good idea. One offers blood, and gives a little of the living world, one maybe pricks a finger and squeezes a drop onto the flute that is a bone of his wing, which is the altar of his memory, and all is well, and one does it again, and each time that it seems necessary, each time that it's all right, it becomes easier, maybe, to think, it won't corrupt and entrap him, not him, my friend, Hedge's dear brother, my near-brother, so resolved, so honourable, so strong and true.

This was not any small willing offering; this was a sacrifice and feast of slaughter flung down before him.

"No," Hedge said more gently. "No, Jinn. Idiots, both of you. Let them go. Arrany?"

"I'm not hurt." Breathless. Shaky. A lot of that going around. "You are. Hedge, Hedge, they shot you and—" her voice cracked and broke. "What is—who is—that?"

"Jinn," said Jinn, and bowed to her, court manners.

"My little brother," Hedge said. She was trying to get a hand around to feel at the arrow, and I was trying to stop her so I could do it myself.

"He's dead," I offered, as explanation. "A ghost."

Maybe I ought to have put that better. Arrany sat down in the road rather abruptly, in that sitting before you fall sort of way. She pushed herself back, farther from the man she had killed.

"He's—" Arrany shook her head, looked away from the dead man, which only brought another into her view. Turned a desperate face to me. "Pony," she said. "Pony, they've shot Hedge." As if I might not have noticed. "Pony—what do we do? Is she—?"

"We stop babbling and get the damned arrow out," Hedge said, and fainted.

Oh, that was bad. That was very bad.

It's very hard to kill a vhalgod. Even an arrow in the back and such a great loss of blood wouldn't necessarily do it. They heal from what would leave a human crippled; they burn off in fever the creeping poison of dirty wounds; their flesh and sinew and bone knit far more swiftly than such injuries do in the creatures of this world. None of that is to say that a vhalgod can simply shrug off such wounding and stagger on, whatever a ballad might tell you. That they don't grow sick and old and die doesn't mean they can't be slain. Slaying vhalgods, the emperor in particular, is, after all, what Hedge is known for. Naskanna Deathdealer.

Me, getting her jerkin off, tearing the linen shirt that was all she'd worn beneath in the summer heat. Me, holding her over my lap in the road, giving Arrany instruction, cold and crisp and clear and not shouting in the least, whatever Jinn said after. Hedge, struggling out of her faint to prove a difficult patient indeed, trying to insist we get off the road, under cover, trying to get to her feet like a damned fool when we'd only just then cut and probed and pulled the arrow—a barbed head, but a light one, not something you'd take hunting bigger game, or the long, narrow, heavy point meant to punch through armour—and were pressing pads of clean towels—really, human women have every right to complain of the mess and pain and utter dreary inconvenience of their reproductive bodies, but there are times the need to travel with such supplies comes in very handy and Arrany had fetched ready what was needed. And Jinn, hovering over us all, watchful for any sign the attackers were returning, Jinn heavy and solid and casting a dark cold shadow, smelling of ashes and bone and fresh blood rather than warm flesh, but that was all to tell you he was not something belonging to the living world.

Well, the arrow wasn't in as deep as I feared, not in to her vitals; no great strength in the draw that had launched it or maybe the distance had been too great. Must have been, for her to have been surprised from behind, turning to face them only after the arrow struck. The bleeding turned to a sluggish seeping, and we wrapped bandages about her ribs to hold the clotted pads of clean linen in place and got a clean shirt and tunic on her and a cloak wrapped over all, for she was starting to shiver. Got the last of the flask of buttermilk into her, and some ale, too, because the body needs nourishment when it's lost so much of its own, and we took the baggage from Dandelion and put Hedge up on the mare, and Jinn, searching among the bodies we'd left scattered, said, "Kanna, where's your sword?"

He had the scabbard in his hand; Hedge had not been wearing it belted on, but only slung from a shoulder crossways over her body, as she usually carried it when we walked at ease. She'd gone to her knees as the bleeding weakened her, but she'd still held the blade then, threat to any who got past Arrany's guard, and then Jinn had fed and taken form and come down upon them as Hedge fell...

We turned the bodies. We searched the edges of the road, where moss and weeds crept over the imperial stones, and scuffed through the roadside flowers, daisies, tall sweetclover and sky-blue chicory pale in the moonlight.

"Leave it," said Hedge. "Fools. We need to get off this road." She clucked to Dandelion, turned her aside, started into the trees of the eastern side.

"One of those scum-crawling human outlaws grabbed it," Jinn said, and I might almost have laughed at the princely outrage in his voice, but he started away as if he would go after them, so I jerked a head at Arrany to go after him. I was catching up with Hedge, a hand on her thigh to steady her, because I was not all too certain she would manage to keep in the saddle, especially as she seemed to be setting Dandelion an uphill course through a beechwood. Arrany, a backward glance told me, had indeed gone after Jinn.

"Um," I heard. "Um, sir, my lord, I think Godling Thallyn wants you to come with us. If—if you don't mind, my lord." And then when he turned that molten stare on her, the look that, aye, in its day, had put vhalgod soldiers on their knees, for it was the emperor's own look in his eyes, for all his were silver, and the emperor's burning gold: "It's just a sword and your sister needs you."

And he gave a huff of laughter and bowed, and said, "Lady Arrany, I'm duly told."

Jinn turned back at her side, but they'd barely crossed the road to us when he whirled, wings flaring, and leapt into the air, and I dropped away from Hedge, horse, for a moment, nostrils flaring, tasting the breeze that came curling up along the road out of the ravine, the rising cool night mist carrying the scent of humans. And vhalgod. Wolf, then, I went slinking fast down to the road, and Arrany strung and set an arrow to her bow with hands that did not shake. Jinn soared out over the bridge, the ravine, and I thought of arrows, and remembered he was dead.

"Stand," he said, and he did not need to shout, only spoke, with command in it, the will of a magus. He alighted on the parapet, spear cradled in his arm, and the handful of people creeping up through the brush all froze, till one stepped forward, up out of shadow into moonlight. Tall, broad, wingless. The stranger held out empty hands toward Jinn—meaning he faced away from me, crouched there, only one leap from seizing the back of his neck. I growled, and saw him stiffen, but he did not turn.

"Goodfriend, we're only farmers of this valley," he said. "No enemy to you, if you are none to us. We're trying to get my wife to some shelter, before her time comes on her. And our house is burned and the robber-queen has stolen our children, so please, let us pass on our way..." And then, "Prince...Jinn? My lord Jinn? No, it can't—"

and he lurched forward, a hand outstretched. Jinn's lance dropped to warn him off and he went to his knees. "My lord prince!" he said, and the others came rustling, creeping, out, a brawny woman very large with pregnancy, and supporting her another human, tall and thin and shaggy-haired.

"My lord, I thought—you were slain, they said you died—"

I was there then, human, offering a hand to help the poor woman along, and of course my fool comrades had come back, and Hedge was sliding down from Dandelion and using Arrany as a prop, saying soft, "Here, put her up on the horse," and Jinn was saying, "Is it—Trooper Zevalash? Of the Fourth Horse?"

"Aye, my lord prince. You honour me. But my lord—"

"I'm brought back," Jinn said, "for a little time. Don't fear me, Zevalash, Please." For the vhalgod had backed up a step.

"No, prince," he said resolutely, and looked around. "Captain Naskanna!"

"Aye, aye," I said, "all old friends here," though I knew nothing of this soldier of the imperial cavalry and didn't much want to. It's all very well to say—and I do say it—that they had little choice, it was serve or die, under cursed Eskandron, but I didn't have to take them all open-armed as my brothers and sisters on first meeting, either. And there were plenty who did run, far to the east or away across the sea, and not a few who died trying. "Can we please get off the road?"

We ended up climbing through the beechwood to shelter in a bit of a dell with, at our backs, a jutting sheer face of stone that leaned out into a slight ledge over us. Not a hiding place, but at least more defensible than the open road, and the woman, Delmara, was glad enough to be off her feet. They were night-chilled, wet from fording the little river, where they'd had to swim at its deepest, and she was scratched and exhausted from a day struggling through the woods as she hid and crept and dodged the robbers who sought to take her. The second human was in worse state, battered and bruised from a beating. One neither he nor she; they were her sibling, Helthew, and from the manner between the three of them, I wondered if the siblings might be sharing not only kinship, but the affections of the vhalgod Zevalash. Their tale was that the robbers had captured Helthew and the two children of Delmara and Zevalash, but Helthew had escaped.

"She won't harm the children, or let them be hurt by her bravos," Helthew said, when this was told.

"You left them *alone*," said Delmara. The telling had rekindled harsh words laid by as they crept through the bush.

"They knew I was going to find their father and come back. They're brave," said Helthew, quiet, looking away. Fingers of one hand splinted and bound together, now. Someone had broken those for them. Maybe apurpose. They had that shocky, inward look that comes from more than mere wounding. Aye, I know it.

"There was no point them watching me die, which is what it would have come to. The only reason Jelagen took me alive from the farm was to have the killing of me later."

"I'm sorry," Delmara said, with a shuddering breath that was the swallowing of a sob. "I know. I know." She put her arms around her sibling. "You kept them from finding me. I do know that."

"Better I'd been able to hide the children in time, too," Helthew said bitterly.

"Better I'd killed her in the east a dozen years since," Zevalash said. "But I didn't, and here we are."

Helthew leaned forward, eyes shut and rocking. "I'm sorry," they muttered. "I'm so sorry. I should have stayed back over the river and not come to you at all."

Well, there was a story there to drag out of the lot of them, but more importantly, there was Hedge wounded, lying half-asleep with her head on my lap and the beginnings of a fever on her, which in a wounded vhalgod is not necessarily a bad sign, and there was Arrany hunting what food we had to share out cold, because we could not dare risk a fire, and all our blankets and cloaks to wrap about the two shivering humans and a couple over Hedge, and Jinn, still visible, still stirring the leaves that crunched with his passing, gone up to the top of the little jutting face of rock to keep a watch over us. Zevalash, seeing his wife and his—marriage-sibling, friend, lover, if Helthew were that, settled and as comfortable as they could be, went up to join the prince, whatever unease he felt with the ghost overcome.

I was not at all easy that Jinn persisted so material in the world. Not when, unless I was very much mistaken, there would be more bloodshed before this affair was over, and every good argument to make on his part, that it was only our need for his embodied aid that drove him to desire it.

The moon set. Eventually, Zevalash came down and lay against his wife's back, arm over her, warming her with his body. Arrany slept. Her head on my lap, Hedge shivered and burned and muttered in unhappy dreams. Dandelion, too uneasy to lie down, slept standing, a hip shot, tail twitching from time to time. Jinn, above, was silent as the shadows, but I did not think he was fading back into them. Only Helthew was wakeful, lying wrapped in Zevalash's cloak and pretending they slept. Their breathing gave them away. Finally I leaned, stretching to reach, and touched their knee.

"The others will sleep," I said. "I'll make it so, for sleep brings healing of heart and mind they sore need. You, though, you need to unburden yourself, for you think the blame in this matter lies at your door, do you not? Sit up and tell me."

"Godling," they said, subdued and obedient.

I did not think any of those three had been close enough to hear, when Arrany named me to Jinn. Still down in the ravine, then, or I'd have heard or smelt them.

"Aye," I said. "Thallyn of Dahres Head, and you are a witch."

"I am. Possibly also a fool." They sat up, and winced, for even in the moonlight when we first encountered each other, their face had shown dark-stained with bruises, and I had no doubt from how they had moved that their ribs were in little better state.

"Tell me," I said.

9

IN WHICH HELTHEW TELLS OF BRIGANDAGE AND OUTLAWRY

"We were young," Helthew began. "And foolish."

"As the young so often are," I agreed.

"We wanted to travel. We wanted excitement, and adventure, and foreign lands. We left our father's mill down in the Garraniash, my sister Delmara and I, and we went over the river, over the Rhunavon into the east, where the kings and queens have been warring between themselves over the name of emperor for a generation."

"Longer than that," I muttered. "As if any of them had any right to that crown, or the folk of this world any need for such a tyrant over them."

Helthew waved their broken hand, and winced, cradling it, but I took their point and subsided.

So this is the tale Helthew told me.

HELTHEW NO OLDER THAN Arrany and Delmara two years younger, they travelled as servants to a merchant, at first, but then took up the spear as armsfolk of a queen, following her banner until she fell to a rival, whereupon they moved on with the captain of their company to the service of another king, and then another. And in time, that captain, a vhalbairn woman named Jelagen, rose high enough that when the king to whom she had most recently sold her company's services died, leaving a child his only heir, she made a try for that crown herself, but was defeated by a rival. (In all this, the child-heir vanished, each side claiming the other had made away with her. Aye, I did ask, and spared a little sorrow for the poor creature.) Jelagen and the survivors of her company, including Helthew and Delmara, and by then, the vhalgod Zevalash, with whom both Helthew and Delmara had fallen in love—

"And that," Helthew said wryly, "is a tale in itself, and not one in which we either of us acted as well as we should, until Zev grew fed up and knocked our heads together and said we might consider that there was quite enough of him to go around."

—went off into a land of forested hills, where they lived, if not exactly as outlaws, then the next thing to it, taking over a handful of small villages which Jelagen ruled as chief, their own chiefs having supposedly asked for her protection against other bands of outlaws that prowled the forest fringes.

"She was no bad ruler," Helthew protested. "No more so than any other chief." Then they made a face, shrugging. "No other chief who thinks their word alone should determine the law, at any rate. But she was better than the ones who would raid a village for the last in their granaries in the dead tail of winter. And we—she had brought us alive, as many of us as she could, through the worst of the fighting in the Landip Hills. You can't imagine..."

"I imagine I can," I said dryly.

Helthew looked startled at that, sat staring a long, long moment, not at me, for the moon had set and we'd dared no fire. Only staring into the dark.

"We followed her," they said, with a shrug. "And there were some good years, then, but the wars quieted down in that region, a strong king holding all that borderland, and he began pushing into the forest, freeing the villages, driving out the outlaws. We were the last.

We were cunning, and wary, and had warning of every move that young king made against us—"

"Jelagen had a witch."

"My skill's more in charms and simples, a little learnt from the old Goodsister of our village. Not so much foreseeing," Helthew said. "Though I dream." They shivered. "Which is not much use, if you never manage to interpret your dreaming, till after the fact."

No proper teaching, I thought, and wondered if Goodbrother Bessamy would want to take on an apprentice twice his own age. "Go on," I said. "The king must have found you at last, or Jelagen would still be ruling her bit of forest in the east and not preying on the road here."

"He never found our stronghold in the hills," Helthew said. "Not till the end, when it was betrayed, and he brought his warband upon us in the night, and in fighting, many were killed, and some were scattered, and fled, and some were out on patrol. Zevalash and Delmara, some others. Del was expecting their first child. We'd been talking, just between the three of us, of leaving. Going home. Zev had been growing—dark. In his heart, you know? Dreaming. Remembering. It was having a child coming into the world. He'd fled the emperor's service in the last days of the Great War because he wanted no more of it, no more of death, no more of killing those so desperate they'd come out with a handful of stones against armoured soldiery. He'd drifted back into the companies in the eastern wars because, he said, what else was he good for, what other trade did he have, he'd been a soldier since he was a boy, and folk would trust him with nothing else, a vhalgod who only knew how to fight and kill, and—well, he'd tell you himself, he'd taken to drink, then, I think to stop himself caring. Until he met me. And Delmara. Met us. But that—we were afraid of that coming back, with the shadows growing darker round his heart. And he was so...anyway." They made a movement, as if pushing something away. "He'd been better, through the years we were together. He was—ah, we loved him, you know? Still do." A look at the sleeping vhalgod. "So we feared his falling back into those old grim thoughts. He'd been wanting to leave, a long time, but Del and I knew we wouldn't be welcome in our home again. Our father, our mother—they weren't the type to welcome home their errant children with open arms; there were reasons we left, reasons we found a mercenary's life better than the mill and the village, and the folk who turned a blind eye... So Delmara argued against it, and I did, argued against leaving Jelagen, who'd given us someplace to belong, who needed us—needed me, anyway, the only witch in the company and one who could at least set a bone and clean and stitch a wound or dose a fever, useful to a band of outlaws, as you can imagine, but the villagers came to us too and the captain didn't keep them from coming to me, didn't expect any payment for it, either, and would have me take none. I did some good, for those folk. I can—your vhalgod friend is wounded, I can take a look, if you'll trust me?"

"Later," I said, and didn't remind Helthew that I was godling and Hedge vhalgod, and that the blessing of my hand on her head and her own healing strength did more than any witch's small charms in medicine and well-wishing, even Bessamy's, which I would trust a lot more than the fumbling of a barely-trained outlaw so knotted up inside themself there was no way their wishes and intentions could flow true.

"But when this king took your stronghold?" I asked, to bring them back to the matter at hand.

"Yes, then Zev and Del decided, that was over, they'd escaped, they were free, time to find a new home. And I'd escaped, as the king's soldiers came searching through the stronghold, killing and burning. The king meant to leave none alive. I escaped and found my way to them. But Jelagen came on us; she'd made it out, wounded, and two dozen or so with her, out of three score of us. And she was in a red, red rage, for her son and his wife were dead, and their two elder daughters, and she'd saved only the little boy, her grandson."

Ah, I knew of that one. Arrany's charming flirt, poor ill-fated lad.

"And she swore we'd been betrayed. She demanded I find the traitor for her, and I said I could not, I had no such skill, and before we knew her intent she had seized Zev and her lieutenant Wolcha had Delmara, put them on their knees with each a knife to their throat, and said, I would find her the traitor, or she would kill them, my lover and my sister, and which did I want to see die first?"

"And did you find her a traitor? Having no skill in such things?"

Gazing out into the darkness, Helthew said, "I was the traitor myself."

"Hm," I said. "You might remember, Goodfellow Helthew,"—they flinched at the witch's honorific, as if they were unused to hearing it given, and doubted, maybe, they deserved it—"that I am a wild godling of this earth, and not so easy as all that to lie to."

Yes, I know, there was that little matter of Arrany's having lied to us at the very start, but it wasn't that I didn't know the lies were there.

Helthew sighed.

"Delmara and Zev had planned it. And not told me, because—because I'd argued so against leaving, even after Del had come round to it, with the baby coming and all. But they'd thought—they'd thought I'd be out on the patrol with them, able to slip off, with them, and lose the rest, and be away. Only at the last Jelagen had set me to another duty. She'd been trying more and more to separate us. I think now that maybe she'd suspected...something."

"So what did you do? Name another?" Somehow I didn't think it.

"I said, it was me she wanted, it was I who'd betrayed her, betrayed the stronghold and the secret way into it, cost her her son and marriage-daughter and granddaughters and her rule of the forest edge and all. And she'd have cut me down there and then, but Delmara began screaming at me for a traitor, and Zevalash, in Jelagen's distraction, flung her off and came after me swinging and saying he'd wring my neck with his bare hands, see if he didn't, and in all the night and the dark and confusion—"

"You escaped."

"Zev and Del were very good," they said. "Very convincing."

"You trusted they were trying to let you get away?"

"Oh yes," Helthew said. "We were always easily of one mind, Del and I." A wry smile. "Save when we weren't, of course, but even then, we both came round in the end." The sharing of their vhalgod man, they meant.

"So you fled. And they were back in Jelagen's company, trusted again, when they'd brought all this about in order to escape."

"A mess," Helthew agreed. Then, grimly, "And a guilt that did not do either of them any good. So many comrades dead or taken to hang, and easier to carry that guilt, maybe, if you don't know for certain it's happened. And they were not so trusted as that. Jelagen was suspicious, but there they were with her, and there I was gone—Jelagen hunted me, a few days, but I made it up into the mountains. Survived." Not happily, I gathered, without sister and lover. "Travelled, mostly. Sold charms and what simples I could brew up at some householder's hearth. Never took up a sword again."

"And Zevalash and Delmara—and their child?"

"Well, Jelagen came west, over the Rhunavon. Said she was too old for a mercenary's life any longer, feeling her age as even vhalbairns do; she fancied making herself a chief again, but from what Zev and Del say, she'd switched who she served so often, there were none willing to take her and her company into service again, and she was finding the kingdoms too hot. Her name was known, and not in a good way. That's really why she crossed the Rhunavon. She found the old fastness in the mines here, that the rebels held against the cursed emperor till he burnt them out, or maybe it was Zevalash found it for her, to prove his loyalty. Recruited all the local ruffians and some wandering ones as well into her band to bring the numbers back up, settled into her brigandage once more, robbing travellers, mostly, and taking a tithe from the outlying farms, the isolated ones, never enough to bring the chiefs of the Garraniash down on her. And Zev and Del had their boy, then, and a daughter next, and they told her, what with the family and all, they'd really like a quiet life, and they persuaded Jelagen to let them go, appealing to her as a mother. So they bought out an old woman's farm; she had no heirs and was going to abandon it, go off to spend her last years with a cousin down in Thurbridge anyway, far from thieving outlaws and their so-called tithing, she said to Delmara after the deal was done."

"Delmara didn't think about going back to your own village?"

"Hardly. She'd have scant welcome at home, less than that with a vhalgod husband and vhalbairn children. But up here, they were well away from crossing paths with our kin. They settled down, and—it was a good life. Del was happy, she says, happier than she's ever been. Jelagen left them alone so long as they paid her their due tax, as she called it, and didn't make trouble—beyond coming down, three times or four in this past year, trying to persuade the boy, the oldest—he's twelve now—that he'd find life a lot more exciting, and profitable too, in her service. Which Zev and Del were not having, but she didn't make an issue of it."

"Till you came back."

"I missed them."

"So you came back."

"Just quietly. Just to see. Jelagen shouldn't have found out."

"She did."

"The boy—my nephew Barris—he told her. Not knowing why he shouldn't. We didn't know—we didn't know, he'd been seeing a bit of Jelagen, on his own. When he took the goats up to the high pasture. She'd ride down and chat with him. Trying to woo him away. Reminded her of her son, she said, her son and her grandson, and she was all alone in the world now, no kin left, but a vhalbairn, vhalbairns as much as vhalgods were meant to lead, not to follow, and not to spend their lives wielding scythe and sickle and pitchfork."

"One of those," I muttered.

"She is," they agreed.

"So she came—?"

"She rode down—yesterday? The day before, it would be. Seems like one very long bad day. I haven't slept. Zevalash was away; we'd had help with the hay from some friends of his in the next village down, with Del so far along and not fit to work in the heat and all, and he'd gone to help them in turn. So Jelagen and a dozen or so came, and I saw them coming and was off into the woods, but I heard the shouting, Del and Wolcha roaring at one another, her telling him that she hadn't seen me, if Barris said so he'd mistaken her cousin Helthew, we were both named Helthew after a grandmother, Barris was mistaken or Jelagen had misunderstood. They left. I didn't much like it. I thought we should all take to the woods. Del said Jelagen wouldn't dare draw the Garraniash down on her by attacking a farm outright. She was telling Barris, too, that he'd been a fool, trusting Jelagen with family secrets that way, and the poor boy saying, what secret, and why shouldn't he talk with Jelagen, why should he be expected to spend all his life herding goats and following a plough, when Del hadn't wanted that for herself, had she—lots of shouting, and sulking after, and tears. I should never have come back." Low voiced, a whisper. "He's not...our Zev, any more. Not mine. They've made a life for themselves, apart from me."

"From the sound of it, the robber-queen would have made a try for young Barris regardless," I said, and did I wonder, a little, about Delmara and the betrayal of the outlaw fortress, and that she did not move the very mountains to at least *warn* her sibling of the coming attack. Intended that Helthew be away with her and Zevalash, aye, I did believe that, but when they were not, and it was not her own doing that it fell out so...a temptation, was it, to throw the dice and simplify a tangle of love and loyalty that was maybe not so content and balanced as Helthew painted it? Wondered, but since Helthew had not said it, I would not, and I don't say it now. I only wonder.

"Maybe Jelagen would have come again for Barris. She seems to have latched on to him as a replacement for her grandson. He was killed by some mercenary who set on him on the road last autumn. But without the provocation of me being with them, it would have been persuasion only, and the family would still have a roof over their heads."

"Maybe," I said, doubtful, because would Zevalash have let his son go to what he had long desired to renounce, if the lad, so young, had said he desired it? And would the robber-queen have taken a no, tyrant that she was, even from the lad's own mouth, having set her will on having him to take her grandson's place? "They came back in the night?"

"Early morning. The cow didn't come for milking, for all the calf's bellowing in her pen. Del went off searching for the cow, didn't want to send the children, didn't want me out to be seen. Came back when she saw smoke, but by then..." Helthew shrugged. "I'd knocked Wolcha out and done a bit of damage to a couple more with a staff but I—don't carry a sword, anymore. I'd sent Barris to get little Marcsy away, and grant the lad, he did what he was told but they ran the children down before they made it far into the woods, and there were enough of them, they'd overcome me by then. Jelagen herself rode down and oversaw it all. They had the children and were driving off the animals—they'd already taken the cow. Setting everything alight, then. I thought," they shook their head, "I thought she was going to have them throw me in, bound as I was and half witless from the beating they'd given me. She thought about it, I'm sure. But she had us all three slung up on horses and headed back to the mine. Bait for Del and Zev. Earth below, you think of Del, watching that and having the control not to come rushing out of hiding, while they drag her children away."

"You got away, though."

"Later in the day. I played dead, near enough. Well, played they'd knocked me out of my senses, and, I suppose you could say nudged? Nudged the woman watching me into dozing off. Something I learnt in my wandering, these past few years. But I couldn't get to the children." Helthew shifted uncomfortably, arms around their ribs. Aye, something awry there beyond mere bruising, I thought. "Found Delmara, scouting around. Then Zev found us. We were—Del's so close to her time, even she didn't argue, when he said he wanted her to head down to the Cove, stay with the witch there—midwife, she is, too, the goodsister there. Leave things to us. It's always a bit of a risk, a human mother and vhalgod father, for all that vhalgods are born small; they'd have had the witch up anyway before the week was out, I think. So we were coming down the ravine towards the bridge in the dark when we heard the uproar, and we lay low, but it seemed the folk who best knew the woods, Jelagen's folk, had been put to flight—I came up scouting, and saw it was strangers, with a horse—"

"Helthew," I said. "With all that, 'Oh goodfriends, we're just innocent farmers hiding from the outlaws'—were you planning to steal our horse?"

"Delmara had already walked quite far enough for a woman in her condition."

I snorted. Even if I hadn't been able to see their face, I'd have heard the hint of a smile in their voice.

"Just as well your Zev recognized Jinn and Hedge."

"Just as well. For us, I suspect."

"Aye. For you. Now lie down," I ordered them. "No, here, by me. I'm not going to shift Hedge so you put yourself on this side here. There." I was sitting with my back against a beech growing close to the sheltering outcrop of stone, legs outstretched and a hand resting on Hedge's cheek. The thick fallen leaves of past autumns were soft and dry, comfortable enough, and she didn't stir as Helthew settled down, obediently lying alongside my legs, their shoulder at my hip. I touched them, just lightly. "You should sleep," I said. "If you will, I can help. Help with the pain, as well. May I?"

They breathed out a long sigh. "I think," they said, "that there's nothing anyone could do, now, to keep me awake. Thank you for—for letting me talk."

For letting them say, I did suspect, things that at least ran alongside what they shied away even from thinking, that there had been a betrayal, a dozen years or so back, and not only of the robber-queen.

"Sleep now," I said, and laid my free hand over their side, where the ribs were cracked, one and two of them. Two fingers broken, as well, though someone, Delmara or Zevalash, had set and splinted them none too badly. "Sleep, and let it bring rest, and healing." Well, it's not only witches, can nudge a creature in the direction they most wish to go.

After a while Jinn jumped down, landing lightly, barely stirring the leaves, his substance gone to shadow and a mere thickening of the night.

He squatted down, spread a wing over us, as if that might be some shelter, some warmth, but the air he brought was chill.

"How is Kanna?"

"Better than she was," I said, and it wasn't a lie. "Jinn..."

"I know," he said. "I won't—but I will make no promises and

swear you no oaths. I won't watch Naskanna slain, even if I must damn myself to prevent it, you understand?"

Some would say he was already damned, but they'd be wrong. He kept himself.

"Thallyn, don't you two go rushing in to get yourselves killed for the sake of a few self-confessed outlaws who can't even keep faith with their own kind and their own kin."

"That's not fair."

"No?"

Maybe he had a point.

"Arrany needs you," he said. "Her brother does. You've taken on a duty to her. This—mess, as your friend the witch there calls it, the three of them brought on themselves, harsh though it may seem to say so."

"She's taken the trooper's children, prince. You'd ask Hedge to walk away from that? You'd ask *me?*"

A long silence, then. "Don't get your little Marshlander lady killed," he said at last. "Don't put my sister in danger, if you don't want me to do—whatever I may need to do—to protect her."

"She's generally fairly good at protecting herself, and all the rest of us too," I muttered. "It's no honourable fight, shooting innocent travellers in the back."

And not a good idea at all, not at all. We'd left a half dozen bodies in the road, to say so. There were some still walking, who had yet that lesson to learn.

10

IN WHICH I GO INTO THE MINES

By dawn, I'd managed to push the hungry, angry craving for vengeance out of my heart. Maybe not scoured myself clean of it, but still, rid myself of the worst of it, breathed it out with the good clean woodsy air and the pale clear dawn. Jinn was gone, faded away some time in our vigil over Hedge, and she and the humans and vhalgods all slept on.

We needed to get into shelter, though. Jelagen would surely have sent out her bravos, or even be on her way herself to hunt down those who had slain her folk. Cold second thoughts said, maybe I'd been wrong, to want to kill those who had fled to ease my heart's fierce rage for vengeance, but still we should not have let them go, and Jinn, who had commanded the emperor's scouts and skirmishers, among other tasks, must have known it as well as I. To take them prisoner, maybe, leave them bound at the roadside long enough for us to flee out of reach—but fear for Hedge had been all our thought, and hers for me.

To kill was no part of a godling's right nature.

What I should be, in myself, was broken long ago, and I'm not alone among wild godlings in that, as you'll have observed by now, listening to this tale. Past remedy, I do think, but Hedge holds otherwise.

She stirred, muttered, flung out a hand, claws reaching—I caught it, enfolded it in my own.

"It's all right," I whispered. "We're safe, we're all here. But we need to be waking."

I nudged Helthew as I spoke. "Up, up, Goodfellow. Time we took thought to save ourselves. The hunters will already be on their way."

Helthew groaned and pulled themself together, drawing in long limbs, rolling to hands and knees, rubbing their face. "Where have we come?" they asked, and stood, taking stock of our surroundings. I forget, sometimes, how little humans see at night.

We woke the others, and Arrany shared out dry oatmeal journey-cakes and some cheese and the little beer we had left while I sniffed over Hedge's wound, which still smelt clean, and though she was feverish, it seemed to me only in the ordinary way of a vhalgod's healing; when I felt beneath the bandaging, the flesh of her back, though hot and somewhat swollen about the dressing, did not have that over-filled-sausage feeling that would have worried me. I left things be; better to let the scabs hold together. She grumbled at me, and wolfed down food, another good sign. When Hedge stops eating, then you know something is very, very much amiss. Delmara moved ponderously, sunken-eyed and grim-faced, and needed the arm of Zevalash or Helthew to rise.

"Not far to the boat," Helthew said.

"Boat?"

"We were making for our boat," said Zevalash. "Barris and a friend from down the river took it fishing up here below the island and the young fools knocked it around in the shallows and ended up with a sprung plank. They made it back to the west bank, hauled it up and left it and walked home, and I never yet had the time to fetch it away. We meant for Helthew to go with Delmara over the river while I went after the children."

"Captain Naskanna and Lady Arrany should go with Del," Helthew said hoarsely. "I'll come with you, and—Godling Thallyn, will you?"

"Aye," I said, though I was not entirely happy about that. But, "At least I can get you your sword back, Hedge."

"Pony," said Hedge, "the sword doesn't matter. Get them their children back. And keep your temper. It's not fighting that's wanted; it's stealth and cunning."

"Aye," I said, resigned that she knew where my thoughts had gone, for all that I'd told Jinn off for the same impulse. Of course the sword didn't matter; a blade's a blade, and vhalmetal or not, there were and are sharp edges enough in the world. But it was Hedge's, and that mattered to me. "Helthew and I will come with you, Trooper Zevalash, and fetch your children away."

And then what? The family would be adrift in the world, no land, no cattle, no roof over their heads, scant welcome from their neighbours, even those friends of Zevalash's he'd mentioned, since they'd be bringing their feud with the robber-queen down on whoever gave them refuge. No, they'd be taking the road as beggars, and they might find work as labourers and fieldhands through the harvest, but winter would come, and they with a new babe atop all else.

Borrowing trouble, maybe, but on the other hand, thinking how you'll cross a bridge before you come to it, when it's a bridge beset by dangers and difficult of approach, does give you a better chance of actually making it to the other side. But first they needed their children out of the robber-queen's clutches. Maybe they might come along with us up into the White Mountains. Maybe a godling putting in a good word for them in some village might find them a warmer welcome than is usually given to vagrant and penniless strangers trying to win a way in on their own. Hedge, who does like to see where she's going, was probably already shaping thoughts along those lines, for the sake of the vhalgod trooper who'd served under her brother in the scouts a time, or so I deduced, for Jinn had never commanded the heavy cavalry that I'd heard.

Well, we found the rowboat drawn up under the shelter of some willows, and water washing about its ribs, but the leaking was in the bow just at the waterline and not so bad as all that, so we tipped the water out. Del and Helthew did a bit of rough caulking with rags torn from Helthew's sleeves and pounded the plank back into place, while Hedge and I eyed one another and grimaced at the noise of stone hammering on nail and timber. Whispered, heads together, while Arrany watched us worriedly and checked over the arrows left in her quiver.

The lass didn't, I would note, argue, over the division in our party. She recognized that wounded as Hedge was, and with Delmara so encumbered by the burden of her pregnancy, she herself was not being got safe out of the way like a child, but set as the strong arm and protection over the vulnerable. Also, breathless as the vast bulk of her belly pressing up to her lungs made her, Delmara was in no condition to do much rowing, and Hedge most certainly was not.

So we parted, once Zev and I pushed out the boat, with Delmara and Hedge settled in the stern so that it rode bow-up and nearly awash as it was. Hedge, having disdained the little wooden dipper they had for bailing, had given Delmara our frying pan for the work, for the water came seeping in along those damaged seams regardless of the repair; she had only grudgingly admitted she was no use to anyone at all and would probably fall flat on her face if she had to walk much further than we had come to reach the boat. It galled her, as you can imagine, that she could not row, nor even bail. Arrany set herself to the oars, her strokes smooth and clean. The river was swift, but calm, save where it curled about rocks below the narrow island that split the channel, and if they were pushed some way downstream that was all to the good, for it put them farther from where Jelagen might look.

We took Dandelion with us, Helthew and Zevalash and I afoot, for we would have need of the horse's strong back to carry the children away, if it came to some fighting retreat. Our plan, such as it was, we made in haste, muttering low, while I strained my ears for warning of other hunters out in the woods.

"Take the flute," Hedge had urged me, before we set out.

"I will not," I had said. I never did like to touch that thing. It seemed—almost an obscenity, to make a relic of Jinn's body so. But it was what had come to Hedge's hand in that desperate bloody moment, an anchor for this banished soul; only later did she clean and polish it, drill the finger holes, shape a beak for the lips. I had carried it, at need, and played it, too, making an offering of my breath to summon him. But if it came that Jinn was the last defence left to Hedge—then he must be that, and not any number of reformed robbers, no, nor even their children, would change my mind on that.

Hedge had given a fearsome scowl, but abandoned the argument.

IT WAS a twisty way that Zevalash led us, avoiding the paths the gang would take, expecting, he reckoned, that he and the unexpected allies who had done the robbers so much scathe would be escaping along the highway with all speed. He set a swift pace through steeply rising forest. I kept an eye on Helthew, who for all that I'd spared them a little of the blessing of healing I had striven all night to shed over Hedge, went with an arm pressed to their ribs. A little before noon we came to a narrow gully, a dry stony springtime watercourse at the bottom of it, overhung with cedar and sumac and wild grape. I led the horse into a thicket of cedar, following a narrow path made by goats and cattle, from the look of it, seeking summer shade. We were close enough to the robber-queen's stronghold that her herds must sometimes graze this woodland. The main track, indeed, passed closer than I liked, for Dandelion might call out, scenting other horses. With any luck all their riders—they kept but a few horses, Zevalash said, though he couldn't say how many that might be—were away hunting us closer to the Rhunavon.

Stand, I ordered the mare, *and keep silent,* though my ordering was not in ways the others could hear, and Helthew looped the leading-rope loosely over a branch. Dandelion was saddled, for we'd always just fastened our bags to various rings of her saddle or strapped them on over it, rather than ever trading for a proper pack saddle, and I realized then we'd left her bridle with most the rest of our belongings, in the leaky boat, and she had only a rope halter for headstall. Still, with luck we'd be leading her away, the children aboard, and otherwise, well, otherwise—I took her head in my hands, forehead to forehead. "You be a good brave wise mare and if they come alone, you carry those children swift as you may, and flee safe down the highway to some human place," I whispered, and it was a blessing strong as I could shape it.

There we parted from her, and went scrambling down into the gully, to follow it another quarter mile or so up to where the land rose into a sharp-edged broken forest of the foothills, with the mountains towering against all the south.

It was pleasant land I would have liked to wander in. Warm, quiet. Though, strangely, empty of any sense that a godling belonged to this land. Higher up, maybe, but here...another victim of the bones-rotted emperor. I shook that thought away. Crickets sang, reminding that summer had begun its slow decline. A black snake basking on the warm rock flicked its tongue and slithered aside. I went softly, fading into tree and stone-shadow, drifting.

"The main entrance to the old workings," Zevalash had said, describing what he called the front gate, back when we made what little plan we had, by the river. "We never made any effort to hide it." A wry twist of his mouth, deprecating his own involvement, maybe, or maybe only the arrogance of outlaws. "Our main hall, the big cavern beyond was, and then there are small chambers made of most of the galleries off of it. We walled off the far ends with logs and rubble, to turn them into rooms and stop the cold air pouring through. The place gets bitter cold in winter even so, with all the drafts. They say if you go down far enough the air's milder—cold in summer and not so biting in winter, but it's dark and rough, a good pantry, but no place to live. She won't have sent the children there. Jelagen's own private dwelling-place is away towards the rear, off to the right as you go inwards, made private with rich hangings to curtain it. The children—Jelagen will be keeping them close. They might be there, if she's kept them within. They won't be—won't be chained up, or anything like that. From the effort she put into trying to lure Barris away, she wants them for their own sakes, as much as to punish us." Their father had been trying hard to believe that, at any rate. "But in weather like this—usually, almost everyone would be outside in the fresh air, living in the summer huts. If she thought we might dare a raid ourselves—but why would she think so? We'd have to be mad."

Helthew snorted at this.

Zevalash ignored them. "No, they'll most of them be off hunting us, and she'll be expecting us, if she expects us at all, to come contrite and begging, trying to make some bargain."

I hoped, for the sake of his children, he was right.

Out of the gully, up over the ridge that ran alongside it and down we went, creeping through the trees—spruce, they were, dark and sheltering—till we came to where they ended in a steep slope of scree, and below as Zevalash had described it, the broad green dell, fenced to the north where the main track ran in, part by old ill-repaired drystone work and part by thornbushes cut and piled, running from one steep ridge to another, so the whole was cradled against the mountain's cold breast by two enfolding arms. A stand of aspens grew halfway up the farther, eastern side, and nearer us, another thickset clump of spruce. Goats grazed the turf, with some cattle and a lone horse. To the south, where the land sloped up to a near-cliff, were the summer huts, some hardly even worthy of that name, just lopped branches leant together, but also a of couple open-fronted sheds and a few more rough cabins built by inexpert carpenters; they all clustered to either side of what Zevalash had called the main gate of the stronghold proper. The mine must have had its beginnings in a natural cavern, for the shape of the mouth was rough, and broad. The robbers had filled it with drystone work but left the top open at its greatest height, so that there was a lopsided and roughly triangular gap about five feet high at its greatest, angling down. The lintel over the double doors was a beam rough-hewn from a massive trunk still showing strips of bark and the doors themselves, of equally rough planks, stood wide open.

"There!" whispered Helthew.

We lay flat on our bellies, except the witch, who tilted to a side to spare their pain.

I saw, as they did. A charming domestic scene. Staged for our benefit? I did wonder.

A leafy bower of fresh-cut boughs. A camp-chair there in the sun, a stump next to it for table, with cups and a sweating jug of something set to hand, and before the chair a blanket spread, and a painted board laid out between the two children, the lad propped on belly and elbows, the little lass sitting cross-legged, frowning as she shook the dice. A regal grandmother, watching benignly over the grandchildren at her feet. Walking stick propped against the arm of her chair, a sword tucked under it, half hidden by the grass. Dice rolled. Marcsy moved counters. Neither smiled, and the lass hunched her shoulders and ducked away when the old woman leaned to pat her head, while the boy scowled. So even if he had been tempted by the enticement offered, the highway robber's life of adventure and wealth and ease, the seduction had not outlasted the destruction of his family home, his kidnapping and the abuse of his kin. You think that's a given? You'd be surprised.

Vhalbairn, Jelagen clearly was—though I thought, likely one a couple of generations removed from a vhalgod parent, and probably not much longer-lived than a hale old human. It's those folk who find themselves most bitter, most resentful of their mortality, I've noticed. And I do wonder, was that behind her craving for these children who were not hers, and were yet vhalbairn? Not mere mother-instinct gone bad, but some greed for a long, long life denied her, that she sought to feed by rearing these children in her own image? Though her lost grandson had been a winsome, generous soul, by Arrany's account of him.

Tall for a human woman, taller than most men, this Jelagen, with strong bones to her face. Her skin was warmly summer-browned, her grey hair, a colour some few vhalgods are born with, she owed to age; though she'd grown her fingernails and filed them to points, they weren't claws. She wore a gown of a rich amber colour with a beaded fringe that brushed the tops of her boots, and a broad belt decorated with gold and enamel plaques. Her fingers, too, flaunted a weight of gold and bright jewels, and her throat, gold chains and enamelwork and gems, ropes of them looped down over her breast, jewels dangling from her ears, more braided into her hair. A fine-looking woman, you might say, and decked out as a great chieftain, but her face was cruel.

Oh aye, how did I see so much, you're asking? What good do you think I'd do, lying there like a stalking cat in the trees above the dell? I was crow and away, floating down over them, perched on the ridge-pole of the bower amid the wilting birch leaves. Barris glanced up and saw me, frowned. I had no way to speak to him, only I clutched in my beak a little length of parti-coloured woven ribbon with which Helthew had tied back their hair. Delmara preferred to trade for their cloth and set up no loom herself, but apparently did do fine tablet weaving in the winter, for trimming and for trade, and she had given her sibling this piece of bright red and blue to bind their hair only days past. I waggled it about, to be sure Barris noted. And then, because sky above be sure I did not want him thinking his mother-kin dead in the woods and picked over by crows, laying it down, I did a little dance, of sorts.

Oh aye, laugh, you won't be the first. I hopped, I turned, I stretched my neck long, wings spread back. I stood on one foot and stared like a fowler's pointing-dog, all at the cloud of spruce on the hillside. Hopped up and down again, looked at him, looked and did my dog imitation once more. Barris blinked rapidly, ducked his chin as the robber-queen asked, "What are you scowling at?"

He shrugged, sullen. She craned around, but from her vantage point there was nothing to see. And anyway, I was only a crow. I hoped the lad might think Helthew had by some witchery bespelled a wild bird to behave so clownishly and carry their message. People who know little of witches or magi either will believe any such thing possible.

Having done what I could there, I took to the air again and flew through the gable-like opening over the mine's open doors.

No bears among the beasts out in the dell. I did notice that.

The cavern within was high and broad as a great tithe-barn. A chieftain's hall indeed, with a central open hearth, only a small cookfire burning there now on a deep bed of ashes, soup cauldron steaming. I saw several long tables of mere rough planks set on trestles, some benches where, in winter, many might also sleep close for warmth. The walls and roof above were blackened by the smoke of years. A nasty fug there must be in winter, for all the gap above the front wall. The place was not deserted, despite the lovely summer's day. I alighted on a ledge about six feet above the floor, a woman again, cloaked in darkness, far back from even the fire's light.

"Well," I whispered to the empty air, "Let us see about this distraction I promised." I had to imagine Hedge's fanged grin, in answer.

Last night, a terror had come on them from above, a vhaldrach in rage, trailing mist and shadow.

Shadow enough to hand here, and darkness for my shaping.

Then, my wolf, for the moment, I howled, calling the pack I did not have. The echoes in that dark place took it up, resounding, and I let them sing. Shadow I gathered to me, and down I leapt, illusory wings of darkness enfolding me. Woman, horse, wolf, vhaldrach—their minds made of me only a thing of terror, and the three people who had sat at one of the tables dicing for farthings, and the woman who'd knelt at the hearth, chopping white summer turnip and throwing the chunks into the pot, were all on their feet. For all her jolt of terror the woman with the big knife flipped it in her hand and threw it, but it passed harmlessly by me. She bolted for the doorway and I tipped the soup hissing into the hot ashes as I circled around the hearth in my woman's form again, snatching up a burning brand on my way, stirring up a wind, gathering shadows into darkness at my hand, flinging them crowding and thick about the walls, as if creatures yet unseen spilled from the high dark crevices and rose from unseen cracks opening onto unimagined depths. The three gamesters couldn't scramble out into the sunlight fast enough.

The farthest chamber, Zevalash had said, belonged to Jelagen. I ripped the hangings away from that tunnel in the strength of my haste, costly brocade though they might be, and flung them aside. No grand furnishings behind, though the bed, for all its rough-hewn framing, looked deep and soft. Chests and barrels and carved boxes were stacked high as my shoulders, and to the roof at the end where the tunnel had been blocked to make the chamber. Fine robes and gowns, enough to make up a queen's wardrobe, hung on pegs pounded into the walls and more spilled from heaps piled haphazard. The several unlit candelabra were of silver and gilt.

One barrel held an assortment of spears, bows, walking sticks, and several swords, none of vhalmetal and most the sort that favoured gaudy hilts over good bladecraft.

As in a tale, a hoarding dragon.

I fired a few of the hanging garments and the open chest of linens at the foot of the bed, then the edge of the trailing velvet coverlet. Turn about, as they say. Worked my way back through the stronghold, tearing down curtains, knocking aside wattle-work screens, setting fires wherever they seemed likely to take. The smoke billowed and rolled after me, stinking of burning feathers as the robber-queen's bed smouldered. Quicker than you might think, it was, for all to blaze up. It might be that my desiring helped it along. A shouting, a clamour rose without. I went cautiously, then, peering around the stripped trunk of a spruce that served as a doorpost.

Most of the gang had come clustering together, the ones who had fled me shouting about vhaldrachen and goblins rising from the deep pits. They were leading the rest back towards the mine at a run, now that they had reinforcements. Spears caught up in hand, an axe, a bow... And Jelagen herself, not running, but striding, with a hitch in every other step, driving herself along with a firm grip on a knobby stick, and the sword—a rather familiar sword—snatched up in her other hand. Smoke poured from the open gable, thick and black. Let them see terrors, hints of wings, of vhaldrachen, of things nameless out of nightmare, let them focus on that and not look around...

Behind them—oh, swift, swift, run swiftly, children...

11

IN WHICH JELAGEN LEARNS THE ERROR OF HER WAYS

So there went the lad and the little lass, Barris and Marcsy, hand in hand, bolting for where the steep mountainside came spilling down to the dell. There was Zevalash breaking from cover, running towards them. Too long a stretch of open pasture between.

Shadows crowded the doorway, but I could do little with them out in broad daylight. I whipped around the doorpost, brandishing my—well, my brand, still smoking, though the flame had gone out. Flame enough there was within behind me now, at any rate. I called smoke after me, set it crawling like a tide over the grass, rising about me to join what poured from the gap above. And I reached and seized on their confusion, their fear, those rushing towards me, those flinging wild glances upward at the half-imagined shapes above in the smoke, and I fed it till it flared up, devouring some, setting them to flight, while others at least checked and faltered in their rush for the cavern. Maybe they saw a woman holding a smoking stick. Maybe they saw something else entirely.

"Fools!" a woman's voice yelled. "It's the traitor-witch's trickery! Get the brats safe inside there!" *There* being the largest of the cabins, by her pointing with—aye, that was most definitely Hedge's sword.

She spun to look back to the leafy bower. Blanket, chair, the game-board, its glass counters scattered…

No children. They were racing for their father.

Jelagen roared. "Barris—!" Began to lope after them. Lame, she might have been, but she forced on through whatever twinges and jabs her ageing joints were giving her. I reached, to try to turn her, draw her attention away to me, to no avail. Her strength of mind and the purpose her self-fuelling anger gave her resisted the burst of fear I'd put on the men and women who hesitated now, scattered and confused. Easy prey for her gang, was how she saw me, and dismissed me. I was not even armed. And Barris was dragging young Marcsy faster than her shorter legs could manage, so of course she fell, and the tight grip between them pulled him down too and they rolled through thistles, scrambled up, he jerking her along before she had her feet under her. Down again she goes, and Barris kneeling, Marcsy scrambling to his back, the lad up and running again, Zevalash running, running, from the shelter of the spruces, and Helthew running behind, bent forward, an arm clamped over their ribs, mouth open, gasping for air, gasping through the pain of those cracked bones whose healing I had nudged a little on its way, but not enough.

Earth beneath, make fleet my feet. I ran. Not wolf but my own proper shape, one of them, swift mare, and you might think, why would I not again be wolf, be some creature large and dangerous enough to offer some threat—but I thought I could serve better as I was. Anyhow, if you think a horse can't be a dangerous thing, I'll take it you've never met one. While I ran, I pushed the smoke to rise, to billow and eddy, to hide the children from Jelagen's eyes.

A cry. A child's shriek, a lad's shout, a roar, deep vhalgod man's voice, crying, "Marcsy!"

I'd come thundering down past Jelagen and she'd barely glanced my way, for what threat is a bolting horse if you're not on its back?

Blighted luck, there'd been two of the gang down closer and I'd not marked which way they ran, when all had been running.

They had the child, the littlest one, hauled down off her brother's back, and he sprawled on the ground again and one stooping, to jerk him up by an arm twisted high behind his shoulders. And the lass screamed and kicked, and then, clever child, she bit, vhalbairn child of a vhalgod father. Fanged, she was, and the robber-woman clutching her shrieked and flung her off and the red blood spattered. But for all her bleeding arm the robber was quick to seize again, by the fat braid of the lass's hair, this time, and set a knife to the child's throat, which stilled the brother, and the father, and me, as I wheeled about, too late, where a moment earlier a few well-placed kicks and a bite or two could have dealt with the two robbers, and a quick-witted pair of children could have been on my back and all away.

I fidgeted foot to foot, snorting, ears swivelling. They were all ignoring me. Baffling, maybe, a stray horse they couldn't account for, wandered in amongst their herds. They didn't count me a threat, at any rate. Then Helthew, fool, doggedly comes trotting up, their breath labouring shallow, all the work of my healing undone by the strain. There's Jelagen, grinning, to show she too has a hint of fangs. Zevalash has the hatchet from our gear raised, as if about to throw, but his hand stays, frozen, for the knife to Marcsy's throat.

"You should thank me," Jelagen says, her face a sneer, "that I'm willing to raise your orphans."

She crooks a finger at one of the men who come rushing up, brave, now that we're held at bay. "Bind that ungrateful boy. I warned him. Hunger will cool his hot blood, if has no care for his sister."

Tears roll down Marcsy's face, the poor thing thinking it's all her fault for her short legs, and a trickle of red, too, gathers and traces a line down her throat from the knife's point, pricking threat.

"Let them go," Zevalash says. "Take me. I'll come back to your service, only let Delmara and the children go away from here safe."

"And where is Delmara?" Jelagen asks. "Not up to much these days, is she? And your other allies, the vhalgods, where are they and their hounds?" She was gesturing to her gathering gang as she spoke, some private hand-sign, but the import seemed to be that they should search up that hillside and through the clumps of trees.

"The vhalgods aren't here," Helthew says bitterly. "Chance met on the road when your fools attacked them by mistake, and no reason to get further involved in our feud now they've had the price of their captain's wounding out of your blood. What does Zev have left to hire their swords with? They've gone. Let Zevalash take his children and go. It's me you want. All was well here between you before I came back."

"Your service is nothing I'd ever trust again, nothing I'd want," says Jelagen. "Not your *service* I want. Traitor."

"I know," Helthew says, very calm and even, their voice, in offering up their life as sacrifice. "Only let Zevalash and my sister and their children go."

"The children, I keep."

"They'll never love you. They're too old to forget. Give up that fantasy, buy yourself an orphan or two in Thurbridge, if children you must have, and take my life for theirs."

In a bad way, Helthew looks, wan and hollow-eyed; their arms are wrapped around their ribs and they bend forward a little to ease their breathing.

Hides, nicely, the sharp-edged rock they clutch in their right hand.

So they throw, hard and true and from close by, and it strikes the woman holding the lass in the temple and she drops, and through Helthew maybe hadn't meant it, she's dead before she hits the ground, and Helthew flings themself to grab their niece and roll away, curling around her. Marcsy gives one shriek, like an enraged woodpecker, and Helthew's hand is bloody on the child's neck, staunching a wound... Scratched, only scratched, by the fallen robber's knife, and the louder shriek is Jelagen, as Zevalash hurls the hatchet and it strikes the robber-queen's stick upraised for shield and Zevalash follows in a rush—but I've my own work, and snapping teeth seize an arm, jerk hard, fling a man aside with the joint of his shoulder giving way within, I feel it rip. Duck my head and stamp my foot, and Barris gets the message, vaults to my back and gives me an entirely unnecessary dig of the toe and thump of the heel to turn me and send me springing for where Helthew and Marcsy clutch one another.

Helthew's got no strength left to heave, but Barris pulls, clinging with his knees and leaning away to balance, and Marcsy jumps, and up she comes across my withers, and Helthew slaps my rump—dear witch, we do not know one another so well as all that, I'd have said, if I'd had time and speech—and I gallop off with the children sorting themselves out, Marcsy righting herself with a leg heaved up and over my neck, and she clutches my mane and Barris clutches her and is trying to turn me, toe and heel again, because I've set myself at the drystone wall—

We fly. I clear it easily.

And we're away.

Into forest, weaving through trees, down along beside the dry gully, into cedars and the scent of a friend, who whickered to greet me. Trotting I came to her and touched noses and shook the children off where Dandelion stood, the end of the rope halter looped over a bit of branch that wouldn't have held her at all if she decided to stroll away.

"Good lass," I told her, shaking my hair from my face, and ignored a yelp and a squeak from the children.

A moment's work to lower the stirrups we'd raised up to stop them banging about when the mare was serving as packhorse. A moment more to tell Barris, "Take your sister and ride. Head downriver—your father has friends there, does he not, in the Cove? Raise the Garraniash, tell them they're fools if they don't seize this chance, with the robber-gang in such disarray, to put an end to their raiding for once and all. If you know a good ford, try it rather than the bridge—"

And setting blessings on them, aye, I was, of swift safe riding, of fleeting by, if not unseen, as close to it as may be. Let them be only a startled deer, only a gust of wind, a darker shadow, cloud and bending tree. The afternoon stretched into evening, shadows lengthening. That would help.

"You—you were—you're a *horse!*" That was Barris.

"Do we have time for this?" I asked.

"No. Um, no, my lady?"

"Good. Up. I'll do what I can, back there. Your task is to have your sister safe away and send whatever help you can raise. And the midwife, too." I flung a thought Hedge's way. "Send her to the island in the river where you nearly sank your father's boat."

"Yes, my lady."

What were Hedge and Arrany doing on the island? They ought to have gone downriver and across, into the wilderness.

Barris mounted. I swung the little lass up behind him. "Hold fast," I told her. "And the pair of you, ride swiftly." Blessing, that, not an order. Or possibly both. "The mare's name is Dandelion and she belongs to Lady Arrany, the queen's sister of the Esrineyn."

"Yes, my lady."

"Is Dandelion a lady too?" Marcsy wanted to know.

"She is no shapeshifter, but you treat her as a lady for all that."

Then I was crow, and winging swift away.

OH, all was not well, back in the dell. No pursuit had set off after me, though one man was chasing the lone horse around, bridle in hand, curses on his tongue. The roan gelding was sensibly reluctant to be caught, and I gave him every encouragement to kick up his heels and not let himself be cornered, while the cattle did their part, catching the general agitation and shifting about in starts and rushes. The goats, being goats, came trundling over to see the fun without my needing to touch their beastkind thoughts, and added their own bit of mayhem.

But the reason the robber-queen's bravos had been distracted from pursuit of the escaping children made my heart lurch. Helthew was down on the ground and Zevalash standing between them and Jelagen. Since he'd thrown the hatchet, the vhalgod had no better weapon than a stick, and Jelagen had Hedge's sword. Zevalash blocked a swing with the staff, and it sliced clean through, but he swerved away and so spared his ribs. Jelagen stumbled, caught her balance. A bad knee, I thought, old injury or the price of age, and it was the robber-queen's own walking stick Zevalash wielded, or two-thirds of it, now. One or other of them must have gotten it away from her, or she'd thrown it aside. Swung, maybe and dropped Helthew first, to save him for some later, more leisurely, revenge? The witch was moving, but groggily. And a man circling about them with a spear came in close and thrust down—

I shrieked warning, more a falcon's cry than a crow's, but Helthew rolled aside and seized the spear embedded in the turf, came up hand over hand, leaning, hanging from it, kicked hard and sent the robber reeling back, and at the same moment Zevalash couched the staff under his arm. Slipping aside from Jelagen's thrust so nearly that it sliced the sleeve of his tunic, he lunged and drove the sharp-sheared end in beneath her breast. She was borne over backwards by the force of his thrust, and down he went, stumbling onto a knee beside her. Swift, he was, to seize the sword from her faltering hand and leap again to his feet.

But she was done, mouth working, silent, words fled, and then still, only her panting and the welling blood, a little trickle of it from the corner of her grimacing lips, coppery eyes staring at the sky. Empty.

Helthew yelped at my tumbling from the air into singing wolf beside them. I circled about, snarling. Still propping themself up by the captured spear, they laid a quelling hand on my head. None were daring to close with us.

Zevalash turned, this way, that, watching them all. Five of them, only five left standing, but there were still those sent out to hunt for us. But the robber-queen's lieutenant had died at the bridge and none of this lot seemed eager to assume command.

Wolf, I was, and then woman. "A wild godling's curse upon you," I said, and if my voice shook, it was with the memory of the rage I had felt when Hedge went down in highway, and the way the child had screamed, dragged by her hair, and the knife at her throat.

Oh, they fell back, then, with their captain, their queen, dead in her own blood at their feet.

"A curse upon you, you who have lived by murder and rapine and theft, who have fed on the suffering and the misery of the folk of these hills and the travellers of the road, and the villages of the eastern forests, too. You who have never even looked aside from your wickedness, as these three your erstwhile fellows have done, nor questioned your deeds, nor sought to make any amend for those deeds by a life lived to better end, as even your chief's heir Jaslyn did, shot down by you yourselves in his act of kindness and mercy and his rejection of his grandmother's all-devouring greed. You, one and all, who stand here, who stole children from their parents, who hunted a pregnant woman through the night, who beat and tormented this good witch, one who by their choice of living now seeks to atone for the harm they have formerly done in your company—you, and those who even now roam the woods and course the highway and search the riverbank, thinking to take us, be you all accursed by my will and my tongue. Let all go ill for you, till seven years you have served what is right and good, and seven years again you have done what it is right and good to do, and seven years more you have wandered, and in every thought, and every word, and every deed, you have striven to make this world a place better than ever it was when you were born into it, to your parents' shame." I snarled, wolfish, and added, setting a fear on them, "Know that the spears of the Garraniash are on their way, raised against you."

They fell back. Two ran, and then the three, and the smoke poured up out of their stronghold and storehouse, a billowing cloud, black and grey, to the sky.

I picked up the bridle dropped by the man who had abandoned chasing the roan gelding, and the horse came trotting to lower his head and snuffle over my face, and the cows and their calves and a pair of big spotted oxen followed, two or three with bells clanking, and the goats scampered round about them.

"Zevalash," I said. "You know this place. Find what passes for a stable, saddle this horse for Helthew, and follow on. I'll be off after your children, to make sure no fool does worse."

The five had scattered, two into the wilderness to the west and three away up the mountainside, each alone. I thought it would be some time before they dared even to come back to scavenge what they should need for wherever their road might take them. There were still those out hunting, though.

I tossed the bridle to Zevalash and took to the air. Aye, maybe my thoughts and my worrying tended to run to Hedge, but what would she have said, if I'd left those children to make their desperate ride alone?

If Zevalash or Helthew thought to strip the robber-queen of her gold and jewels in passing, well, I suppose the impulse was a practical one.

12

IN WHICH ARRANY HAS FURTHER BOATING MISADVENTURES

While Helthew and Zevalash and I were working our way, secret as weasels, through the woods towards the robber-queen's fortress, Arrany and Hedge were facing problems of their own. Arrany, indeed, was feeling that Hedge was one of those problems, and no small one at that. Pony, she was saying to herself, might be all very calm and offhand about it, and insist that it was perfectly normal for a vhalgod's face to go the colour of a dead fish's belly, with the skin about eyes and lips standing out like livid bruises, or for her body to throw off heat like a hearth, when she was so gravely wounded, but despite Arrany's vhalbairn ancestry she had no such knowledge herself. She did not trust but what I was making light of matters to stop her worrying over what she could not mend.

Perhaps. A little. But for all that it was true enough, that the fever went with a vhalgod's healing.

Arrany rowed. Delmara, grunting with the effort and her face flushed red, bailed. Hedge, who had first watched the way ahead over Arrany's shoulder to guide her around the rocks below the island, sat on a thwart slumped over her knees, and her breathing was swift and shallow, like a wounded animal's.

There was water rising up the sides of the secondhand boots

Hedge had bought Arrany after Rhunavon. They leaked, and a foot was growing cold and wet.

"Delmara..."

"I'm doing my damnedest," that woman said, through clenched teeth.

"I know, but—" And then Arrany yelled, "Down!" and they all tumbled together in the sloshing water, six inches deep now, it was, and more along the keel, as the archer she had spotted on the shore shot and the arrow sped hissing over.

She groped for her own bow, while Delmara grabbed an oar that was sliding through its rowlock.

"Stay down!"

"I'm staying down." But she couldn't, not if she meant to stop that archer. She popped up, sighted him, had to drop again but was fitting arrow to string, and rose to a knee to loose, the fool robber not having shifted his position, just standing there yelling, "They're here! They're here!" back into the woods.

So down he went on the rocks of the shore, not slain, but an arrow in his shoulder and something to yell about, anyhow, and better, he'd dropped his bow into the shallows, which was not going to do his string any favours.

"I'll row, you shoot," Delmara said, scrambling up to the rower's thwart, so Arrany scooted to the stern, nocked another arrow and drew, kneeling low and watchful, crowded against Hedge. Delmara puffed and groaned and dragged at the oars, digging deep, catching crabs. No water-woman, even at the best of times; she must have left the fishing to Zevalash. The boat moved in wallowing jerks, nosing deeper, with Delmara's greater weight towards the prow, and the water rose, creeping past Arrany's ankle, up her shin.

Hedge shifted, trying to sit up.

"Down," Arrany said, and tried to push against her, but it was like trying to shift a boulder.

"We're all going down," Hedge said. "Take us upriver, Delmara."

A long groan was her only answer, but the boat wavered, turned.

"Give me the bow, Arrany. You row."

"You can't—" Arrany would have protested, but Hedge took the bow from her hand. It was a light draw for her, or would have been, but her arms shook and it was with teeth clenched that she pulled it at all.

"Vhalgod!" someone ashore bellowed, as she rose up to her knees to shoot, and there was a rustling and crashing, a flicker of shapes vanishing away under trees. The reputation of the great vhalgod warbows was enough, it seemed. For a little while. The man with the arrow in his shoulder, abandoned by his friends, crawled into a thicket of red-barked dogwood.

Hedge sank back on her heels and Arrany traded places with Delmara again. Arrany leaned to the oars, but the water was flowing in faster than anyone could bail with a mere saucepan, the rough caulking torn away by some scrape over rocks as they set out, I suspect.

"Island," said Hedge through clenched teeth. "Out of sight."

Arrany said nothing. That was already her intent. They certainly weren't going to make it to the farther shore. A struggle, she had of it, fighting the current to bring them up again into the rough broken water around the island, where rocks thrust through to make curling white plumes or lurked beneath the surface, swirling eddies the only warning. A bump, a scrape, the current pushing them back, caught and twisting, growl of stones under the keel. The boat wallowed deeper, so that waves sprang over the top strake, all awash.

"Out, out!" cried Delmara, heaving a bundle to her shoulders as the keel grated again. She clambered up to crouch on a thwart, peering uncertainly at the swirling water. She sat heavily, slid out into the water—it came partway up her thighs. The force of the current rocked her and stones shifted underfoot, so that she had to cling to the boat to keep her balance.

The others followed, Hedge growling at Arrany when she would have taken all the burden of our packs and saddlebags onto herself. Hedge, I may say, denies the growling.

Rocky, slippery, uneven footing. The lightened boat, though sluggish and still filling, tugged to be free and nearly had Arrany away with it. She let go in haste and grabbed at Hedge's arm while the boat wallowed out into stronger current, the deep channel, riding lower and lower, until without any great splashing it slid under like a turtle and was gone.

They made it to the island's shore, clinging together, climbed up through stones and scrub-willow bushes and dogwood tangled with wild cucumber vines. The island was long and narrow, like an upturned boat, a stony ridge its keel, and without debate they made for this, Arrany slashing a way through brush and vine and tall pink balsam-flower with her sax, Hedge and Delmara supporting themselves somehow along behind her. Delmara was muttering under her breath and gasping; Hedge had gone grimly silent. The going was easier on the steeper, drier ground, above the level of spring flooding, where ancient maples and elms spread broad canopies, shading out the brush. Hedge dropped the saddlebags she had slung over her good side and sank to the ground between the roots of a great-grandmother of elms, shivering, head in her hands. With a groan, Delmara joined her, cradling her belly.

"Can you think of a worse time and place to be having a baby?" she asked.

"No," Arrany admitted. She considered that. "Are you?"

"Possibly."

"Soon?" Arrany says she didn't squeak. I suspect she did.

"These things," Delmara said, and you can imagine the twisted sort of smile that went with the words, "usually take some time. But I won't be swimming, if any of Jelagen's accursed crew come after us. Tonight, maybe. By tomorrow, for certain, if the other two were anything to go by. It's—begun." She shut her eyes on what Arrany took to be a cramp. "I want Zev." But that was a whisper, not meant to be heard.

"Flute," said Hedge. "Arrany." She was breathing as if that took all her attention. "If they come. Call Jinn. He'll know—what to do."

"Call him...?"

"With the flute. You probably won't be able to see him, or maybe you might, but—he'll come. He'll do what has to be done." She meant to offer her own blood, of course, and the shape she was in... but she didn't think that Arrany understood that.

"All right." Arrany agreed only reluctantly, not so much out of unease with the magic involved, but with the idea of summoning a ghost at all, too vivid a reminder of the slaughter we had effected at the bridge.

"Good." And Hedge laid herself down, curled on her side and shivering. Delmara was shivering too, after her wetting, for all it was a hot summer's day, but exhaustion and the river's mountain-born chill, little sleep and less food and the terror for her family—all those things were taking their toll.

Fire? Arrany couldn't decide what was best. Jelagen's people might assume they had made it over to the farther shore; the boat had not been so obviously sinking when fear of Hedge had put those watching to flight. A fire, if she kept it small, if she found only the driest wood to burn, might be safe enough, might not paint the sky with its banner of smoke to summon their enemies.

Or it might.

Or Hedge might sink into some deathly chill. And Delmara's baby was coming, and she all draggled and begrimed with river-water and river-mud and the dust, and was that not the first thing that midwives demanded, that all be clean, clean, clean? She'd never been attendant at a birth, not of a human, at any rate, though she'd been around at enough lambings to have a vague idea of what might need doing. Humans, though, were a trickier matter. And humans pregnant by a vhalgod...

If there'd been an offering-stone about, she would have been pouring out a libation and a raft of prayers for my quick return, she told me, afterwards, even if all she had to offer was river-water.

Fire, she decided, was worth the risk, if she made it with care, so she unrolled those blankets that had avoided dunking in the river, which was one and part of another, and wrapped them over Hedge and Delmara together. Hedge's skin, for all her shivering, felt hot and dry. Delmara was muttering under her breath, charms, Arrany thought, or prayers, her attention all drawn inward, anyway, and she only nodded distantly, raised no objection, when Arrany said, "I'll make a fire."

There was plenty of dead wood under the maples, much of it rotten, though, and growing shelves and scales of fungi. Down along the waterline of the spring floods Arrany had better luck gathering dry branches stripped of bark and polished smooth by much battering. She lugged armloads of it back, small stuff that she could hope was dry right through and not harbouring some smoke-feeding damp at its heart.

Her third trip down for driftwood, or maybe her fourth, she heard a yell. A human man's voice. Arrany dropped her armload of wood, drew her sax and ran, dodging through the trees, leaping fallen branches. Came to a stumbling halt with her arm about a tree. A man there, his spear levelled at Hedge, who was on her feet with Arrany's bow drawn on the man in turn. Delmara, sitting with her back to the tree still, knees drawn up and knife in her hand, was braced as if to leap, though he would have known she could not.

And the bears. They stood one to either side of the man, dripping, heads lowered like wary dogs, drawing in scent, considering, little ears swivelling about. One reared up taller than a vhalgod, yawned as a dog might in unease. She dropped down again, shook herself, spattering river-water over them all, like a dog again, and shambled across to sniff at Arrany. Arrany stood very, very still.

"One word," the man said. "One word from me and they'll tear you limb from limb. Shoot one, and the other will eat your heart."

"No," Hedge said. "Not again. You do wrong to make these beasts of the wild your weapons and already I owe atonement for such innocent blood."

Well, Arrany didn't know what she meant by that about innocent blood; Hedge, after all, was happy to hunt for our cookfires and was not one of those philosophers who forswear the eating of meat. She hadn't told us about the she-lions that lion-man godling had set on her, you may recall. I might have said that a warhorse ridden into battle had even less choice about being there, and less understanding of the argument between army and army, than those she-lions, who attacked Hedge because she seemed to their godling to be an enemy of their pack. Or pride, or tribe, or whatever it was they were. Hedge would say I was being argumentative to no purpose and her feelings were her own and not subject for debate in such a matter.

But for my part, I feel the horses are more to the pitied than those lions, or those bears in that moment. The wild beasts were not compelled against their will; they were free to recognize themselves overmatched, to turn submissive or withdraw. A warhorse, no matter how caught up it may be in the excitement of the charge, is not.

Hedge would say—well, as you may gather, it is a fireside debate that arrives at no certain conclusion. Best to abandon it and let everyone keep their temper.

"They don't obey you, Nairk," Delmara said. "Remember, I know you. Remember, I was there when Jelagen ordered the slaughter of the bears in their winter-sleep and took these two nursling cubs to rear as her pets. It's Jelagen they hold as dam in their poor muddled beast-hearts. True enough she let Jaslyn and Wolcha command them. But not you. You've only ever been her stable keeper."

"Who do you think they love and obey better, me their groom or Wolcha, who only ever shouted and beat them as much as he offered honeycomb? Wolcha is dead and I doubt they mourn him. They carried me over the river to you willingly enough. Lay down your weapons, or I set them on the vhalgod."

The bow trembled. Hedge was near the end of her strength. But the air was chill, and Jinn was there, unseen, a shadow and a shifting in the corner of the eye, a coldness striking deep. The bears knew him for an uncanny thing, and growled, and ducked their heads, and backed a little, while the man himself took a step away, unsure of what it was he feared.

And Arrany, freed from their attention, slid under the belly of the nearest and rose, and thumped the man Nairk on the back of the head with hilt of her sax gripped in both hands.

Down he goes, dropped like a falling stone.

"Good," said Hedge, and not quite so swiftly, folded up on her knees.

WHAT'S to tell of the rest of us, that evening and the day that followed? We had a wild gallop through the woods and down the highway, Dandelion and I, matching pace for pace, till we came to the village called just 'the Cove', and a young woman went riding off on a fresh horse to the bigger, walled village of the chiefs another few miles downriver. I, seeing Barris and Marcsy safe enough at Valyn Weaver's hearth—her husband was nephew of the midwife-witch Valestia—left Dandelion to be praised and fussed over by Valyn Weaver's young son, to go flying along above the messenger. Aye, I had my say to the three chiefs gathered.

You can imagine, it was not cream and honey that was in my mouth.

So, thus spurred, and heartened by knowledge that Jelagen herself was fallen along with many of her bravos, they summoned such folk of their trained bands as lived nearabouts, and set out well before dark, with promise of more to follow and a couple of boats of eight and ten oars apiece to patrol the river, and furthermore to set some help, the midwife-witch among them, on the island where I did know Hedge to be.

The finding of Zevalash and Helthew encamped among the ruins of the farm and debating whether to try to build a raft and set out over the river in search of Delmara or to wait, trusting that the farm would be the obvious place to which all would return, was an easy matter. All the cattle and goats I had set to follow them were spread out through their pasture, grazing contentedly. Garraniash beasts for the most part, no doubt, and not likely to be left to Zev and Delmara as compensation for their losses, but perhaps there might be yearlings among them born to the robbers' herds, and perhaps a word or two on my part with the chiefs might see them left with Delmara and Zevalash. They'd lived peaceable enough once they forswore their life of brigandage, and the tribe had done nothing to oust Jelagen all the years she'd squatted on their borders. It was Zevalash, after all, who'd slain the robber-queen and rid them of that menace. Some recompense might be in order.

Leaving aside the question of whether they'd thought to rob the dead.

Once I'd assured Zev and Helthew that Delmara, and Hedge and Arrany, not that Zevalash asked after my two, were safe and on the island, nothing would do but that they join them. Off we went, Helthew riding the roan gelding, which no one of the Garraniash spears had tried to claim. A quick matter to hail the Garraniash boat that had landed Goodsister Valestia on the island and have it come to carry us over.

What did we find? Hedge, wrapped in a blanket, lying with her face to the fire and a bear sprawled as windbreak along her back. Delmara, pacing slowly back and forth, clutching an apparently solicitous she-bear by the fur of her great shaggy neck, while Goodsister Valestia made faintly worried noises—about the bears' interest in the proceedings, for there was nothing obviously awry with Delmara thus far—and prepared those things she might need. A robber, glum, resigned, and suffering rather a bad headache, sitting with his hands bound and tied to a tree, a Garraniash spearwoman keeping a close eye on him. Arrany, on her knees, tending to the several fish threaded on greenwood skewers leaning over the fire and the bannock that was just starting smoke.

"The children are safe!" Delmara cried first of all, having that news from Goodsister Valestia, as if I might have forgotten to mention it to her husband and sibling.

"Jelagen is dead," said Zevalash, wrapping her in his arms. "The chiefs have set the trained bands to capture those who ran." There would no doubt be trials, and all too likely executions, and we might hope that would dampen young Barris's enthusiasm for an outlaw's life if his abduction had not.

"I could have done without this diversion, really, Pony," Hedge muttered, when we'd settled ourselves a little apart, we and a second fire, though we didn't have it to ourselves long, as the Goodsister chased away all who had no business in Delmara's current undertaking.

"It wasn't my fault, this time." So often such diversions are, I admit. I soothed her, her head in my lap, my hands running over her, shedding the blessing of healing, of strength, of peace and sleep. She did sleep, and her fever faded, and Arrany slept, and the men and women of the Garraniash who'd stayed to keep watch over us and our prisoner...well, they slept, too, and the prisoner, it transpired, was improperly tied when they moved him away from what had become a birthing-place, for he slipped his bonds and went off to take his chances swimming to shore. He hadn't been at the fortress when I'd laid my curse, but I'd had a few words with him apart that seemed well-set in his mind, and thought it likely he'd do no further harm to anyone, but spend his remaining days seeking to live a better life. I do know he passed safe through the Garraniash hunters and never came back to those parts again.

Past noon when Helthew, fear standing in their eyes, came from assisting Goodsister Valestia to fetch me. Nearer the supper hour, when we between us finally brought a new wailing life safely into the world, saw it washed and wrapped and clutched tight to Delmara's breast, and she herself could sink into exhausted sleep, weak and pale, but with every hope of recovery. I overheard Valestia and Helthew muttering together, planning stern admonishments, that Delmara and Zevalash had three healthy children now; there was barrenseed, and there were charms a strong witch such as Valestia could make (and would) for them to wear, and Delmara was not to risk any fourth such pregnancy, so there. And that would be them told. There might not, Valestia said, be a godling by, next time.

Aye, it very nearly did not go well. No, you don't need to know the details, that's nothing that's any business of yours.

A FORTNIGHT PASSED SWIFTLY, Hedge resting, and healing, and Helthew and Delmara too, back down in the village called the Cove, in the house of Goodsister Valestia, and Arrany and I lending our help to the raising of house and outbuildings, and cutting hay in the high meadows, to get Zevalash and Delmara a start on preparing again for winter with a larger herd to feed. There was a field of buckwheat that had escaped burning and trampling, and one of yellow winter turnips; with the charity of their neighbours, they would come through, and at least there'd be plentiful cheese, for as I'd hinted to the chiefs' captains, the couple were owed some recompense for all their losses, beyond the return of their own beasts. In addition to a yearling heifer, an extra weanling pig for the smokehouse, and several goats, they'd ended up with an unclaimed milch-cow, calf at heel, more than they started with.

Helthew would not be wintering over with their sister's family. A few long talks, we'd had, Goodfellow Helthew and I. Before second harvest began and the year turned to autumn, they were going to take their roan gelding and set out north. I thought a year or two under Goodbrother Bessamy's tutelage in Smithsford might be what Helthew needed, for the cultivation of their skills as witch and healer, aye, but even more, for the healing of their own soul. Bessamy was young, indeed, but had a wisdom beyond his years, and a deep calm and understanding that was soothing as the contemplation of quiet water. It would be well.

Finally, in a morning with the dew lying heavy on the grass and the crickets singing of coming autumn, leaving the little household waving from their still-ashy dooryard, we set out again, Hedge and Arrany and Dandelion and I. This time, we had no adventures crossing that bridge.

The bears? Ah, I'd forgotten the bears. It seems they had adopted Delmara as their new human and the baby, named Helthara, as their own cub.

13

IN WHICH A BROTHER IS LOST

So. Again, we were on our own, as we took the old imperial highway up into the foothills of the mountains and then swung to the east, following a road that climbed and wound through steep forests of pine and spruce. Small villages and scattered log-built farmsteads clung to the slopes above narrow white-churning brooks that rushed away to join the Rhunavon, which in these upper reaches of its waters flowed out of the east. The closer the mountains had drawn, the more silent Arrany had become, till now as we hiked over their very knees she seemed fallen into a mood entirely dark. She was not sleeping much, either, tossing and turning, growing shadow-eyed and wan. I wondered if she fretted at our delay after the affair of the robber-queen, through we could hardly have pushed on before Hedge was fit to march again, or if our nearness to the end had set her to brooding fruitlessly—as she had before—on her brother's peril. She shrugged me off when I tried to ask, turned snappish as a dog in pain, so I left her be.

Perhaps I should have been keeping a more watchful eye on her.

We made camp at dusk that last night of march along the mountains, planning to wake in the early hours and set out under the waning moon, to come to Under-Ice in the pale dawn. Arrany's suggestion was that we might find one or other of Spider and Penryl going out alone to tend the goats, and thus be able to lure the lad off to some safety where we could defend him against the witch while we worked to get the god-collar off him. Though we'd often been sheltered in the sweet new hay of some kindly family's harvest, that night we would be sleeping under the stars, rolled up in our blankets under the pines. It was a pleasant camping-place, with the sound of the wind soughing through the boughs and a small brook rushing and gurgling down in its rocky bed nearby. Not far off, a pair of owls called to one another.

I had that restless feeling on me, you know how it is, when there's action impending, and Hedge, too, was all wound tense. We'd have gone on, I think, and lain up without fire or supper where we could spy out the cottage in the dark, only Arrany was flagging with day's end, and her plan seemed the better one for human eyes.

Arrany offered to make the supper, though it was Hedge's turn, and after we had gathered wood enough for the cooking we left her to it and went wandering together. There's something about a pinewood that lifts the heart, don't you find? I sniffed out some early white pine mushrooms, which we carried back, to fry up in a bit of salt butter from the last farm and serve alongside the thick pottage Arrany had made, red lentils and onions, and shavings of smoked dry cheese, all flavoured with fennel seed. It was an excellent pottage—Arrany's cooking had improved greatly over the course of our travels—but she ate little, for all our urging that she must set her nerves aside, she'd need her strength, she'd do her brother no good coming in to his rescue with her belly empty and growling and we'd have no hot breakfast, only an oatcake to nibble. But she couldn't, she said, she'd be sick, and sick enough she looked, all hollow-eyed and grey, not so much in the face as in the soul. It was no hardship to finish what she left ourselves, and I thought, well, tomorrow she would make up for it; once we had Penryl safe in our keeping Hedge would make something good, tempting soft buckwheat pancakes, and maybe we'd carry away some cheeses, good hard keeping cheese, but to pique weakened appetites some potted creamy fresh white cheese, too. Or we could plunder a milch-goat entire, since likely we'd want to lie up in shelter for a week or two while Penryl got his strength back; with a goat to milk we could make clabber, good invalid's food for the pair of them.

Arrany was restless in her blankets again, over at the foot of another great pine, but she settled, in the end, and Hedge slept, a deep and peaceful sleep, for travel kept her from brooding, as I'd noticed before, and the bad dreams come only rarely when we're on the road. And I slept, snuggled in to her side, human, with her arm over me. And the brook burbled and babbled and sang and chimed, and the wind, and the owls...

I woke on the grey edge of dawn, with a bit of moonlight slanting down, for the moon was in its last quarter and stood high overhead at that hour. I yawned and stretched, and sniffed the air, thinking something was off, something was—not there that should be, and it was Arrany, and the mare, scent gone chill, not the fresh warmth of their presence.

Hedge stirred, not quite waking at my stirring.

Fire, embers banked in ashes before we slept, for it was a warm night and you really don't want a spark going astray in a pinewood. Our bundles, there where we had left them, the pot and pan and bowls all packed away ready to go, because we had meant to be off without delaying at this very hour in the morning twilight.

Saddle—no.

So I put a hand to Hedge's shoulder and squeezed it, and she opened her eyes, swift-waking.

"What?"

"Arrany."

Hedge rolled to her feet, shook out her shoulders, stood on one foot, the other, putting on socks and boots, then the tunic she'd laid aside for sleeping. "Well, now."

No immediate danger in the air, Hedge read that from my posture, didn't have to ask.

"She's been lying all this way, Pony. Jinn did say so."

"Aye, of course. But now we find out *why*." We'd expected something. All this way, that lie, whatever it was, had been waiting, and we'd neither of us thought it was merely the little matter of her not wanting to confess to being a lady born and a queen's runaway daughter.

"You didn't hear her leaving." It wasn't a question.

"I did not."

"Hrm," said Hedge, a deep rumble in her chest.

"The brook is very loud, really," I said, in my defence. "And you couldn't ask for a softer cushion to walk on than a forest floor of year upon year of pine needles slowly rotting." From which I had considerately picked up nearly all the dead and broken sticks like to crack and betray.

"Hrm."

"Well, you didn't wake, either, Hedge, my love."

"That I did not."

I might have made a noise then. Not quite a growl, not quite a groan. Hedge put her arms around me and I thumped my head a few times gently against her chest. "No fools like old fools, as they say."

"Do they say that?"

"If they don't they ought to."

"Compared to you, Thallyn of Dahres Head, I am really quite, quite young. So. I would suggest we remove ourselves to someplace else, and quickly, lest Arrany be on her way back with company."

"Aye." It was sensible, but I felt tired, and angry, to be agreeing. Not angry with Hedge. Not even angry with Arrany, not then. Just—a small, quiet, anger, at there being betrayal in the world.

Hedge shook out her dragon-scale coat. I did not dissuade her. Helped her with the buckles.

"Take the track?" she asked. "Or go around?"

It wasn't like we didn't know where Arrany had gone. The prints of Dandelion's hooves, newly shod again before we left the Garraniash, even a town dweller could have followed. She had been led quietly away over the soft mould of the forest floor, down to the track, still at walk, fording the noisy little brook, and then there was some shuffling around under a tree that showed Arrany had, I thought, either carried saddlebags and saddle away first and then come back to lead the mare away, or the other way around, before she saddled her and rode. When—by the scent, I made it a couple of hours, no more.

Speaking of scent, it was dried valerian root in the pottage, of course, taken from the little bags of useful this and that which Goodbrother Bessamy had sent us off with so long before. And I ought to have sniffed it out, but what with fennel and onions and old cheese, and then my own addition of the strong-scented white pine mushrooms frying…It's not that it will knock you out like a witch's sleeping draught in a ballad, only it does give you that gentle nudge over the edge into a sounder sleep. I should have known it, if not by the scent, by the odd little dreams it gave, the sort that don't distress you but leave you a bit puzzled in the morning, asking, where did that come from, why should I dream that Ilyu and Hedge and I were wandering through the coffee-houses of Gowanesh far away in the southeast of the old empire in search of someone to sell us a goat, a special goat, white with russet ears, though what we wanted it for none of us seemed to know.

And it was—good, in a soft, quiet sort of way, to have a dream of Ilyu that left me only a little affection, a little sorrow, rather than the nightmare grief of his death relived and my own helplessness, and lost Iliya.

But I didn't have leisure to think about any of that then.

So, "Oh," I said, "let's go around by the heights and come down on the cottage from some direction they won't expect. It's a nice fresh morning for a walk in the woods, and we don't have the horse to cumber us. I can perch on the eaves and do some proper eavesdropping." It was a matter of six or seven miles to the valley of Under-Ice, Arrany had told us, and then perhaps half a mile up the valley to the witch's cottage. "We might even come there before her."

"Pony," Hedge said then. "*Pony!*"

"What?"

"The flute. She's taken Jinn's flute."

The sheathed flute on its baldric had been set safely aside with

Hedge's sword, propped against the bole of our sheltering tree within reach of a vhalgod's long arm. And that the sword was there, untouched, and the hatchet, we'd seen at once, of course, the eye running over those larger shapes, skipping what was missing.

"Aye," said Hedge, and her voice was grim, all benign toleration fled her. "Go. I follow."

14

IN WHICH A BROTHER IS FOUND

Six or seven miles, Arrany had said it was, to the valley of Under-Ice from where they camped by that loud little brook coursing down in its rock channel. A lie. It was a matter of only two miles along the track, and then a half a mile further up the valley to Sikassyn's cottage. She had been worried lest Pony's sharp nose detect even at that distance the scent of the witch's hearth. Worried lest they wake, in which case she meant to creep away afoot, if she must, but she very much wanted to have the horse with her, and as it turned out, neither godling nor vhalgod woke. The coarse-pounded valerian root had been easy to identify by its smell even though she had not recognized the symbol inked blurrily on the little linen bag among a handful of other packets and jars in Hedge's leather satchel of cooking herbs and medicines. She'd seen it, put the thought of using it away with the already half-formed idea of how to handle the return to Under-Ice, back when she was helping Pony hunt out salves for the wounded, after the fight with robbers. She'd been surprised it worked on a godling at all, but it was a small thing, something that could easily slip by her defences, not some malevolent poison, which a godling would surely notice and bring all her powers to fight against. Too, she thought that her miserable nights, unable to fall asleep despite what should have been the pleasant weariness of their days' marching, must have grown them used to her tossing and turning and moving about; she had chosen the campsite for the cheerful noise of the rushing stream and what cover that would give her. Still, in the end it did surprise her, that she had been successful in creeping away, horse and all.

Or lucky.

Did she wish that one or other of the pair had woken, had sat up, called her back, asked the question...?

Aye, maybe she did.

No traitor ever came to a good end. Arrany did not suppose she would.

Riding at a walk; then, half a mile safely behind her, at a trot, the moon risen to light her way, and she knew it well enough, having been sent foraging for mushrooms for Sikassyn all through that first autumn she'd served the witch.

If she could only get Penryl safe away, with no harm come to Hedge and Pony, then whatever their contempt for her, she knew that they would not leave her brother, ill and broken, to die alone and lost on the road. Whatever she herself had done, whatever price their just anger demanded from her, they would care for him and see him safe to some refuge. No matter how they hated her. Only, her heart ached so.

Trotting, even risking a hand-gallop, the track clear in the moonlight. The more ground she put between them, the safer she felt, but the flute, its baldric slung over her shoulder, its slight weight bumping under her arm, felt strange, warm as a living thing, and growing heavier, but that was her guilt.

Out from beneath the trees. The one trodden rut of what had once been a cart-track was now just a shallow depression overgrown with grass and buttercup. The path plunged downward past a shattered offering-stone for some lost godling. Arrany had used to climb up the hillside and pour out a little milk there, when she could, asking whatever virtue might still linger to open Penryl's eyes, to end his infatuation with the witch. She'd had no idea, then, of the powers at work binding him.

In the east, no touch of light was yet greying the horizon. The waning moon still climbed towards its noon. She reined in a moment to look back beneath the dark trees. No pursuit. Was that regret? It might have been.

Down the track, slanting along the valley side. Narrow goat-paths curled and braided through a landscape of humps and sunken green pits, overgrown with bushes run wild, vast patches of raspberry and tall tangling blackberry canes, apples and pears and plums long unpruned, and clumps of wind-seeded spruce and birch. Creeping tides of pine tumbled down the valley sides from the forest. Walls, too, there were, fallen to heaps of mossy logs, here and there the stone courses of a foundation still rearing up through the raspberries. The ruins of the village of Under-Ice. It has been abandoned in the years after the wars, Sikassyn had told her, too many of its folk gone away to fight, and the ones left behind dwindling, as the ice crept nearer from the valley's head, until the last few old women drove their goats away to other hamlets where the spring came earlier and winter's shadow did not fall so heavy. And so it was deserted when Sikassyn herself came, to make a home where she might pursue her studies in peace, serving the folk of the nearby valleys without dwelling among them.

A nice tale. Arrany wondered if it were true, or whether the folk of this place had weakened and wasted and died with the witch as their neighbour, if it had been only when there was no one left that Sikassyn had begun feeding out her rumours, to lure in young vhalbairn witches.

Not that I find Spider in any way defensible, but I think she was probably innocent of the slow death of the village, at least. She enjoyed her young men, she really did.

Dandelion forded the shallow, rocky stream that snaked along the valley from the south, chiming and burbling, mirror-gleaming, and not so cold as you might expect. It had its birth somewhere deep under the glacier, some hot spring, and gnawed its way steaming through the ice till it found its way out into the valley. It stained the rocks it flowed over yellow and rusty brown, and stank of rotten eggs, but it was a healthy water, so Sikassyn claimed, though the goats would not drink it. The witch bathed in it every morning, and drank it, too.

Arrany dismounted in the dooryard of the one house still standing. Well removed from the ruins, it was. The air struck cold, the ice that filled the valley higher up seeming to breathe out winter.

She felt weak-kneed, sick in the belly. If Sikassyn had given her up for dead, or thought she had abandoned her brother to his fate, never meant to return...

No. She would not let her mind walk that road.

The little house was log-built and steep-roofed, with a fenced kitchen garden to the side, dovecote and a long low shed away behind it. Was there a gleam of light within, a candle lit, in the workroom? No, she had imagined it; nothing there now. She led Dandelion around, let her drink at the water trough by the well, then took her behind the goat-shed, out sight of the house entirely, and left her tied there to a post of the dovecote, hoping it would not be for long.

She noticed her hands were shaking.

Back to the front of the house, the gable end, and up the two steps to the porch that ran the width of it, under the outflung roof.

Hesitated, then lifted the latch without knocking and slipped inside.

All was as she remembered it, the table spread with a fine cloth, the three-legged stools, the witch's painted chair with its fleece-stuffed cushions, the pots and pans scoured clean hanging in a row. Either the witch had found a new servant, or she was minding her own housekeeping. Or putting poor Penryl to work.

The door to the back room, the workroom, was open on darkness, the door to the lean-to larder and dairy closed fast. The side panels of the carved cupboard-bed were folded back in the summer warmth. And the wind through the open shutters of the windows blew fresh and cool. Maybe, maybe...oh, a last desperate wish, that she might coax Penryl from the bed and draw him away without ever waking the witch, be gone, back to Hedge and Pony—

"One step more, and I split you crown to crotch."

"It's me," Arrany said. "Arrany."

A word, and a candle sparked to life, the witch stepping into the doorway of the workroom. Magus-skill, that, not a gift of witchcraft, though Arrany still didn't know the difference. Sikassyn's threat had not been an idle one; she bore a hatchet in one hand, the pewter candlestick in the other.

"Ah," the witch said, and set not her weapon but the candle aside, coming into the front room. "I was beginning to think you had abandoned your brother."

"I wouldn't. You knew I wouldn't."

"So. Well done." Spider was already—or maybe it was still—half-dressed, goatskin breeches and a linen shirt hanging loose over them, her glossy chestnut hair swinging in a braid over each shoulder, barefoot. Up late studying, or had Dandelion's hooves on the stony bare path been enough to alert her? Too late to think now she should have left the horse further off. Spider padded softly towards the door, as if suspecting ambush lurking without. "Where did you leave them?"

"You don't need them," Arrany said hastily. "I found out—I have what you want. I brought it with me."

"The death-token?" Spider almost hissed. "The amulet? Oh, well done, girl. Give it here. Give it!"

"It isn't an amulet."

So heavy, the weight of the slender bone, when she took it in her hand. "Where's Penryl?" Eyes on the bed, deep in night untouched by the weak candle's flame over on the mantelpiece.

"Asleep," Spider said, dismissively. "All he does now is sleep. Humans burn out so quickly. I told you to make haste back."

"I hadn't even found them yet, when winter set in," Arrany protested. "They were half the world away." Not at all true, but Arrany's world then was yet a smaller one than ours. "Let me see him."

"Give me the relic."

Arrany tightened her hand on the flute. "I want to see Penryl."

"Look, then, fill your eyes with him. He's no more use to me, and certainly none to Duke Atana or the prince." Spider had opened the door, warily, peering out, hatchet at the ready. Nothing stirred. Well, we were still sleeping deep under the pines. Though not for too much longer. The moon was high, the little dog casting a black shadow on it. Soon the first grey would seep over the eastern horizon. Spider tucked in her shirt, finished her dressing with stockings, boots, a leather jerkin over all.

Then, "Give," she demanded, but Arrany was at the bed, the flute pressed to her chest all unawares, as if in it she held her own dear, the candlestick shaking in her hand.

What she saw. An old man, he seemed, an old man wasted away to death. A skull, skin the colour of parchment stretched over cheekbones, lined and crackled, eyes hollow and ringed black. His hair, long and unkempt and in knotted mats, his scruffy beard, white alike. He lay propped up on a heap of pillows, mouth hanging open. Hands, on the quilted coverlet—the gift of some grateful patient, for be sure Sikassyn did no such work herself—were all gnarled and knobby, clenched like claws, with broken, ragged nails. The body beneath that quilt looked far too sparing of flesh to be even her lightfoot, slender brother.

Arrany went to her knees then, and what escaped her was not so much a sob as a howl. If Spider had not snatched the candlestick from her she would have dropped it and set all alight.

"Stupid girl."

Arrany clutched at her brother's hand, dragged it to her cheek, and—warm, it was warm, feverishly so. Sikassyn would not leave a dead man lying in her one and only bed, of course she would not.

"The death-token?" Spider demanded. "The relic with which they've enslaved Prince Jinn?" She twisted a hand in Arrany's hair, jerked her head back to make her look up.

"It's the flute." Did the words choke her? I think maybe they did. "They use the flute, to call him."

And she fumbled at the baldric, but Spider was before her, snatching and dragging it off over Arrany's head. She drew the flute out a little ways, enough to see that it was carved of bone, not wood, enough to see the stains and know them for what they were.

"Ahhhh," she hissed, and hung it about her own neck like the amulet she had expected, tucked within the breast of her jerkin. "Clever. I wouldn't have expected that subtlety of work from Naskanna. That should satisfy the duke. But my poor Jinn, so long enslaved." A few strides took her to the doorway, where she paused, hefting the hatchet's weight, testing it.

Dry-mouthed, Arrany reached around for the hilt of her sax at her back. Could she draw it, springing up, and come at Spider before the witch hurled the little axe? She did not think so.

Spider snorted. "You had better not be here when your friends show up," she said. "Naskanna Deathdealer is not known for her mercy."

And she threw the hatchet. It thunked into the woodbox by the hearth. Arrany flinched. And Sikassyn was gone, closing the door softly behind her.

"Pen," Arrany whispered, and she would not deny that his hand was wet with her tears when it turned in hers and feebly gripped, and he stirred, and mumbled, and weakly rolled his head to see her.

"Arry?" he asked. His voice croaked, broke, as if it had been long since he had spoken. "Am I dead too?"

"Are you—*too?* Sun bless and sky above, Pen, did she tell you I was dead?"

He frowned in what seemed almost a baby's puzzlement, horrible on his old man's face. "You were gone. She said, she said...she said you were sick, you died, that I'd forgotten you were sick." His other hand came reaching like a claw, tangled in her hair, trying to stroke. "I forget so many things, now."

"She lied," Arrany said fiercely. "She lied, Penryl. Sikassyn—Spider, they call her Spider and I can see why—she lies, and lies, and lies."

He fumbled at her hand, didn't seem to know what she meant. Clutched her fingers.

"We have to get you out of here," she said.

Penryl shook his head, tried to push her away at that. "Don't. Don't be jealous. I'm so ill. The white death, it is. I haven't long. She's done everything she can, but there's no more even she can do."

"You're—" For all she knew, it could be some disease had done this to him, but "—no," she said. "There's no disease would age you so, turn your hair white like an old man's. Penryl, Spider—Sikassyn—she's more than a witch. She didn't draw you here out of some great desire to teach you. She's a magus, a wicked, wicked one. She's *old*, Pen. She was in Ghedhaynor in the Emperor's time. She did this, she was a magus serving in the library of the university; she seduced students, vhalgods and vhalbairns, and drank their life slowly away, and they died, and only when she tried it on a prince, a student-magus himself, then they discovered what she was doing. She was condemned to death for it, but she escaped and vanished in the wars."

When had Arrany learnt all this? Well, we'd spoken of it, a little, as we came along after we left Helthew and all behind.

"Think, Penryl, think." And she didn't say, for once in your life, which I think was very forbearing of her. "Why would she lie to you about me? Why would she tell you I was dead? She sent me away. She told me, she would kill you, she would keep on drawing away your life to keep herself young and beautiful, until you were all eaten up to a husk and died, unless I brought—brought some old enemies of hers here to her, and a thing they carried, and I thought—I thought they would be killed, the one she calls the duke means to kill Hedge, I'm sure of it—"

"Who?"

"Hedge, my—a vhalgod, the one I went to find. The one the duke wanted me to bring here, they were going to kill you, if I didn't. You remember, they came last summer? The vhalgods? The duke, and the magus, and their soldiers?"

But Penryl only shook his head weakly.

"The vhaldrach, you remember the vhaldrach? She came and sat at the table, there, eating bread and cheese, and her wings all furled up behind her like a great roosting bat?"

Again, only a puzzled look, which faded. "I dreamed of flying," he said softly.

"I know you did. It was dreams put into your mind by the witch, Pen. Only dreams." A sob escaped her. "They're going to do to Prince Jinn what they did to you. Or something worse. And he was so—I thought it couldn't matter. He was dead, and you weren't. I could still save you, and—he was so—a person, still. And kind. And I've betrayed him, betrayed my friends, the ones who set out to help me, to save you."

"Sikassyn wouldn't."

"Do you remember, when we came here? Do you remember what she looked like?"

Penryl frowned.

"She was old, Pen. An old, wise woman, we thought her, white-haired, standing in the door of her cabin leaning on her stick. Do you remember?"

He shook his head weakly. "I don't—she's a vhalbairn, Arrany. One of the first generation."

"And even they grow old and die. Her hair was white, when we came her. Do you remember? And now it's brown as a glossy horse and yours is faded away to cobweb."

"I love her. You don't need to be jealous."

"You don't! It's some beguilement, some wicked magic. And I'm not jealous. I was jealous of Tairna, because I was a stupid child and I didn't want to share. I was jealous because my whole life, that's all I'd been, Penryl's twin, Penryl's shadow and echo, there to dog your heels and talk us out of your trouble when I could, and take the blame and the blows when—when our mother was angry but we all knew it couldn't be your fault, because you were so precious to her. And if you grew up and took a wife where did that leave me, who was I then? A stupid child's jealousy, and you—you left Tairna behind without a thought, without a word, and I was mean enough to be glad of it, to think it meant I mattered more, and not to see—not to see how it meant something far, far worse, that you'd forgotten her so easily."

"Tairna," he said vaguely and blinked, his eyes focussing on her with a little frown. "Is Tairna...did she...?"

"Tairna nothing, you went off in the night and never mentioned her from that day to this. Did you think of her even once, since the night we sneaked away?"

The frown deepened. A tear. "You'll tell her...Sky above, Arrany, will you tell her...?"

"Tell her what?"

He shook his head.

"You can tell Tairna yourself," she snapped, angry suddenly. Furious. "Explain, when we get back, why you left her to go off chasing some two-hundred-year-old life-drinking hag!"

"I'm dying, Arrany. Don't cry."

She batted away the hand that tried to stroke her face and he gaped at the rejection. "You're not going to die. You're horribly, stupidly ill, but you are not going to die of this, I won't let you, not after all this, not after I—I betrayed my *friends* for you, the first friends I ever had for my own, who weren't yours, I lied and made them like me, they helped me, they saved me more than once, all we went through together on the road and I lied from the start, I lied every step of the way and then I betrayed them and she's got Jinn now and—and Hedge is going to kill me for that, her brother, I traded her *brother* for you—and you are not going to cost me all that and die like some stupid feeble hero in a ballad."

"Your friend's brother is with Sikassyn?" For a moment, Penryl looked—no, not jealous himself. He was terrified, and his silver-blue eyes with their vertical cat's pupil were awake and understanding. "She'll—Arrany, what did she do to me, oh sea and sky she was so beautiful and she said, she said, I wanted, I could almost see the way of, the way to change myself, to be—and she was so beautiful and I couldn't think, I couldn't—all the words in my head went away, so far away, and the world was so distant and strange and I could not remember—Arrany, I couldn't remember Tairna. I couldn't remember you." He started to cry in earnest, then. "I wanted to fly away from it all and I couldn't, I couldn't find the way. I want to go home, Arrany. Don't let her have me. Don't let her take me back."

"I won't, I won't, hush, I won't. Now come, we need to get you out of here."

Easier said than done. He was struggling, now, as if the bed were some trap he had to escape, but he could hardly stand on his own. She made him sit, flung open clothes chests—of which there were several, Spider's acquisitiveness not being limited to young men—until she found wide-legged trousers in an eastern style which, with a tablet-woven sash to cinch them in, would do, and a shirt and a long embroidered wedding-tunic. He was only wearing a threadbare nightshirt.

His tears dried, as a little child's grief does, and bewildered, obedient, he let her dress him. Managed a watery smile, a joke, that he had no drawers. Sikassyn had apparently not kept such mementoes of her victims. Arrany found socks and moccasins for his feet, wrapped him in a bridal-shawl of soft goat's wool, some villager's fine weaving.

"Come on, then." She got Penryl's arm over her shoulder and he was no weight at all. She thought she might almost have carried him swung up in her arms, only he was taller than her and his limbs would have dangled ridiculously.

Out the door, and Arrany had to leave her brother sitting on the steps while she fetched Dandelion around, thanking the dark and Spider's haste that the witch, wherever she was headed, had not thought to look for the horse. She had to help Penryl to use the height of the porch for a mounting-block, and guide his feet into the stirrups, steady him there as she led the horse away. Not back down the valley, but up past the goat-shed.

Penryl was looking around him, blinking as if the fresh air stung his eyes. The dawn was breaking in a pale duck-egg blue, a tinge of pink along the slope of the next mountain. A cold breeze blew down the valley from the south, rolling off the mountains and the ice. He was managing his feet and hands, not looking so much like a badly balanced sack of turnips, so she mounted up behind him and set them off at a trot, reaching around to hold the reins and steady him within her arms.

There was a well-trodden track from the witch's cottage, following the course of the brook through the stained stones towards the narrowing head of the valley and the ice that filled it, and a rutted cart-track that ran up the valley as well, through all the green. And more, that same track bent and crossed the sulphur-brook and went away eastwards up out of the valley, where before there had just been the faint trace of the wheels of the witch's goat-cart. Arrany reined in. She had thought the stranger-vhalgod and his company must have taken themselves back off to the big village to the east, Ramsleap, taken over the old ruined imperial tower there, as they had spoken of doing, but clearly there was much coming and going to the ice—

What stranger vhalgods?

—oh, you see, there was much and much that young Arrany had not told us—

—and Sikassyn was still in sight, striding up towards the boulder-field. Arrany turned back to the west, to the steep valley side down which, some half a mile north, she had ridden in the dark. Haste, now, because Hedge and Pony must soon be coming, swift and angry, and she wanted to be into the woods before they came out of it.

Well, we had abandoned our intention to go around through the higher slopes of the forest, had come running on the straight track, Hedge afoot and I on my four good hooves. I might have flown ahead scouting, but I did not want to be out of reach if some ambush fell upon Hedge as at the robbers' bridge, and Spider, expecting us, would know to hide herself from a bird's spying. Even so, Arrany and Penryl made it into the shelter of the forest before we, passing by the offering-stone to some lost godling, left it. Things might have gone rather differently, if we'd met up together in the woods.

And by then Spider had vanished from sight.

In the valley, where there was a clearer view, I flew up, circling over Hedge, over the ruins and the clumps of young trees, an aerial scout. She kept up her steady run.

No smoke rising from the chimney of the one house still roofed. We didn't bother with stealth. Up the steps in one bound—that was Hedge. No hesitation. One blow, and she had kicked in the door, tearing the latch from the jamb. I swooped in past her.

15

IN WHICH ARRANY MAKES A DECISION

After that brief flicker of strength in the sunlight Penryl was shivering and sagging again, slumped against her. Arrany began to fear that even at Dandelion's smooth walk he might fall and take her down with him. Then her mind began to throw up the thought that he would die in her embrace from his weakness and chill.

Go on, stay, find shelter. Put the miles between, then find shelter. Turn north to the valley of the Rhunavon, find some farmstead or village and a witch. Seek out a town where there might be physicians. Maybe all he needed was rest and food and warmth. Maybe Hedge and Pony would come looking for her. Maybe the vhalgod Duke Atana, lacking Sikassyn's mercy, would send out his soldiers to be sure they did not live to tell whatever little it was that they might know...

Penryl's weight was all on her, of a sudden, and before she could rebalance him he was tilting over to the side. She caught herself, caught him, turned it to a rough slither to the ground that had Dandelion sidling, ears back and eyes rolling.

"Sorry," he muttered. "Sorry, sorry, Arry. I can't—just let me rest, just a little—" and other like things, but his whole body was shuddering, his teeth jittering together.

They were in a steep place where there was more spruce than pine, all growing amid a jumble of great ice-rounded boulders. Shelter, a niche where one huge stone had come to rest against another; Arrany got Penryl into it, wrapped in the bridal shawl and the blankets of her bedding. It took little time to scrape back the thin growth of clubmoss to bare earth and lay ready a fire of dry twigs and cones, far enough out that the spitting sparks wouldn't alight in his wraps, near enough that the boulders should catch and hold the heat. Dry enough there would be little smoke, she hoped. There was plenty of old lichen for tinder and she got it burning almost at once, filled the one small pan, her own, from her water flask, set it close to the flames. She hadn't been able to extract much food—it would have meant too much rummaging and risk of waking the sleepers, the valerian she'd dosed them with notwithstanding. But she had a bit of dry sausage, and she hacked off chips of that for the pan, crumbled in some oatcake, and threw in a handful of raisins, too. Call it an oatmeal soup, she told him, like the spiced bread-milk-and-honey soup the cook of their mother's hall made when they had taken a chill. (She quite, quite forgot, at that moment, that their mother was dead and her brother did not even know it.) She stirred it around till it was warm and as thick as a thin gruel, and she gave him her horn spoon and ordered him to eat, eat it all, while she went in search of more wood.

Came back, a great bundle of broken sticks tied up in her scarf, to find he had in fact eaten it all and fallen asleep, leaning against the stone at this back, slumped over a little and his head at an angle on his shoulder to give him a stiff neck. He woke when she tried to settle him curled up on the ground, muttered something she couldn't make out, and went back to sleep clutching her hand, so she sat there and broke up sticks with one hand and her foot, and fed the fire, and watched Dandelion grubbing up the thin wiry grass and browsing on spruce twigs. Penryl's skin felt warm to the touch and his shivering had stopped. His face, too, had a better colour, a flush of pink. But still, so old, skin drawn thin over bones. She felt sick just to think of it, to think of the beguilement laid on him, to think of Pen in Spider's arms, Pen making love to the old, old vhalbairn, while she sucked the strength and the life of him away, spider and fly, he wrapped in her toils and so bespelled and besotted he could not see how she devoured him.

And now they had Jinn, who had been Spider's once before, Arrany had gathered that much, but she did not think, no, she did not think Spider would have had much chance of luring him to her bed again even had he had a living body to be seduced, but what Duke Atana intended—

Did she even know? No. She guessed. She...spun together scraps, words dropped half-understood, for they had always spoken the vhalgod tongue in the old imperial way, and the common traders' speech was drifted from it.

She'd done a terrible thing. She did know it.

"Oh, Pen," she said, and for a while she huddled there, and maybe she rocked herself, and maybe she had a bit of a cry, because you need to remember that for all her year and more of adventuring on her own, and her travelling with us, and the dangers we'd come through, and all her hard edges so hard won, she was but a youth still, who should not have tempered in so hot a fire so soon and sudden.

I SUPPOSE you want to know the truth of how and why Arrany set off west to find us. You might even be wondering about the when, and all her tale of a hard winter's service in that chief's hall. And Duke Atana —you might think on old tales, and say, Pony, wait, do you mean *that* Duke Atana? The cursed emperor's companion, Prince Tavris's counsellor and foster father? But he died when Ghedhaynor fell.

Or maybe those songs and his very name have been forgotten by now. It's all he deserved, in the end.

Certainly Arrany had known nothing of him, beyond his name. I don't think she had even heard the tale of Prince Tavris that Bard Burnett told in The Emperor's Head, before she was kidnapped and carried off. If she had, would it have made a difference?

So, summer had faded into early autumn and the miller's boy came all in a panic to fetch Goodsister Sikassyn, for his mother was in labour with a baby coming wrong and the witch and the midwife of Ramsleap despaired. And Sikassyn packed her bag and off she went with the boy, for as even Arrany would admit, she was truly a witch of long experience and no little skill. She took pride in her skills in healing and more pride in the respect it won her from the folk round about, if she did little else that was expected of a witch with a true calling by way of care for the folk among whom she lived. At least she'd had the honesty not to settle among folk, to invite their turning to her for advice and comfort in their troubles, as is the burden the gift of a witch-talent brings if you don't choose a hermit's life.

And Arrany went into the back workroom to argue with her brother, and saw, with Spider's attention and her glamour withdrawn from him, how ill and wasted he had become, and the madness of his obsession, the deranged scribblings that were his supposed studies.

What she did not see was a golden collar about his neck.

But all else fell out as she had said; their arguing, how she tried to make him see his own decay in Spider's silver mirror, how he raised his hand against her.

Only she did not abandon him. She took the hatchet from the woodbox where it was left convenient for slivering kindling off the firewood and waited for Sikassyn's return.

That was a long day's vigil, and a long night, in which she tended the goats, and tended her brother, and ate her heart out with worry and fear and anger all seethed together, and it was noon of the second day after that before Sikassyn returned. Arrany expected to see the miller's boy bringing her back on the white horse.

She meant murder, so she did confess to me, in a long, long talk we had in a later time, if threat alone proved not enough to force Spider to release her hold on Penryl. But Spider returned in company, and not with the miller's boy.

Oh, you want to know about the miller's wife? Birth is a perilous passage. I don't know that Arrany ever knew what came about there. She had other matters on her mind. So did Spider.

But Arrany, waiting hatchet again in hand and sweating cold with the fear of what she meant to do, heard a horse, then realized it was horses, and peered out the window. Not the Ramsleap miller's white cob but four of the big heavy horses the vhalgods still breed, under saddle, four riders and Spider pillion behind one. A team of the same breed pulled a high-wheeled, canvas-covered wagon; a small company of foot, a dozen or more, all vhalgods or vhalbairns, rough-looking types in leather and mail, armed variously with bow and spear and sword and axe, followed them. Circling in wide lazy circles overhead, a winged shape greater than eagle, greater than vulture, greater even than the great bone-devouring lammergeier.

Smaller than a dragon, though. Not that she had ever seen one, to compare.

Vhaldrach.

Arrany just had the wit left to put the hatchet away and grab the broom, so that she was innocently sweeping when Spider pushed open the door, saying something in the vhalgod tongue. Welcome, Arrany thought it was, and "my lord duke." "High magus," she heard, too, a title which, like duke, she knew from tales.

A vhalgod man in a dragonscale coat and winged, gilded helmet was the first in, glowering around, hand on his sword's hilt. Arrany ducked her head when his gaze fixed on her. She got the feeling he expected her to bow outright. Penryl had come to the door of the workroom, leaning there. It might look casual; the glamour had returned and he seemed only a bit thin and pale. She thought he was needing the doorframe to hold himself upright, though. His face lit at sight of Sikassyn.

"You were gone so long," he said, as if the others were of no account at all. "Come and see what I've been working on. I think I've found a piece of the puzzle..."

The lordly man gave him a look that was more sneer than scowl, curling his lip, and turned his back as if from something unsightly, but Penryl barely seemed aware of any of them, his gaze following Sikassyn the way a sheepdog would watch its master, alert for command. Sikassyn flapped her hands as if she were shooing hens. Penryl turned and vanished obediently. He'd not so much as glanced at Arrany and her bruised face.

Close on the vhalgod captain's heels had come a vhalgod woman, her long silver hair in many braids, wearing a full-sleeved black gown, rather tattered about the hem but belted with a cord of silk, its ends, which were long beaded tassels, clicking and ticking as she moved. The beads glittered and gleamed, some polished smooth, some faceted, some gemstones, some fine enamelwork over gold. They might have told Arrany much, if she had possessed the skill to read them. Such beaded tassels, as you've likely heard, proclaim the wearer's rank, the college of the university at which the magus has studied, and to which orders or circles they belong; also, some strands may themselves encode spells, or hold ones latent and waiting. Given the gems and quality of the work, that particular array would also have told an educated reader of them that this was a magus who sprang from high family rank and wealth— or at least, that she possessed the latter, valued its display, and wanted you to assume the former. Like the lord, the magus swept a disdainful look around. Arrany, oh so meekly, swept her scanty accumulation of dust into the fire and retreated to the narrow doorway of the dairy.

A silver-haired but younger vhalbairn man in the robe of a magus followed the first two, his robe as tattered but his beads less gaudy, and a vhalgod woman wearing a coat of mail.

And after them, the vhaldrach. She was a woman, black hair cut uncommonly short for a vhalgod, lean and lightly built, as vhaldrachen usually are, and her eyes pale gold. She wore a long, high-collared but sleeveless dragonscale tunic in the style meant for vhaldrachen, with the long slashes down the back so that it might drop either side of each wing, her broad leather belt girdling it together again. She was barefoot, wearing leather leggings and vhalmetal vambraces; her only weapons seemed to be an assortment of knives. Unlike the others, she stared about with catlike curiosity.

That was it. The rest stayed outside. Mercenaries, Arrany suspected, for everyone knew that there were soldiers of the old imperial elite vhalgod companies roaming south of the White Mountains, hiring themselves out to the mostly human rulers and councils of those lands. They stood closed up around the wagon, eyes flicking warily to the cottage and all about. Vhalgods, with a handful of vhalbairns among them.

"Don't gawp, girl. Fetch the good wine." Sikassyn's glower said Arrany had better play the meek and dutiful servant and hop to it, or else, so she found the sealed jug that had sat untouched in the dairy for as long as she'd known the place, the fine green-glass cups that were never used, and a tray to put them on, and played servant with a deference Sikassyn seemed to know full well was mocking, from the sideways glances she gave. Happy Sikassyn was not, with her guests, Arrany thought. Well, why should she be? Remember, she had been tried and condemned to death for her wicked abuses of her young lovers, for working spells to influence their minds and drink the life from them, and these were great folk among the vhalgods, the rank of duke belonging only to those nobleborn commanders who had crossed with mad Eksandron, and a high magus.

The younger magus and the woman Arrany thought of as the duke's under-officer brought the fireside bench and a couple of stools over to the two chairs already at the table and all settled there, putting their heads together in some intense, low-voiced discussion over the bread Arrany had baked that morning and a large pat of fresh soft cheese. Sikassyn did not send her out to wait on the soldiers, and Arrany did not offer. There was the well, if they were thirsty.

Penryl drifted to the workroom door from time to time, looked at them with a faintly puzzled frown as if not quite sure they were even real; he went back to his mad jottings each time the witch noticed and waved a hand. Arrany took him wine in an earthenware cup once, and a slab of bread spread thick with cheese with green herbs sprinkled over, and she whispered, "*That's* a vhaldrach. How do you think you can ever become *that?*"

"You're not supposed to be in here," Penryl had said. "After everything Sikassyn's done for me, Arrany, I wish you'd stop going out of your way to defy her. It just makes you look like a child."

"Sikassyn says you're to eat this, all of it," was her answer.

He'd taken a bite or two and set it aside, already lost in his book again, by the time she left.

Eavesdropping would have been more profitable if she had spoken the language. The prince, she thought she heard. The ice. The name of Naskanna Deathdealer. Mountain, maybe. "You'd better make a start on supper," Sikassyn told her. "Are there a dozen squabs fit for eating? We'll have pies."

Which meant building a fire in the stone oven built in beside the big fireplace, killing and plucking and cleaning the squabs, and seething them with some carrot and onion from the garden, and picking the meat from the bones, making pastry, making a gravy...and a dozen was nearly all the young pigeons there were, a huge sacrifice from the little flock. Sikassyn very much wanted to impress these visitors, and yet, it would hardly be enough to feed the dozen big vhalgods outside...but going out to climb the dovecote ladder, she found the soldiers had slaughtered one of the kids, which were penned by the shed while the milch-goats were out grazing, hung it from an apple tree to bleed (wasting what would have made the blood soup often eaten in those lands), and were building a fire pit to roast it whole.

She didn't know why that disturbed her so much. It would have been the fate of at least the little bucks come winter anyway. Maybe it was that they'd done it in full view of the other kids. Or maybe that she had the feeling the soldiers would have cared as little, and asked as little leave, if they'd decided to cut her throat instead.

The discussion at the table went on, while she worked. At one point Sikassyn, the younger magus, and the duke went out, Sikassyn putting on her boots and flinging a shawl over her shoulders, though it was a warm day. Arrany, with a foray to the kitchen garden after herbs as excuse, watched them stride off up the valley to the south, collecting a pair of the soldiers from their theft of Arrany's firewood along the way. She was still watching, wondering what they were about, when she realized the vhaldrach had come out to the porch and was leaning against a post to watch her in turn. She scowled and made a show of stretching a stiff back before bending to her snipping of thyme and oregano again. The vhaldrach, Tesh, they named her, chuckled, took two long steps out into the garden, and leapt into the air.

That, Arrany might watch with cause. Maybe a bit of longing. She was just as glad Penryl had not seen.

Sikassyn and her companions returned as the sun was falling into the west. There was nothing to the south but the mountain rising into ice and barrenness, and little enough, if you went aside, but the dark forest of spruce and pine that scrambled amid the stones of the steepening slopes. Nothing to hold them so long. Even if there were some forgotten pass through the mountains to be reached that way, their wagon would never manage it.

Her supper, served late, with dusk falling, pleased them—at least the vhaldrach Tesh praised the pie and winked at Arrany as, her own meal snatched in a corner in haste, she went out to drive in the goats for milking, uneasy in the gathering dark, and wolves singing away to the west. The bleating of that one doe after her missing kid was hard to endure and though she'd eaten little of the savoury pie, the smell of roasting meat in the soldiers' camp didn't tempt her. It wasn't like she hadn't slaughtered a dozen pigeons herself that day, not to mention having helped Sikassyn with the winter butchering. It was the way they'd gone about it, she decided. Or that she felt her situation to be more akin to that of the goats than to that of the soldiers.

She wondered, knowing it was madness, about stealing one of the big horses. It could easily carry her and Pen riding double.

To outrun an angry magus? To outrun a vhaldrach?

No.

The soldiers had tethered their horses and pitched two small tents and one larger, but it was clear now they were keeping guard over their wagon, one at each corner. The canvas cover on its hoops was drawn tight. They said something, mocking, a bit threatening, as Arrany skirted around them. Inside the house, food and wine had not mellowed the discussion. Voices were raised. The table was thumped. Sikassyn leapt to her feet at one point, upset, outraged, Arrany could not tell. Was soothed by the officer, while Tesh laughed and the two magi scowled and the lordly commander—Atana, his name—leaned back in his chair, claws tapping together, and smiled, as if he had achieved some victory in the witch's loss of temper.

Even Penryl, sitting close against Sikassyn's side on a stool, noticed something amiss. When Atana spoke again and jabbed a finger in Sikassyn's direction Penryl leapt to his own feet, leaning forward, fists on the table, about to open his mouth on some angry defence of his beloved in this argument he could not understand, unless he had been learning the old vhalgod tongue in his so-called studies. Sikassyn and Arrany—standing behind with a jug, still playing the good servant, though they were on to the homemade rowanberry wine by then—pushed him back into his seat.

Whatever the disagreement, they wore it out, and the discussion turned to—Arrany was not happy about this—herself. At least, all those glittering, metal-sheened cat-slit eyes, bronze and copper, gold and silver, fixed on her. She took a step back all unawares, clutching the near-emptied jug, and the white-haired high magus seized her wrist. Her claws did not bite, but her grip was a vice nonetheless.

"I expect," she said, and that was the first, Arrany said, that any of them showed sign of having any human language at their command—the trade tongue heavy with the cadences of the lands south of the mountains. "I expect that you'd like to see your dear brother out of Spider's bed and in command of his wits again, would you not?"

Penryl frowned, as if he did not understand at all that it was himself under discussion. And Arrany had no idea what to say to that. Her gaze flicked to Sikassyn (stony-faced, she was) and away.

Spider, Arrany was thinking, for this was the first she'd heard that name, was all too apt.

The vhaldrach laughed. "She's thinking, Orosyn, that she'd like the whole boiling of us consigned beyond the Rift, never to shadow these broken lands with our presence again."

"Oh, are you going to involve yourself after all, Tesh?" The lesser magus spoke, a deep rumble. "I thought you had, what was the human phrase you used, other fish to fry?"

The vhaldrach shrugged, a movement that made it seem she might be about to flare out her wings, making the high magus, seated next to her, flinch aside.

"Perhaps. Perhaps I might take an interest, look in on matters from time to time. But I've little wish to spend a winter freezing my —" she coughed delicately, grinned wickedly at the magus. "—my behind off, squatting on the ice keeping guard on a lump of frozen meat. So aye, it may be I'll find other fish to fry."

"Find the Deathdealer for us and save us all a mess of trouble."

"Oh no, meddling with Naskanna I leave in Duke Atana's capable hands. I'm sure he, and the young lady, will manage it between them."

Arrany, as the only young lady present, felt a definite chill at that.

"Look on it this way, Spider," said Tesh. "You'll have had all the good you're ever going to get out of him by the time the child returns to demand her due reward anyway."

Sikassyn only sniffed and looked away.

The magus Orosyn released her then, and their talk resumed, incomprehensible once more, and milder, until the duke pushed back his chair and his whole party went out to their tents. Sikassyn explained nothing, said nothing beyond a curt command to tidy the place up, and towed Penryl, heavy-eyed and stumbling, off to their bed.

Though Arrany was still clearing up long after, it was longer yet before sleep came to her, curled in a blanket by the hearth, not daring to risk the goat-shed with the soldiers about.

In the morning, Sikassyn, with the duke and magi and Tesh looming to witness, made the bargain with her.

Fetch Naskanna, and the death-token she carried of her brother. A lock of hair in an amulet or some wooden charm carved with his name, perhaps even stained with his blood—something of that sort. Naskanna would most likely carry it close to her heart, and Arrany was not to try to steal it, for that would surely lead to failure and her own death at the grim captain's hand. A fell magic inhabited it, for Naskanna, though no great magus, had some tutoring. She had worked a wicked, wicked magic and by it enslaved her brother's soul to her service as a ghost. Far in the northwest, she was rumoured to have settled, with a wild godling, one Thallyn, a shapeshifter often seen as a horse. Seek, and Arrany would surely find word of them as she drew nearer. A royal dun, a lake beyond, the highlands that approached the western sea—rumour gave little enough to go on, but enough, if she were diligent and determined in her searching. Theft would surely fail, the witch repeated; but cunning would fetch the Deathdealer to where those warriors better able to face such an enemy might overcome her. Arrany's task was to be the embodiment of innocence, to spin truth and lie together.

"Make fear for your brother your truth," the high magus said.

And the vhaldrach gave her the story, not even knowing how close to the truth it ran, how she had seen her brother, the glamour on him forgotten in Sikassyn's distraction—

"There is no glamour on him, he is perfectly well, and the girl had no business—"

"Quiet," snapped the high magus, and Sikassyn was quiet.

How she had seen the golden collar, the god-collar, mention of which was sure to convince and enrage Naskanna and her godling, who might not, they seemed to think, feel a mere mostly-human vhalbairn worth rescuing for his own sake...

That detail, the vhaldrach, who seemed to feel she was the best teacher in such matters, had Arrany repeat; had her tell the whole of the story over and over, until in her fear and growing panic at being sent away without Penryl and no way she could see out of that, it began almost to sound like truth in her own ears. And how did she learn that Naskanna was the enemy Spider most feared, why did she go so far, risk so much, for Naskanna and her godling, and them alone, when the world was no doubt full of heroes waiting to help a young woman alone on the road?

The wandering folk, a seer, mystic advice that she must seek this one hero only, that sorted well, that would do, tell it over, and over...

And the vhaldrach, with the younger magus helping, amused herself putting together a bundle of all that Arrany might reasonably have taken, if she had been so cravenly desperate, or desperately craven, as to abandon her brother to chase across half the world to find a rescue for him. The sax, relic of some former victim of Spider's, was part of that, with a mere hour or so of instruction...

"You've had some training in arms," Tesh observed, with perhaps unflattering surprise, to which Arrany says she offered no explanation.

"She'll be dead within a week," the younger officer said in disgust. "A child like that? Dead, or taken and set to slave in some chief's kitchen, or their bed."

"She came this far, or they did, the pair of them together, and younger then than they are now," Sikassyn said, unexpected defence.

And she gave Arrany an amulet, a charm against notice on the road, to help her come safely to journey's end.

Well, we know how long that lasted.

"I still say we'd be better sending a party well-armed and fearless, and Tesh with them, and taking what we need from Naskanna's hot corpse."

"I still say, I'll none of that," Tesh said. "I've no wish to find my head sent after the emperor's."

"Blessed Eksandron," the high magus murmured, as if it were a prayer, or some invocation of protection, and the duke and the younger magus echoed her.

Sikassyn rolled her eyes. "I mislike this plan entirely," she told Arrany. "But Magus Orosyn is right when she says you'll take Naskanna and her godling by stealth, and that the woman's wicked enough, fell enough, she'd destroy what we seek rather than allow it to fall into anyone else's hands or lose mastery over her brother, even in death."

And thus was Arrany set on the long road to Smithsford at Dahres Head.

THERE IN THE shelter of the boulders and the dark evergreens, the dawn was still fresh and clean when Arrany freed her hand gently from Penryl's grip and tucked him up under the blankets. She'd ceased to feed the fire; now she knocked the coals apart and smothered it in its own ash, and scraped damp earth up over it as best she could, with an anxious eye on the smoke. Pen was warm enough, and she couldn't risk a spark. She left all neat and orderly, caught Dandelion and tied her to a tree. No paper. With a bit of charcoal, she wrote on the stone above his head:

Start for home. Will catch up. Thing I must do. A.

Then she kissed her brother's cheek, patted the horse, and set off afoot through the trees.

16

IN WHICH WE COME TO THE ICE

"Nobody home," Hedge said in disgust. I'd forestalled her rush into the workroom by bursting through that door myself, so she'd flung open the door to what proved, as Arrany had described, to be the dairy and pantry. No place to hide amid the shelves of provisions and ripening cheeses, no Spider cowering beneath the scrubbed worktable.

No Arrany, no feverish ensorcelled lad tucked away in the cluttered workroom, either. I was already making a second circuit of the whole place on four legs, sniffing. They'd been here. They were gone.

"Hedge." Human-seeming again, I perched cross-legged on the fireside bench. "There've been others here. Vhalgods, or vhalbairns near enough vhalgods to have the scent of them. Various of them, half a dozen or more, off and on, over quite a long time. As if—well, in a village I would say, as if they're neighbours, in and out, you know. And...familiar, a couple of the scents."

"Who?"

"Not sure. Not anyone we know well, just...known."

"Where do we know them from? The road?"

I considered. "Ghedhaynor, maybe?"

"So long ago?"

I shrugged, springing for the front door again. "You see if there's any more to learn in here. I'll take a look outside."

We'd rushed in without any heed to what the yard might tell us, not that there was much to read, save the obvious signs and scents: that Arrany had come, riding in haste; that Dandelion had been tied behind the goat-shed; that Arrany had come out of the house with her brother and they had ridden off together, angling away to the side of the upper valley, while Spider had gone afoot, more directly south following a path that itself followed the stony course of the sulphur-reeking stream.

There seemed to be a cart-track running that way as well. Not one in daily use, but still, someone, I thought, was back and forth with a wagon often enough to make a rutted road. It did seem peculiar, that anyone would be taking a wagon up towards mountainside too steep for even a ridden horse, and the valley locked with ice besides.

Big, heavy horses, too, by a couple of deep rain-softened hoof marks that were not Dandelion's.

The goats, shut in their shed, were bleating in what had passed from disapproval to pain. I did not approve of that myself, and went to free them, turning the whole herd out together, to let the kids take care of the milking their mistress had forgotten. And I filled their water trough, too, though no doubt they knew well enough where to find better water than the sulphurous brook.

"They left in haste," I said, meeting Hedge coming out from her—probably violent—search through Spider's belongings. I surmise the violence, for she seemed to have settled into a grim calm, her rage, no less deep, not burning so close to the surface. "Arrany and Penryl mounted, Spider afoot, and not together. Arrany's gone to the woods—" I pointed the rough direction. "And Spider up the valley. So?"

"A book or two that she's better off not owning, but nothing much in there beyond what you'd expect. She's got more coin stashed about than a village witch generally manages to keep put by. Running-away money, I'd think it was, if she didn't seem so comfortably settled."

"Did you take it?"

Hedge gave me a look.

"That's my good dear. Did you find that book she'd supposedly written?"

"On the fire," said Hedge. "Seemed best."

"Aye. Do you want Spider or Arrany?" I pointed out the directions they had gone, and Hedge, adding two dark-bound books, rather musty smelling, and a purse that indeed looked promisingly fat, to the bundles she carried, considered.

"That cart-track—is it the vhalgod neighbours, do you think? What's up there to need carting?"

"A mine?" I wondered. But that would result in a bare and stony road worn away through the valley, surely, from either many wagons, or packhorses. "Maybe there's someone carting ice down from time to time—there may be some town further east, down in the valley of the Upper Rhunavon."

"Somehow I don't see Spider inviting some little clan, even a vhalgod one, who've set themselves up to trade in ice, to share a friendly cup by her fire in the evenings. You go after Arrany, Pony, just in case. I'll take Spider."

"Aye." I took to the air again, crow flying fast and high, scanning the rocky valley and the clumps of brush and conifers for sign of anyone laid up in hiding, but there were only the goats scattering out, the kids frisking wild in their unwonted freedom. At the stony forest's edge I landed and went sniffing on four legs again, to most swiftly find where Dandelion had entered the darkness of the trees. Horse, I was, running that trail, not to affright her, which scent of a wolf well might have done.

But then I smelt her, strong amid the resinous trees, away to my left, and moving, coming back towards the valley, so crow again I went, dodging and darting through the dense dark, and came soft and silent, alighting on a swaying branch over the track the mare followed, a narrow path made by wild things coming down to the valley.

Dandelion, plodding weary, and weary the rider slumped and swaying, but he had Arrany's bow strung, an arrow clutched with it. I might have thought him an old man, for the lank hair tangled on his shoulders and the thin beard were white, but he came alert as I plunged down before him, and in the pale gaunt face his blued-steel eyes, the only vhalbairn thing about him, were fever-bright.

He dismissed the crow as any threat the same instant he saw me, which meant Arrany had not told him of us, or not enough, so I stepped down and took the bridle, and took the bow from him too, as he flinched away and nearly gave himself a tumble, while Dandelion snuffled my hair in greeting.

"Where's your sister?" I demanded.

He righted himself, tried to take back the reins.

"Is your name Hedge?" he demanded in turn, or at least, probably he meant it as a lordly demand. It came out rather thin and desperate.

"No. Be glad of that. Hedge is in no good temper. Nor am I, for that matter. Where's Arrany?"

The flute was not with him. This close, I was sure of it.

"She left. She told me—I was sleeping—she left a message, written in charcoal on stone. She told me to go home, that she'd catch up on the way."

"The Marshlands are that way." I pointed away northerly, being helpful.

He scowled, to show me just what he thought of that. "And leave her to go after the duke and—and *her*, alone?"

"What? Which duke?"

"Sikassyn's—I don't know, I thought, a lover, I'd have killed him..." He frowned in puzzlement over that. Shook his head. "He's welcome to her. But I knew soon enough it wasn't that. Ally? In what cause, I don't know. He came—last month? But it was—no, it was autumn, they were here last autumn, all the winter, I remember the sound of their axes away in the woods to the east, the horses going by, dragging logs. That was winter. So long?" He shook his head, his gaze gone hazy, distant. I thought about slapping him, but I've never been certain that's as helpful as some humans seem to think. His attention returned to me. "There's a magus," he said. "She's—I'm afraid of her. Even Sikassyn—is afraid of her. But Arrany—I thought she'd died, you see, died long ago, years ago…" Shook his head. "It's like a dream. How long have I been here?" He held out his hand, which trembled, an invalid's indoor pallor, dry and seamed and frail as ancient vellum. Shook his head again. "*Arrany*," he said, and focused his mind with an effort. "They sent her away and I thought, when I remembered at all, it was to be rid of her, because she sulked so." A sidelong glance at me again. "I know it was her worry about me, really, I know, but that's what I thought, that's what it seemed like—but that anyway didn't make sense, because Sikassyn had to tend her own hearth again. Arrany went, all alone, but that was a dream, too, you see. I didn't—none of it was real. Sometimes I thought, I believed, the magus had killed her. She looked at me like I wasn't even a thinking being, worse than an animal, some—some dirty thing, some piece of rubbish a servant should clear away." I didn't interrupt, to ask the name of the magus, not then. His thoughts were scattered enough already. I just nodded understanding, and he went on. "But it was, they sent Arrany to do something for them. Find something and bring it back? And she said, she said it was a bad thing, what she had done. And now she's gone, and I think she's gone to Sikassyn, to try—whatever it is she's done—to undo it. But the duke, the magi—Arry doesn't know what they're like, not really. She doesn't understand. The high magus, she'll kill a human without a second thought, like swatting a mosquito, if she's in the way. And the vhaldrach—she laughs, and she doesn't care. And Arrany's all alone."

"So what are you doing?"

"Going after her, of course. She's my *sister*." He frowned. "My best of friends." His voice trembled.

"Your best of friends. About time you remembered that. Lad, can you even draw this bow?"

That stung him. "I've been hunting since I was a child."

"Not what I asked. There's not much more left of you than a puppet of sticks and twine, is there? Put it away. Vhalgods, you say. I don't want you shooting at *my* vhalgod by mistake. There's been enough of that already this summer." I unstrung the bow as I spoke, strapped it away and returned the arrow to Arrany's quiver. "Now, I'm going to ride with you, and you're going to tell me everything you can remember about this duke and these magi: their names, their numbers, what sort of place it is they dwell in—"

He protested he had no idea, only they had cut much timber, but some of that might have been small stuff for next winter's firewood.

"Guess," I said. "Tell me everything about what they've been up to here, every chance word they've let fall that's given you a guess. And as for your Sikassyn, I'll thank you to call her Spider, to get her own right nature fixed in your mind. Your way is out of the woods and then up along towards the ice, and I'll let you know where we should go from there."

Crow again, I flapped up to his shoulder. Like clutching a skeleton clothed in rags. I felt the lad stiffen under my talons, but he didn't flinch. Not till I tweaked his ear, to spur him into nudging Dandelion into motion again.

ICE. Ice there was, even in high summer. Ice and snow on the mountain peaks, blazing white in the sun. Ice in the deep ravines where midsummer's noon never reached. Ice pressing, a vast weight of it, down from the high valleys in slow, cold reaching tendrils a thousand winters old. Hedge left the rocky path along the stream and crossed it dry-shod, stone to stone, went aside and made her way like a hunter in the cover of this thicket, that copse, those clustering spruces growing near sideways in the push of winter winds. An eye, always, to the path, and the cart-track beyond, where nothing moved, only the white goats bright against the green. An eye, always, towards the south, and the ice rising there.

The valley rose into a steep barren slope of broken stone. The ice—see it in your mind's eye. You are a mouse, a toad, some little creeping thing, and you crouch at the base of a great and ancient elm. See the rough and fissured texture of it, rising above you, not in a flat or evenly rounded wall, but the thrusting buttresses where roots rise into trunk, the undulating folds of it. That's the ice. White, grey, seamed dark with grit, with the stone it has gnawed from the higher valley and chewed in its slow, slow crawl down to this crumbling edge. The draggled tide of rubble at its toes gleams wet and you hear the summer-ceaseless drip and trickle of water, but summer is brief, and the retreat of this ice as brief itself. Come winter, it will find its way down, over the stone, crawling, grinding, maybe even so far as those first low seedling spruce. Till spring comes, to strike it back again. For a little. A yearly tide, the ebb and flow of the ice. Perhaps will come an age when there is no retreat, and the ice crawls, season by season, to overwhelm the whole of the valley, crush trees and ruins and all beneath. Perhaps an age will be when it will see the ice's ebb tide, summer by summer, a retreat up the valley, up the mountain's flank, and the trees and the green will follow, their own tide rising.

Hedge made a wary crossing of the barrens below the ice, close in its cold shadow. She was not so exposed there as you might think, for when I say rubble you should understand, it was the rubble of a mountainside. There were boulders the height of a vhalgod, boulders the size of a great bear or an aurochs, or even the woolly elephant that you have probably never seen. She'd put on her hooded cloak, undyed grey wool from the hardy sheep of our fells, and so she passed, swift movement from cover to sparse cover, freezing to become no more than just another lumpen stone while she watched for watchers, and moved again. For a few moments she hid in the ice itself, where the warm waters of the sulphurous brook, springing from some source deep beneath the ice, came burrowing out through a smooth-walled, dripping tunnel. Stinking steams drifted there, as if a dragon might sleep within, but there was no sign that any living creature did make use of it. She crossed back over the brook on the yellow- and rusty-stained rocks, continued her stalking. Up a rise, and she flattened herself down amid the boulders. Hidden from the lower valley behind the southernmost finger of the evergreens, there was a log-built hall, with a squat square tower rising at one side of it, spotted pigs roaming around and a herd of half a dozen horses grazing. The rutted cart-track, of course, led to it; another path, not fit for wagons but worn bare with much use, climbed higher, crossing the bit of pasture and twisting up through stone, to where it might seem to vanish under a rockfall from the cliff above. From Hedge's vantage point, though, she could see that in fact the path turned sharply around the ridge of fallen stone, and passed into a black mouth.

Difficult to reach, by daylight at least, unseen from the tower. And Spider might have gone into the hall. Maybe. No, Hedge didn't think the hall was the heart of this mystery, but even camouflaged as she was, to head for the cave mouth in daylight seemed to be inviting another arrow in the back, and dragonscale coat or no, well, no one likes setting themselves up as an archer's butt. Hedge made for the hall, circling it, stealthy as a stoat about the henhouse.

No guard at the door of hall or tower. No windows save one high at each gable. The tower did have windows in its upper two storeys, small and squinting. They'd built for defence despite the lack of an outer wall. Habit, perhaps. It didn't do them much good, what with the utter absence of guards. Hedge went in the front, through the hall, the great room with its chimney-breast of undressed fieldstone, a pair of smaller chambers at the far end, and two lofts above, one at each end, linked by a narrow gallery along the side where the tower stood. Cooking, sleeping—they passed most of their time in the great room. The small chambers belonged to people of higher status, though even there what little furnishing the rooms held was of rough-hewn planks or logs stripped and worked green. A couple of books that belonged to the magus, though nothing of as much interest as the two she'd taken from Spider's hoard, a few jars of imported wine, hints of finer clothing, that sort of thing. What there wasn't, was a single living soul. So through she went, swift and growing both more puzzled and more angry, and into the tower, up and down, and outright kicking open the door to leave it swinging as she stormed out—

Dandelion shied. You may wonder where she found the energy. Penryl said an unlordly thing and grabbed at her mane. I flew up from his shoulder. We'd both been hesitating, considering whether to ignore the hall or search it—though I had the advantage of knowing

Arrany was somewhere beyond, up the mountain, and had been about to shift and tell him so.

"They've gone!" Hedge roared across the green at me, and the distant horses pricked their ears, and the pigs looked up from their rootling.

Penryl shortened the reins and asked, "Lady godling?" I hadn't given him my name, and he clearly hadn't paid much attention to whatever his sister and Spider had discussed in whatever plot they'd laid, to learn it from them. I circled back and flew to Hedge. Penryl took the hint and followed over to meet her.

"Deserted," Hedge said, as I alighted on her helmet. She raised her left hand so I could hop to her gloved fist, like a tame falcon. "Don't clamber about up there, bird. It makes my hair stand on end. There's a cave up the mountain, where the track goes. Where's Arrany?"

"She—said she had done something she needed to put right," said Penryl, before I could speak, though I'd bounced down to my human toes between them. He was eyeing Hedge with a lot more respect than he'd given me, well-mingled with a bit of fear. "Lady Naskanna?"

"Captain," Hedge corrected absently, then frowned. "Hedge. My name's Hedge, this is Pony, you're Pen, good, here we all are. Where this side of the blasted Rift has your sister gone with my brother's flute? Where's Spider?"

"With Atana and Orosyn," I said. "There's a cave up there, hidden, intentionally or not, behind a ridge of fallen rock. That's where the track goes."

"Orosyn? *Duke* Atana? I thought he was dead in the fighting—they buried him, didn't they?"

"Not deep enough," I muttered. "The body was—not in particularly good shape."

"Not his, you mean. And Orosyn was lost at sea."

"Aye. And the sea's spat her up."

"What are they doing here? And with Spider? Orosyn—she'd not count a vhalbairn like Spider, a disgraced scholar, a coward, a condemned criminal, fit to wash her feet."

"Tesh has been here."

"Oh, that's just what we need. How many more?"

"A dozen or so, Penryl here thinks, but they come and go, fetching supplies from the villages eastward, so we should keep in mind their numbers may have increased since they first arrived."

"A dozen, maybe sixteen? That might suit with what I saw there." Hedge gave a nod towards the hall. "No idea what they're up to?"

"Not a clue."

"Lord Penryl." Brisk and efficient. "You ride back to the woods where the main track from the west comes down. We'll send Arrany after you once we retrieve her." No, we neither of us thought we'd have time for the tongue-lashing she deserved. "Head away on the western road. We'll catch up when we can."

"No!" Penryl protested.

"You're no use as you are now." Hedge was merciless. "You'll be something we have to defend, not a help. I do not need you for a weight on my sword arm. Go."

He scrubbed at his face, looked up, lips set. "Fine," he said. "I'll go back and wait at Sikassyn's—Spider's house."

"No. The road."

"They'll take me," he said. "If you fail against them, they'll take me, on the road or in shelter. I might as well get something to eat. Get some supplies together. Do *something* of use, however slight."

"If we fail, they're not likely to bother much with you, if you don't bring yourself to their attention."

Pale-lipped fury, held tight and cold. "I'm going nowhere without Arrany."

"Go," I said. "We don't have time to argue."

I might send Dandelion to the road, but he'd simply dismount, or fall off trying to. I could put a compulsion on him, but what a wicked thing, to take that choice from him, when he was fighting his way out from under a far weightier loss of will and trying to choose, for himself, to do right. To atone, even, for how he'd used his sister.

I'd have to trust him. Trust his better sense.

That...had not been much in evidence, so far.

But he nodded, anger and shame both in his face then, and turned the horse.

"Tesh," muttered Hedge, and cast a look at the sky. "I wouldn't have expected her to throw her lot in with Orosyn and Atana."

"No. No friend to us, though."

"No. Ah, Pony, this is not going to go well."

"Soldiers, Penryl says. Atana and an aide, an officer whose name he's never heard, a younger magus with Orosyn. The rest soldiers." That might be some comfort.

"Atana's soldiers."

"Nevertheless. Soldiers do like to have an officer over them. They find it reassuring, to be told what to do. Captain."

"Traitor," she countered. "What I was before that, they'll have no respect for."

I thought she was wrong there. I hoped she was. "Like the robber-queen, sweetheart. Take out the keystone, the arch collapses."

"It's another cave, you said? Let's not talk of collapsing stones."

Hedge divested herself of the packs and bundles she carried, and my harp, hid them down under the low branches of one of those wind-sown spruces, squat and dark against the brilliant summer green, that pushed the forest out into the valley. She squared her shoulders, settled her helmet, checked the draw of her sword. "Well then."

"Well."

Banking now and then to cast an uneasy look at the clear sky, I flew ahead, scouting, but they'd set no sentries lower down. Only around behind the rockfall, where it had been cleared back to make a half-enclosed bay at the cave's mouth, were there half a dozen soldiers waiting. Watchful. Nervous. Expecting us. Three were armed with crossbows, scanning the sky, but I'd flown high and far off and seemed to go up the mountainside, and I'd seen them track me, and dismiss me. A crow was no uncommon thing.

No sign of Arrany.

I had a moment to make a choice, myself. Hedge might, as with Trooper Zevalash, be able to command them, by old authority, by reputation, by respect, even. But these followed Duke Atana, and after the fall of the thrice-accursed emperor, it had been plain that no few among the soldiery of the empire had been as sickened and weary of his rule as, well, not as much as his human subjects, but as those officers and scholars and magi who'd turned against him, and they'd been glad enough to lay down arms and scatter to find lives of their own. It might be that any still obedient to the commands of a Duke of the Crossing were most likely to be ones to name Hedge traitor and see taking her head as fit vengeance, even justice, for her betrayal. He'd been outright worshipped as a god by as many as hated him even in those last years, Eksandron, and it hadn't all been due to fear.

Or maybe it was habit, and fear of a high magus. Was I willing to risk it, to say, why don't you put down those bows and just stand aside for now, and go your own way after?

So I chose, and as when I'd so lost my temper and all decent sense in the city of the heron-godling, I came back down the mountainside like a thunderbolt from the sky, and two discharged their quarrels, which meant two frantic working to span and reload when Hedge came over the rockfall upon them—they didn't have the numbers to hold both their tower and the cave, but I still shake my head when I think they'd kept no watcher up on that berm of stone. They must have thought that, obviously the godling will spot us, and we'll spot her, coming from above, and that's all the warning we'll need, and none of them had wanted to be the one lying up watching atop the rocks, the sacrifice to my first attack. Bunched up like sheep, they were, so I took the one most like an old grandmother-ewe, the one standing just a little apart, watchful, with the bronze badge of a section-leader on a chain about her neck. Struck her down from behind, practical. Horse, I was, as I dropped out of the air, and she wouldn't be getting up again, and I'd kicked out and knocked the last arbalester, if you'll allow me the word, flying while Hedge swung and put one, two out of action, slashing wounds to arms and legs, where her vhalmetal blade could have taken the limbs right off and she'd chosen not, and cut the cords of the bows. Then I was wolf at her back, singing a snarling warning, and we were two, and they were two, and two wounded, and two, dead or dying, and those were mine.

So, "Yield," Hedge says, and it's an order, not an invitation.

The man still on his feet, clutching his bleeding arm to his chest, pushed a toe at the spear he'd already dropped as if to protest that he had. The one on the ground, hamstrung, was curled up whimpering and would likely bleed to death if the others gave her no aid. Hesitation from the two yet unharmed. Neither willing to be the first, either to strike or surrender.

Waste of time. I lunged myself, seized an arm. Did not bite off the hand at the wrist; I was determined not to let slip my self-control, this time, though I tell you vhalgod soldiery in remnants of imperial uniform raised my hackles even without their needing to raise their weapons.

The arm dropped its sword; the vhalbairn that arm belonged to, sweating, threatened to follow it. I let go and she fell to her knees.

"Captain," she said.

The last one lunged. Hedge dodged, swung; the spear grated off the plates of her dragonscale coat; the vhalgod spearman's head fell severed.

"You," Hedge said, to the woman who'd surrendered. "Tend those two, and you all three might live. Where's Spider?"

"Down below, captain. With the duke and the high magus. In the ice."

"Why?" I asked, and the wounded man still on his feet jerked back and fell, as if, human, I were somehow more fearsome than wolf. "What are they doing?"

The kneeling soldier shook her head, mouth clamped shut.

"The witch came to the hall. She had the death-token of Prince Jinn, finally," the wounded man said. "The high magus didn't want to wait."

Hedge made a hissing sound, like a snake or a smallish dragon.

"What are they *doing* with it?" I asked. "What do they want with this...death-token?" Because surely, surely they could not know the truth of it. Sky above and stone below grant they did not know the truth of it.

Even the talkative wounded man pinched his lips shut, and then, head jerking up, wide-eyed, tried to scramble back while sitting on his rump. Crunch of steps coming around the stone.

But it was only Penryl, afoot.

Of course it was Penryl. He glowered at us, and helped himself to a fallen sword, though his arm trembled with weakness.

I sighed. Hedge shrugged.

I didn't like leaving that scatter of weapons for the soldiers to rearm themselves, but there was only one fit to fight and if we tied her, we might as well have cut the throat of the woman with the freely bleeding leg wound and had done with. If someone could get the bleeding stopped, vhalgod as she was, she still had a chance, though she'd be lamed for life.

Hedge jerked her head, sword never wavering. "Tend them," she said again, to the uninjured one. "Penryl, stay close by Pony and when we tell you to stay put, you do it, because you may very well cost Arrany her life if you get in the way down below."

"Yes," he said faintly. Trouble taking his eyes of the severed head at his feet. I took his arm and gave him a tug on past.

And so we went into the dark.

17

IN WHICH ARRANY MAKES ATONEMENT

Arrany, you're wondering. What had become of Arrany? Had she really gone with Spider into the cave?

Well, she found the hall and tower deserted, as we had, duke and high magus having rushed off in grim excitement as soon as Sikassyn strode up with her treasure, taking all their hangers-on with them, to have all their little force guarding the one place that really mattered. So she followed, and made no effort at stealth. She knew there'd be no sneaking past any watchers at the cave's entrance.

"Please," she said, approaching, and at that point there was one of the soldiers with crossbows up atop the earthwork that looked like a rockfall. "Sikassyn wanted me to come to her after I'd seen to my brother's needs. Is she—down there?"

Nicely judged. Wary, reluctantly obedient, not liking the thought of following the witch into that dark mouth one bit.

"Yes," said the section-leader.

Arrany waited, but that was all she was getting.

"Can I—she's expecting—is there a lantern?"

"There's light enough," the woman said.

Arrany gave an awkward little bow, sidled timidly past the soldiers and went into the cave. Someone spoke, words she didn't understand, and another snickered. High enough for a tall vhalgod to walk comfortably, broad enough for three vhalgods to walk abreast, and the floor trampled grit and rubble. Frequent use, that cave saw. A little ways it went level, the walls grey stone smoothed as if by water, or the passage of some great creature rubbing as it went along, and then it dropped, plunging steeply downward, bare stone rather than rubble-floored. Careful footsteps were silent now. A cold wind blew up to meet her.

Darkness, but a glimmer of light relieved it. Arrany went warily, keeping to the wall, her left hand lightly touching to guide her, to catch herself if she stumbled, eyes straining.

Heart pounding so loudly it seemed that anyone below must hear.

Down, and down, and, she thought, angling to the eastward. When she looked up and back, there was no glimmer of light from the entrance. She was not in utter darkness, though. Torches burnt at intervals—rare intervals, but there was just barely enough light to see the dark shadows that might have been gaping fissures and turned out almost always to be the shadows of ripples and humps and other uneven places in floor or roof or wall. Once or twice was there some dark crack or crevice, but these were small openings into which she could barely have crammed herself, no passage for a vhalgod. The air grew winter-cold and smelt of smoke and pitch and frost. Black ice, a slick of frost over stone, and her feet went out from under her. She fell hard on her elbow and would be feeling it for days, but not a sound escaped her. Back to her feet and onward.

A whisper, a distant voice, she thought she heard. Ice seamed the walls, filling cracks, thick on ledges. She walked on ice, now, and there was ice above, clinging to the rock, icicle-fangs thrusting down to meet ice-daggers rising. Many were broken, damaged by much coming and going, and the stone of the bare rut worn down the centre of the passage was slick with the frost's attempt to reclaim it. Carefully, now. Carefully.

Arrany had no idea what she might do. Her unconsidered thought had been only that she might sneak in to where they had made their shrine, or whatever it was, and there hide, watch, steal back the flute, this death-token, as they called it, of the famous prince, blood-stained Eksandron's most beloved and favoured son—most beloved, and thus most hated in his betrayal. Songs and histories told how the emperor had been worshipped as a god in his temples and even in shrines in people's own houses; she had the vague thought that these vhalgods, holding to their imperial pattern of life, wanted this relic of Jinn for some such veneration as Eksandron's son. That being so, she needed a place to hide until they were done whatever it was they were doing. Some ceremony, perhaps, some ritual of dedication and remembrance.

Down, still, went the passage, narrowing, the ice thickening. The cold bit through her clothes, made her hands stiff. She wondered if they had burrowed into the great ice-river itself, but I don't think it could have been so, for that ice shifts and moves, restless as, though slower than, water. No, this was an ancient, ancient cavern, down under the roots of the mountains, and if once it had been the place of some dragon or dragon-godling, they were long, long forgotten. But the duke or the high magus, or maybe the vhaldrach Tesh, must have heard of it, and found it fit for their need, and Spider, well, Spider, and a harmless human agent to send off to fetch Hedge and what she carried, those were a convenience that fell to their hands. Without them, I suppose they might have sent the vhaldrach in search of us, and who knows how things would have gone then?

Arrany might wish for the treasures of the magi, a ring or helmet of invisibility. She had nothing but her caution, and the inattention of those she stalked, who had surely not discounted Hedge and me, but were overconfident in their six guards above.

Too used to the long years of knowing godlings as weak and broken things, the cursed emperor's favourite slaves. Too used to thinking us powerless, passive, sullen, servile. And before Eksandron taught us to be otherwise, we wild godlings were not beings of violence.

So Arrany crept, not like a mouse, which anyway does not creep but scurries swift—crept like a stalking cat, and the tunnel was all ice, beginning to glow blue and pearly in the spill of light, and abruptly it opened out into a larger cavern.

She crouched down, to be less a human shape. Shadows hid her; the cavern itself was a little better lit than the near-darkness though which she had passed, with its occasional torch fixed to the wall. Cressets filled with pitch burned on tall poles sunk into the icy floor, shedding a reddish light and filling the air with smoke, which stained the ice dark. Not many—only four, not away by the walls but centrally, set near, but not too close, to the four corners of a long, low mound of ice, waist-high and longer than a big horse's length. Maybe some boulder or ridge of stone, swallowed by the ice. An altar, she thought. She'd read of such things in the temples, and in the east, in the land of which Jinn's mother had been a queen, they made temples where folk came together to dance and sing for the ones they call the Grandmothers of the Land, and burn incense on their altars, as one might pour out a libation at a godling's offering-stone.

Occasionally there was the drip of water, as the heat from the cressets rose to melt the ice above.

So they were carrying on a secret worship of the emperor, as she'd thought, and they had wanted his son's relic brought here for that. Well, she would creep back and find some dark niche to cram herself into, and once they had finished their prayers, or whatever it was folk did in worshipping the memory of a beheaded tyrant, and took their leave...

The high magus, wearing a white veil over her hair, held something up high and sang a verse. The younger magus, his hair also veiled, held up empty hands and answered with another. They stood one at the head, one at the foot of the altar, and the duke at one side. The others—Spider, the under-officer, eight soldiers—stood a little away, respectful and attentive, though Spider's face was sour. No friend to Atana and Orosyn but rather one whose quiet retreat and private entertainments had been very much disrupted by her chance encounter with them. Or perhaps they had always been coming to that place, and it was her misfortune that she had chosen this particular valley in which to settle. You remember there was an old imperial tower in the next village east; Under-Ice was not a place unknown to imperial maps.

Anyway. The magi sang. At some points the watching soldiers and the duke himself sang, some expected response, a repeated chorus. Spider did not sing, though she mouthed the words when the under-officer turned a frown her way. Arrany's eyes adjusted to the murky light, not so fire-bright and dazzling as when she had first come to the cavern. It was the bone flute that Orosyn held aloft, of course.

Arrany thought she saw, just the faintest shadow forming in the smoke, the shape of a vhaldrach. Of Jinn. Struggling, she thought. So slowly, he turned and writhed and flung up hands as if in denial, wings spread and beating, but slow, slow, slow, as if he struggled in thick tar, or time moved differently, every breath of his four, five dozen for her watching. But it was only the hint of him, a gathering of smoke and shadow

Arrany thought she saw that the ice of what she had taken for an altar was not humped up over some roughness of the floor, but held a more regular shape. A low—bed, she thought. A narrow cot. And a long lean shape laid there, folds of a black cloak on either side...

An ornately carved bed, a catafalque, a body laid out on it. A vhaldrach, the wings folded but spread to the side, and all encased, it must be by magic, in thick, clear ice.

The high magus sang again, her voice rising, words strident, demanding, barking harsh, and following the lead of the younger magus all gathered there bowed, even Spider, and Orosyn laid the flute over the breast of the figure in the ice. She spread her hands above, not touching. Her voice dropped low, no longer singing but speaking words, and the ice—it began to melt where the flute lay. The ice seemed to sink in on itself, water trickling. And the slow-writhing figure in the smoke took on more substance, but still he was smoke, and shadow, and—fear, Arrany saw. She had not thought there was anything Jinn might fear, or (he always did have that effect on young women, human and vhalgod alike) ever might have feared.

It was not thought, even; not any considered thought.

Arrany leapt down, raced across the cavern floor, snatched up the bone—it lay in a hollow of cold water and her fingers touched something hard beneath, frozen, and yet stiffly yielding; shroud, burial gown...Orosyn shrieked a denial. The ice shattered, a great billow of fog rising, roiling—she spun on her heel, just avoiding the grasping claws of the younger magus, darted between two of the soldiers, swifter of reaction than their fellows, who lunged for her, and bolted for the tunnel, futile hope.

But she had the beak of the flute to her lips, and managed, not a tune, but a frantic bleat of breath, running as she was.

"Jinn?" she called. "Jinn!" Offering enough to call him, shadow drawing shape from the tendrils of fog that followed her, and they had already drawn him partway there, for all his struggling against.

Form but no substance, he was, cold ghost chilling the air, drawing more fogs about them both, new frost-flowers blooming on the walls from her rising breath as she passed.

Pounding feet behind. No, she hadn't had any hope of escaping, no hope even of hiding in some dark niche of the tunnel, not now.

And the duke's officer seized Arrany, jerked her backwards. But Arrany had her belt knife in her hand...

Across her forearm she slashes, and the well-honed blade bites deep, deeper than need, but her desperation is great, and this is all she has to give.

"Jinn!" she cries, and that's her third summoning. "Please...take my life, if you need one, save Hedge and Pony and Penryl from them. Save yourself." And looking up at the vhalgod officer, who has flung her down on her back and has a hand about her throat, crouching over her, and a hand prying the flute from her faltering fingers, she says, "You won't have him now."

Shadow over her, and cold, cold, cold the touch, Jinn's mouth on her hot wound, drinking deep of what she offers, and cold, cold, cold the kiss of his bloody lips on hers, salute of her courage, or her folly, and in the same moment he's rising, driving the under-officer back against the wall, a sharp blow of the side of his hand and the officer sinks down, that's her finished, no breath passing that ruined throat, though her eyes watch wide, disbelieving, a hand reaching as if to plead, but the light goes out of her, and he's drawing Arrany aside, tucking the flute safe into the breast of her shirt, folding her arm close with the hem of her tunic bunched up against it—muttering any number of soldiers' words, closing her hand over the swift-soaking cloth. "Hold this," he says. "Hold hard."

The place is too narrow to spread his wings. There's no seizing her and flying her away to some safety.

They're on him, then, and he turns on them roaring, calling his spear to his hand. Rings are burst asunder and the long leaf-blade pierces the mailed breast of the foremost. Vhalmetal, the spearhead, and he jerks it free and in that narrow place the soldiers see their doom...

Heroes of lays and ballads might stand, face doom in a narrow place, offer up their lives for their love, their chief, their land, their kin. I've known them to do so, vhalgod and human alike. These were not such, their duke not so loved, their cause not so dear. Quite sensibly, they fled, the two of them still standing, back to the cavern, where their commanders, thinking three soldiers and an officer quite enough to fetch back one young woman, were showing more concern for salvaging their ritual than for what might be taking place above.

Jinn's more concerned with getting Arrany out of there, and alive, than with Orosyn and her chanting. He's slashed away much of the skirt of her tunic, thrown away the sodden fistful he first used to try to staunch the wound, wadded up a cleaner clout and bound it firm—and if he drank again, well, he'd say, it was blood flowing anyway and took nothing but what she was shedding, nothing but what she'd freely offered, and the more strength he drew to himself the better.

Sitting with her back to the wall, she watches him. So close, so intent. So seeming alive. She fumbles her other hand to touch his face. Cool, but firm flesh, solid as her own.

"Was that—you?" she asks, and suddenly, tired, afraid, she thinks she's done something wrong, not right, done something even worse. "River and sea forgive me. Are they trying to—bring you back?"

She forgets how he struggled against Orosyn's chanting. Everything feels so faint and far away.

"All the palace was my pyre," Jinn says. "No. It's not my body lies below. But—I don't know what they intend."

And then, for all the strength, the life she's given him, he flinches, and for a moment is smoke and water-reflection again, wavering; the cold air that rises up from the ice cave shivers and is drawn down, as if the cave itself inhales, and like a current it tugs at him.

They have taken up their spellcasting again, desperate, intense the words, the summoning, and no need now for the token of bone, for he is here. It drags, it sets hooks in him—

"You will not," he roars, and he is gone from her, not obedient to summons, not resisting it, either, but gone in a rush, leaping out into the cavern. Caged bird, he is there, able to spread his wings, but no scope for flight, only a frantic-flapping low space to rise, to twist and turn, ice enclosing—he stoops on Orosyn as the heart of the matter, spear seeking that heart, and the duke himself—oh, Jinn knows Atana—flings his body between, vhalmetal point grates on dragon-scale coat, grates and skids and finds a weakness, thrusts through. But the ice, the ice is reaching for Jinn, long reaching tentacles of fog and where they touch, ice coats him, chills him, freezes blood and limb, weighs him down. He stumbles from the air, crouching, holding himself up, a bare foot, a knee, a hand braced, over the cold body from which the ice has now melted fully away, but still he has Orosyn the prey fixed in his vision; he's dragged his spear free of Atana's ribs, holds it couched now, trying to find a way to her, but the duke's swordpoint is pressed to his throat for all the man is leaning his weight heavy on his other arm, supporting himself against the head of the catafalque.

See the dead man's hand rising to grasp Jinn's wrist, and the spear falling from his grip.

18

IN WHICH, YET AGAIN, A BROTHER IS FOUND, AND A BROTHER IS LOST

For a moment, they stared into one another's eyes, Jinn and the dead man—the other dead man. Silver, and silver alike.

"Jinn...?" It was barely a whisper. A breath.

"Tavris..." A whisper. A breath. Horror. Grief.

Hand left his wrist; hands seized his throat. But he was fading, Jinn was gone to insubstantial fogs and shadow, firelit, and every gasping breath that Tavris took drew him in, ribbons of smoke and light unravelling. Jinn was sinking, fading, drowning in his brother, and his brother's arms wrapped him now, clutched him close for all he struggled, as if for Tavris alone he remained a thing tangible, to be embraced in those dead arms. Embraced, engulfed, imprisoned. Two made one.

On his knees in the cold water that puddled over the ice, the duke let fall his weapon. Blood stained that water, black in the torchlight.

"My lord!" Orosyn cried, leaving off her chanting. Tavris pushed himself up as if he might rise from the sodden drapery of the catafalque like a man rising from his sickbed. A horror, you'd have found it, to see him move like the living. Whatever spells they had laid on the corpse to preserve it all these years, whatever help they had thought sealing it in ice might give, could not keep the testimony of death hidden. His skin was pallid, dull, stiff as old parchment; his flesh sunken into the frame of his bones as if he had died starving, thought that was only his vhaldrach's lean build and the drying of his body. And now he was entangled with the smoky form of Jinn like some misfortuned twinning doomed to die.

"My prince!" That was triumph, but the high magus screamed then, shrieked denial, falling backward to the icy floor. And she died, arms flung wide, while the sword that had arrowed across the cavern to pierce her through and pin her there still quivered.

"Tavris!" Jinn yelled, and whether it was horror or heartbreak, I don't think he could have said, but he struggled, merged as they were chest to chest, pushing, wings beating but stirring no air, and then he tore himself, a thing of ragged smoky tatters that should have had no substance at all, from his brother, pulled himself free like a butterfly leaving its paper-frail husk.

He reared up and away, standing over Tavris, who had fallen back, wings, arms drooping to the floor.

Jinn...let me go. But perhaps he did not hear that at all, perhaps it was only his imagining.

Jinn's spear was in his hand again. The sacrifice of Arrany's blood was spent, though, in his great effort, and he had no form and being against our enemies but their fear of him.

Hedge leapt to him, and her own arm was slashed and bleeding, no such rash act as Arrany's but considered and careful even as she ran, the pulling off of her gauntlet, the laying of the vhalmetal edge against the back of her left forearm, a small cut, but deep enough.

"Drink," she said. "We're too few here and that young fool may die if we don't get back to her. What was she *thinking?*"

No need for an answer. Jinn did drink, and caught Hedge as she lurched and almost fell to her knees, struck from behind, but she turned that lurch to a spring past him to drag free her sword, a boot planted on the ribs of the late high magus, leapt back to join Jinn, who'd claimed the catafalque as their high ground. Back-to-back, straddling the long-dead body of their brother. Son, as you will probably know from the songs, of a vhalgod wife, a Duke of the Crossing who died of the terrible wounds of the soul sustained in that passage not long after giving birth. Tavris was never so fiercely loved as Eksandron had loved Jinn, youngest and dearest, but remained a faithful son till the end. Lord-Commander of the Golden Guard. Beloved brother. Beloved enemy.

It was Jinn who had slain Tavris, stabbed him through as they grappled in the air over the burning ships of the harbour. He had gone from that grim victory to Hedge, and with her, to face the accursed Emperor.

Back to back, and the man who had thought to strike down Hedge was down himself, Jinn's spear striking snake-swift and up again, and Hedge's sword sings—one falls, another, and they keep their distance, the four soldiers remaining. They circle, watching—watching, too, the vhalbairn magus, the last of those with the authority to command them.

"What have you done?" Jinn demanded of that surviving magus. "This—obscenity...this—" No, he could not find the words. Grief, it was, and horror.

"Traitor," was all the answer he got from the magus. "Murderer—kin-slayer! Not all the torments you suffer in your damnation can be vengeance enough for your crimes, we'd not have freed you from them even if that were possible, but this—this way you'd have served the empire one final time, made some atonement for your great treason, given life to Blessed Eksandron's true heir, let him return to lead us."

"Oh, that would have turned out so well, to trap me in my brother's body. Was he ever anyone's puppet? Was I?"

No, I wasn't there or I'd have answered that. Just a whisper, to remind him. *Spider.*

"Did you seriously think Tavris would ever have danced to Duke Atana's piping, let alone Orosyn's? Did you think he could be commanded? Or I? Who did you think would get up from that bier, if you'd managed to force my ghost into his body?" And his words were a scream, then, a roar of rage. "He's here—you fools, you've trapped

Tavris here, all these years, bound him in your spells, bound him in your ice, trapped him and left him suffering here—"

The magus shouted something, a rapid running phrase that sent a wash of white fire from his outflung hands. Hedge didn't see it coming, facing away as she was, but Jinn shoved her off the catafalque, cried a word of his own and raised his spear in both hands as if to block a blow. The fire splashed as if against an unseen wall and washed back like a wave. The magus stumbled away, his sleeves burning.

Aye, you'd forgotten, hadn't you, that Prince Jinn was a magus before ever the emperor set him to command of his scouts and his spies.

"Captain," one of the soldiers was saying. "Captain, we—My lord prince." Not very coherent a surrender, you might say, but that one set their sword down, and another her spear, and then they were all four of them on their knees, and their weapons laid on the ice.

But the magus cried, "Traitors!" and rushed, robe burning and dagger upraised, and Hedge spun on her heel and took his head even as Jinn's spear bit, and that was a swift death and doubly sure.

Water pattered like rain over the body of Prince Tavris. The heat of the torches, which must have been lit only very rarely in all the year this cavern had served as his tomb, was gathering at the roof with the smoke, and now the gown of the magus and his hair burned bright, flames rising high, heat striking out as if they had lit a brazier.

A chunk of ice fell, as when the late winter sun warms the south-facing eaves and the icicles give way.

"I had nothing to do with this," Spider said, and like Hedge and Jinn, you had probably forgotten she was even there. Cowered back into a corner, she had, when the fighting started, and had been inching her way towards the tunnel. "They were in Ramsleap at the old tower there, last summer's-end, scouting for a place to lay the prince in ice again, after they were driven from their stronghold up in the snows above the Lammergeiers' Gate. They came, I couldn't stop them. They wanted Prince Jinn. It wasn't anything to do with me.

Jinn, darling Jinn, you know I'd never do you harm, for the old love between us. I told them—"

"Get out," Jinn said, without looking at her. He was folding the wings in close and wrapping the wet silk sheet, on which the corpse had lain, about it. When he took up his brother's body, it was not stiff, but limp as a sleeper. He carried him careful as life, head cradled against his shoulder. "Go on, out, out, out, all of you, and death to any one of you fool enough to raise hand against Captain Naskanna or any of these under her protection. Out!"

They scrambled to their feet, those kneeling soldiers, and went in a rush up the tunnel. Hedge called, voiceless thought to mind, *Pony! Four survivors coming, disarmed. And Spider.* And she pelted after.

The chunks of ice falling, and the stones rattling down with them, as Jinn came last of all with his heavy burden, were no small ones.

~

WHERE WAS I, while Hedge and Jinn were facing Atana and Orosyn in the ice-bound cavern?

Where do you think?

Swift, yet wary, our passage down the tunnel had been, Hedge and Penryl and I each as urgent as the other, and when I heard, with ears better even than a vhalgod's, the shuffling footsteps, the shallow quick breath of a creature in pain, I ran ahead, and was there to catch Arrany when she folded up on the stony floor. She'd been making her way up the tunnel, with no more thought left than to get out of the dark and cold.

"Jinn," she told me, through chattering teeth, when she realized I had her. "So sorry...Jinn..."

Sorry, aye, we could deal with that later, but Jinn what, she was in no fit state to explain, though the arm she clutched to her chest told its tale. It had soaked the wadded dressing and her face was near-vhalgod ashen.

"Get her out of here," Hedge said, and she dodged around and kept going. "Penryl, stay with Pony!"

Stay with his sister; he had no other will, down on his knees with a cry of grief, reaching out as if to take her from my arms where she lay over my lap.

"Up," I said, "and then take her a moment." Up he got, and took her, and as I thought, the weight of her nearly brought him down again, but he propped his back against the ice-seamed wall and understood my intent, which I may have forgotten to mention, when I shifted. He got her onto my back, and I saw him eyeing the roof, which was rather closer over my ears than I was happy with. No, I wasn't planning to risk even a trot, to bash poor Arrany's head against some low hanging ridge of stone.

"Hold tight," Penryl told her, and she got a one-handed grip of mane and then, feeling the roof far too low over her, scooted back towards my croup and lay down along my spine, her wounded arm tucked under her and her head on her upper arm. Then she pushed herself up, let go long enough to fish out the flute from her breast and hand it over to Penryl, and lie herself down again. Pen tucked the flute down his own shirt, and the care with which he took it said he had a notion what it might be. I flicked an ear, bobbed my head to ask, ready? It seemed we were. So long as Arrany didn't dig a toe unexpected into the tender places before my hind leg she would do very well, with Penryl resting a hand on her shoulder to steady her and make sure she didn't slide off over my tail. Going up, with that a consideration, there seemed to be a far steeper incline than I'd noticed on the way down to where we found her.

Walking, but a swift, smooth walk, and maybe I was taking Penryl's weight a little as well, by the end, but the warm sunlight seemed to reach in to meet us and then we were out into that enclosed space between the cave's mouth and the high bank of fallen stone. The vhalgod and vhalbairn soldiers were alarmed to see us back so soon, but they'd been laying no ambush. The dead were carried aside, their faces covered with scarves or coats against the flies, the woman with the severely injured leg was lying like the dead under a coat, but apart, her leg bound up and the man with the wounded arm fanning the flies from her face and the bloodstained bandages with a switch of rue and his good arm. Of the other, there was no sign. Fled, or gone for some help, though I certainly hoped there were no more imperially-minded vhalgods round about.

"The Duke?" the soldier asked, and Penryl must have learnt something in his studies after all, because though the man spoke the vhalgod language, his brief question easy enough to understand for any with any dialect of the road, Penryl answered, haltingly but correctly, in the language of imperial Ghedhaynor that we had found his sister. An answer that avoided what was asked, and we all knew it.

The vhalbairn soldier settled back on his haunches, gave me a sullen glower when, Pen taking my standing still, ears and tail flicking, as instruction, the lad pulled his sister down into his arms again and I was able to shift.

"I'll fetch Dandelion?" he asked, setting Arrany against some sun-warmed rocks, trying to angle her so that the dead were not the most obvious thing before her.

"Do." I crouched over the lass, took her arm in my hands. I did not want to disturb Jinn's rough bandaging, not while it still seeped.

"Stupid," I muttered. "Stupid, stupid, valiant stupid lass, there was no need for such grand gestures." And I settled myself close against her, leaned head-to-head, and tried with all in me to check the bleeding, to set the wound to clotting, scabbing, the flesh to knit clean. The pain, too, to ebb, for it was great, I felt the echo and throb of it in my own bones, holding her so. A song, I found, of healing, of rest, and I sang it, putting my healing into it as much as it flowed through the warmth of my hands, and Arrany went soft and unresisting against me, like a babe in arms, and her eyelids lowered and her tight face slackened into peace, and she slept.

Sleep, too, took the wounded woman, the wounded man, for all he fought it. Penryl came back yawning, leading Dandelion, squatted down by me while the horse, after a welcoming whicker at me, fell to grubbing up greens from among the stones, hardly rolling an eye at the dead.

"I feared the soldier might have taken her," Pen said softly. "For all she's not up to a vhalgod's weight for long. But I saw that woman trying to round up a couple of their horses. She's alone," he added, before I could break my song to ask if there were any sign of some vhalgod reserve coming out of hiding, so I nodded well-done to that report and went on singing.

Rounding up a team—maybe a wagon for the wounded, wagon for the dead, wagon to haul our inconvenient corpses away when the duke and the magi had finished with us?

Song trailed into silence. Arrany slept. Penryl, leaning on my other shoulder, slept. The wounded soldiers slept.

Pony! Four survivors coming, disarmed. And Spider! I did not so much as twitch an ear. Human, that's tricky to do, anyway.

All's well enough up here, I told her.

It was some time after that when Spider came sidling alone from the tunnel. I growled at her. She scowled, looked at Penryl, opened her mouth to speak, looked at me, turned on her heel and stalked away to the track down into the valley, not quite running.

Dandelion grazed on dandelions. I wouldn't have minded a few mouthfuls myself.

Beating of great wings, rush of air.

"Well now." A vhaldrach woman crouched on the stone berm, folding her wings. "Godling Thallyn. You're a long ways from home."

I said nothing aloud, just the silent warning, *Tesh!* to Hedge, but the tension that ran through me woke Penryl. He scrambled to his feet, hefting his scrounged sword, and put himself between Arrany and me and the vhaldrach. A noble impulse, but not where I wanted him.

"I suppose Captain Naskanna's down below?"

"Sit down, Penryl," I said. There wasn't much he could do against a vhaldrach, the weakened state he was in, and for all I mistrusted everything about her, direct violence was rarely Tesh's way. "It's all right. She only wants to talk. Isn't that so?"

Tesh settled herself cross-legged. "What shall we talk of? I know! I seem to recall—doesn't your captain owe me money?"

"No."

"Oh, she does, she does. Someone picked my pocket, on the road to Gowanesh."

Trouble? Hedge asked.

No, I don't think so. She's just perched up over us, being chatty.

"Hedge is hardly likely to have indulged in pocket-picking," I said, "no matter how hard up we were."

"No, but I hold her fully responsible for what her pet gets up to." Tesh flashed a sharp-toothed grin. "A drink. The pair of you owe me at least a drink, admit that."

"I'm sure there's wine enough in Atana's pantry."

"I fear not. Hard times all around, these days."

"It must be so, for a Duke of the Crossing to be reduced to ice-mining, and a high magus with him."

"Ice-mining? Well, there are more dishonourable trades for those once high in the emperor's favour to fall to. Necromancy, for one."

I hissed like an angry cat. It just slipped out. Tesh's bared teeth were not so friendly, that time.

"Naskanna is no necromancer, and Jinn's ghost no bound slave."

"But bound he is, if the tales that came to Orosyn's ears be true," said the vhaldrach. "And here you are, and Spider's young errand runner, whom I did not truly ever expect to see back in Under-Ice, brother or no, and where is Captain Naskanna and the death-token she bears of her brother?"

"Here," said Hedge. "Quite safe and well, the pair of us."

Stumbling, nervous, a handful of vhalgods keeping close together. Two, three, supporting a fourth. No, they hadn't laid some ambush on their way out, but one had taken a bad fall in their haste, turned an ankle.

And Hedge behind. Bloodied sword in hand, and grim her face, blood-spattered, wet and begrimed by soot and grit from the melting ice and crumbling roof. Tesh bounced to her feet, but didn't snatch for any of her knives, of which I was certain she had a fair few. She usually did.

"Ah, the wanderer returns," she said. And she did flinch, then, for Jinn came out of the dark behind his sister. A step, a wing-spread leap, and he was up beside Tesh, seeming flesh and bone as firm as her own, and carrying Tavris still in his arms, wrapped in the silken pall on which he had lain. I didn't know what it was he carried at that point, of course, only that it was another vhaldrach, and even in human form my nose is better than so most, so I smelt he was long dead, and yet not rotting, and not bone, and wrapped round and round with spells of the magi to preserve him. And I saw, too, or maybe it was that I smelt, the shadow and echo of him, the threads of his soul, still clinging to the corpse from which they should long ago have pulled free, the—call it potential—of a ghost, lying still bound within.

"You," Jinn snarled. "You, to be involved with this."

"My lord—" Tesh actually took a step back along the berm, wings rising, as if she thought she might need to flee. "My lord—" Held up her hand, placating. "He was dead, laid quite respectfully in the cold hallows of the crypt of the magi's Jade Circle, bound with the spells of preservation reserved for only their most honoured high magi. Hope of his resurrection, since they found him, has kept Orosyn and Atana from greater mischief for a good few decades, now. Surely that's worth a little—"

"How many dead in this place?" Jinn asked. "And how many more on the road that brought you here? How much pain and suffering for these human children you've abused in your scheming—"

Penryl blinked. He wasn't used to be called human, given the exaggerated respect his vhalbairn eyes had commanded in his mother's hall. Nor was he used to being dismissed as a child. But he bowed his head, seeming to accept it.

Tesh shrugged again. "But they might have summoned more soldiers, lord. Never doubt there are more, among the mercenaries of the middle lands between the mountains and the southern sea, who would answer, when a Duke of the Crossing called. More who would rally to the promise of a prince of great Eksandron's blood awakened to lead them again. Atana and Orosyn might have summoned a company, sent it marching north after rumour of Captain Naskanna, Naskanna Deathdealer, to take from her what rumour said she carried, the death-token of her brother to whom she and her wild godling lover had bound Prince Jinn himself through their wicked necromancy—"

"I had nothing to do with it!" I protested, indignant.

"A company, to fall on the lands of the northwest, the little tribal lands about the Dahres Water—"

Jinn didn't argue, which I think was what she wanted. He only turned his shoulder on her, flared his wings, sending her scrambling back as he took to the air, not bothering to give her further ear. Hedge leapt up to the place he had vacated, watching him go. Still sword in hand, and if you think she wasn't watching Tesh as well, you haven't been paying attention to much.

It looked to me that he was circling down already. Even dry and light as the corpse was, Tavris was no easy burden to carry in flight. Heading for the hall, I realized. As good a place as any, to lay a body.

"Well," said Tesh. "You seem to be on top of things here."

Hedge gave her a look. Tesh backed another step.

"Captain Naskanna," she said, with that annoying little bow. "Godling Thallyn." A frown at the remaining soldiers. "Consider yourselves discharged," she said. "Go away. Don't talk. Don't cause trouble. You don't want Bloody Naskanna coming after you. You don't want me." And smiling again, a vague wave of her hand to Penryl and Arrany. "Human children. Charmed to have met you both."

She leapt, great brown-black wings beating hard, till she had the height to soar. We watched, both Hedge and I, to be sure she was not going after Jinn, but she rose higher and higher up over the valley, and then swooped away eastward. I watched till she was no more than a distant dark fleck against the sky, which could have been eagle, lammergeier, vhaldrach, or dragon. Then I lost her in the dazzle of the high snows.

"Spider," said Hedge, like a curse, and oh, aye, it was me who'd let Spider wander off, but I'd wanted her well away from Penryl, with her spellcrafted gyves on him so newly frayed. "And where's the damned god-collar that this whole thing was about?" She glared at the soldiers, who eyed one another uneasily and—since that had worked so well for Tesh—shrugged.

"There was never a god-collar," Arrany said, waking to force herself weakly away from me. "There wasn't—it was a story. The vhaldrach said, make it real in mind, tell it over and over, that will bring them, surer than any other thing. I'm sorry. I'm so sorry. She was killing Penryl and I couldn't find any other way, he wouldn't listen, he wouldn't come away with me, I told you how he hit me and that was true, I tried, I tried more than once to get him to see, to get him to understand, but I never could, and they said she'd let him go if I brought you—"

"I'm sorry, Arrany," Penryl cried. "I'm so sorry, I'm so—" and he squeezed me out of the way and they clung to one another, weeping, and it was all very teary and touching and no doubt did them both a world of good, but such a quantity of guilty weeping and wailing grows quickly tiresome, so Hedge and I left them to it—I had every intention of pointing out at some later time how very foolish it had been of Arrany not to trust that she could have just told us everything. Surely by the time we had travelled so far as Rhunaberg, with all the affair of her abduction and the rescuing and the fighting in the city, surely by the time we'd come to the robber-queen's lair, and the rescue of the children, when she'd learned of Jinn's nature, fought beside him, spoken to him, she might have trusted, and told us the truth, and left us to deal with Spider and have Penryl safe away, no matter how many dukes and magi and imperial soldiers lurked about the valley of Under-Ice.

Hedge, her anger long forgotten, says, Arrany was hardly more than a child, and youth do so often make such bad decisions, with such strong emotion and so little wisdom to guide them. It's why so many die young heroes, rather than growing to old sensible plodders like us.

Speak for yourself, I say, and she says, aye, sensible is not a word anyone is apt to lay on you, love.

Outcry, down on the wagon-road.

"Better see what that's about," says Hedge, and off she goes, leaving me in charge of weeping Marshlanders and gloomy, fearful, grieving, and possibly repentant, soldiery. And it seemed the day hadn't yet taken its full toll of bloody deeds, for the soldier who'd indeed gone to catch and harness a team to the wagon was coming up the road with it when Spider was running down, and the witch had apparently decided that a good high-wheeled wagon and team was a better means of hieing herself off to greener pastures than the little goat-cart she used for her marketing, and she'd chosen to contest ownership of it with the soldier.

She'd never been a woman of her hands, Spider, choosing to think herself a scholar and above such things, though both Jinn and Hedge were testimony the emperor had not encouraged such division in the education of his own children. Her attempt to wrest the reins from the soldier and oust her from the driver's bench, despite the help of a sharp stone with which she had tried to beat the woman's head in, had not gone well.

The soldier had a badly bruised shoulder. Spider had a dagger in her ribs.

It was about bloody time, was I suspect Hedge's only opinion on that.

19

IN WHICH HOME IS STILL BEHIND US, AND THE ROAD IS STILL AHEAD

"And of course that would have turned out so well, to trap Jinn's ghost in Tavris's body, to give him some semblance of life," I said.

Jinn's ghost, or at least that part of his being which could still be drawn into this living world; it was his damned and banished state they meant to use, the prisoning of his soul in its outcast hell, that meant he could not fade and pass on through to whatever it is that lies truly beyond.

And how did they think to keep that body, thus given some perversion of life, animate, even if only from time to time?

To feed it on other lives, as Spider had fed on her lovers? Sacrifices, young women, young men—Tavris had been fond of both, in his day—to live and die to keep their new emperor alive?

Not only had they very much miscalculated in thinking that if they could anchor Jinn's ghost in Tavris's body, it would somehow be Tavris who rose and walked and spoke, but they had, I very much suspect, misjudged Tavris.

"He spoke to me," Jinn said. "Kanna, he did. He knew me, and he was—he thought we were fighting, still, as we'd been when he died, and then he knew me. I think—the Grandmothers grant he didn't know, didn't remember, all the years of being bound—"

"He's gone," Hedge said, and rubbed a hand over her eyes. Weary, she was, and the smoke was stinging. "He's gone now. He's safe beyond, no longer trapped. He's free."

Whatever the magi of the Jade Circle had done to prepare his body before they interred it, perhaps even while it still bled, his last life fading, fished from the harbour while his soul yet lingered—had they, all unknowing, trapped Tavris's soul there, on the border between life and death? Trapped him, bound him in spellwork? And then Orosyn and Duke Atana had learned of him, stolen him away, carried him from one secret hiding place to another, seeking always the deep ice and the dark to aid in his preservation, travelling through the mountains, making an unholy relic of him till rumour came to them, somehow, of another relic, one holding a ghost still strong and vital. And all along they already had what they wanted, the trapped soul of an heir of the emperor, a bound ghost. Only they had never tried to wake him, to find out.

Just as well, really.

Though I did wonder about the rites with which those high magi of the Jade Circle had been interred.

Not, at the moment, our problem.

We had taken a table for a bier, laid Tavris on it in the hall the vhalgods built. With their axes we hacked down doors and the shutters of windows, to lay all that splintered timber about him, and all the furnishings, and beneath the table we tipped over the small barrel of pitch from which they had fuelled their torches.

Hedge and Jinn, I left alone with him to say whatever final farewells they needed.

Then we lit it, Hedge and I. Retreated, watched, as the flames rose red to light the windows, smoke billowing. Jinn watched with us, ghostly, shadow-suggestion, shape of eddying smoke himself. He faded as the smoke rose black against the stars.

Still we watched. No new ghost came to us. Tavris was gone. Free, faded out of the world to whatever fate it is that follows. Eventually the roof caved in, and the tower fell, and still the burning lit the night.

It was a worthy pyre, Hedge said. Me, I had no great love for the Lord-Commander of the Golden Guard. No particular personal cause for enmity, only the general. But he had been their brother.

Epitaph enough. The rest of the dead—the surviving soldiers, or those still fit for labour, dug a grave their dead might share. I was all for leaving them, Orosyn and Atana in particular, to the ravens and wolves, the hyenas and lammergeiers, but I was overruled, and anyway, it turned out those who had died in the ice-cave had already their burial, for most of the roof had come down, ice pulling rubble with it, in the heat of the burning magus. It was only Spider and the soldiers we'd killed at the cave's mouth and in the tunnel whom the survivors gave to the earth, and Spider they buried face-down beneath the rest, with iron nails through her feet, which is both an insult and an intention to be sure no ghost finds its way out of the ground.

THINGS WERE DIFFICULT, for a little, between Hedge and Arrany.

"I've forgiven her," I told Hedge. "She thought she had to choose between us and her brother. She should have known us better; she should have trusted us further, she was foolish, she thought as a child and not a grown woman—but, Hedge, she thought it was a choice between us and her brother. I've forgiven her. I'm pretty sure Jinn has. So can you."

"No," was all Hedge said.

"Hedge," I said. "Sweetheart. My great and terrible and most wonderful love. Naskanna. I've forgiven *you*."

Hedge flinched, and turned her back on me, and walked away. But I saw her, later, go to where Arrany was sitting, a little apart, cleaning Dandelion's bridle, awkwardly one-handed. She squatted down on her heels beside the lass. I don't know what was said between them. I don't need to.

~

PENRYL TOOK over Spider's pantry and hearth, proving himself a fair cook when he put his mind to it, turning out kettle after kettle of nourishing soup and pottage, hovering over Arrany while she ate, urging more on her till she protested she would burst, though it was he who most needed feeding up. We lingered a fortnight while they both got their strength back and Arrany's arm healed—helped, I may say, by my stitching as much as my well-wishing, and aye, I patched up the wounded soldiers, too. Though Pen had taken over Spider's hearth and stores, I insisted we sleep in the goat-shed, or out under the stars. That room, that bed, was no healthy place for Penryl to dream.

The soldiers trailed about, uncertain whether they were prisoners. One vanished in the night, but they took only their own gear and one of the big horses, so it was no great mystery. The one crippled by Hedge's sword made herself a crutch, but more often drove about in Spider's goat-cart, till one day she and the cart and the four wethers who pulled it—an improvement over the previous year, Arrany had said, when she'd had only a team of two—also vanished, along with a number of Spider's cheeses. She reappeared several days later with a cask of plum brandy and some sacks of flour and groats.

"Looks like we'll be here for the winter," she said. "Someone had better learn to make proper bread, and I'm the one most housebound." She didn't say what the plum brandy was for.

Arrany taught her to manage the oven and the lump of motherdough.

The soldiers themselves took to sleeping in the house, since we didn't seem inclined to claim it. How they all fitted into the bed I didn't enquire. Hedge had another look through the workroom and extracted anything more we thought we would rather vhalgods of possibly imperial inclinations not get their hands on, though the writings of the magi are notoriously difficult for the uneducated to unravel. Still, the books and paper made good tinder. No, she didn't burn the two rarer volumes she'd already taken. Jinn would have given her what-for when he found out.

Hedge also seemed to have claimed a couple of the big horses, a fine bay gelding with white feathery stockings and a buckskin mare, the pick of the remaining herd.

"Where are you going to put them?" I protested. "They'll hardly fit in the door of your old cow-shed."

I did begin to wonder, when she made no answer, only shrugged and said, "I like them." Wondered more, when I found she'd given Spider's purloined purse into Arrany's keeping, and separated out her gear from our own.

"Where are the twins off to?" I asked. "Because, you know, our road and theirs lie together a good long way, even if we do want to avoid Rhunaberg and the heron-godling.

"Thurbridge," Hedge said. "The university there. Penryl, anyway. He thinks he might seek work in the library as a copyist if he can't win a place as a student."

"Not apprentice himself to a witch?"

"Not yet, at any rate. Though there are witches enough all through the Lowlands, if he decides to follow that calling in the end."

"Time to heal, I suppose." I didn't think there was much in the library of the university of Thurbridge, a relatively new and mostly human foundation, that could lead him back into the mad dreams in which Spider had ensnared him. "Is Arrany staying in Thurbridge as well?"

They'd been talking a lot, apart from the rest of us, Arrany and Hedge. Much to say; much to understand; a fair bit to forgive, it might be, but they seemed easy with one another again.

"Arrany's not so sure she'll stay past the spring, but she'll see him safe and settled, at least."

"Not home to the Esrineyn?"

"There's nothing to go home for," said Arrany herself, coming up across the garden to where we sat on the wall eating the soft-fleshed early apples and throwing cores to the soldiers' pigs. "I thought—there was a girl, he left behind, Tairna. But he says, he won't go back to her like this. In a year, two, then, when he's made himself a man worth waiting for, he'll go to see her, and if she doesn't want to wait till he's through at Thurbridge and found himself a place in life, then fair enough. I expect," she added, consideringly, "that the two of them are grown so far apart already, it'll never come to be, but who knows? But no, we're not going home to stay, ever, and not even to let them know where we've been, not any time soon. Our mother's dead; Penryl has no wish to be Queen Esmissal's witch; Missal's never had any use for me but to marry me off to some alliance. We'll find our own way."

"We could see you safe to Thurbridge, at any rate." I eyed Hedge. "Or—not?"

"I met a wild godling on the high pass over the fells," Hedge said. "Vinya, his name. The lion-man."

"Oh?" Those very sharp thorns that she had walked into and been clawed up by in the night. I did remember.

I took my harp, picked out a tune, slow and tentative.

"A mad godling. Soul-wounded. Murderous. He'd been killing vhalgods." And she told the story then, while I drew out rippling water-music, high dancing swallow-music, and did not let anger kindle, that such a thing might be. A wild godling become like a mad animal, killing without cause.

Aye, maybe I felt that wind blow too near my own shoulder.

"And you didn't tell us?" Arrany protested. Blushed, when we both looked at her, hid her face in her hands. "Never mind."

"The thing is," Hedge said slowly, "I think I know the godling his sister. Lion-woman, as he is lion-man. Lavinor. I know Lavinor is not dead, or she was not, when last I saw her, and that well after the war's end. And since he is bound in sleep unwaking till she come to free him, and there can be no healing for him, in that sleep...I would like very much to find her, and at least, to let her know of her brother's state."

"Where would the world be, without all you sisters looking after your brothers?" I asked, for it did seem to have been rather the theme of that summer. I tried to make it a thread through the music, but it needed words, and the time had not then come to make a song of Arrany and Penryl, though in a later time I did, and you may even have heard it.

"But Pony," says Hedge, "you could see Arrany and Penryl to Thurbridge, keep them out of trouble, and head on back to Smithsford. I'd only be—well, if I cross over the mountains before the winter comes, I could find the lion-woman Lavinor and be home again before next harvest. Maybe even before midsummer."

"Or you could get lost in the mountains, or be buried under an avalanche, or run afoul of another band of imperial soldiers looking for someone to make emperor."

"Sky and sea prevent! Pony—"

"Or meet another crazed godling out to kill vhalgods—"

"Half the folk of the lands south of the mountains and about Ghedhaynor are vhalgods or vhalbairns. Someone else would have noticed. Pony—"

"Or run into Tesh again."

"*Pony!*"

"What?"

"Do you want to come with me?"

"Of course I want to come with you! Why on this good green earth would you think I wouldn't want to come with you?"

Hedge shrugged. "We've been away so long."

I snorted. "Half a year? You're the one I thought would be pining for your ducks by now."

Hedge sighed. "Ghedhaynor," she said.

"We don't have to go to Ghedhaynor. There's lots of land south of the White Mountains that *isn't* Ghedhaynor."

"We might. Heart of the empire, once we cross the mountains, and that's where I last heard of the lion-woman. Imperial lands, imperial tongue, and every second person vhalbairn."

"I don't mind. It doesn't bother me. How could it bother me? Look what I sleep with!"

Arrany had gotten up again and slipped away sometime during

that conversation. Just as well. I stared at Hedge, wondering what I'd meant, really, wondering why I hurt so.

"Ah, Pony." She wrapped her arms around me and I buried my face in her breast, felt her holding hard, holding tight against all nightmare, and her breath warm, gentle, nuzzling into my hair. "No picking fights with city godlings."

"No," I agreed, somewhat muffled.

"No picking fights with magi, if we have to go talk to them at the university."

"All right."

"No getting into fights at all."

"Highway robbers. Brigands. Tesh."

"Tesh doesn't want to fight with us."

"She wants something."

"Undoubtedly, but it isn't a fight with us. So you'll come?"

"Aye. I will."

"Good." Hedge sighed into my hair. "I really didn't want to go alone, and I don't dare call Jinn again. Not when he's—oh, Pony, Arrany lost so much blood."

"I know." I'd kept a watchful eye on him, as we kept vigil over the great pyre we'd made of the vhalgod's hall and tower for Tavris, but Jinn had shown no sign of trying to prolong his presence in the world, and he had not returned of his own accord at all since his fading. That, in itself, did worry me, a little, that he had not come, mere faint chill and shadow, to join us when we walked or sat alone, if only to ask how Arrany fared. I wondered, did he fear to tempt himself?

"A mountain crossing," I said, brightening up. "At least, if you're taking that big brute of a horse, we'll be able to supply ourselves well with cheeses. And I hid away the last jug of Spider's own plum brandy, before the soldiers found it."

"Two big brutes," she said happily. "One to ride and one to carry the cheeses. And the brandy."

"One's for Pen, surely? Dandelion can't carry Arrany and Penryl both all the way to Thurbridge. She's had a hard summer."

"Pen's taking that pretty skewbald. Don't make that face. I'm leaving the soldiers a team for their wagon." She laughed. "They have the goats, and the pigeons, and the pigs. They're going to plough up a field for buckwheat, and make cheese and cart ice packed in straw down to the towns in summer."

"Or set themselves up as robber-chiefs over Ramsleap."

"No," she said. "We've had words, on that subject."

"Have you, indeed."

"After all, we might pass this way again, on our journey home."

"We might, at that."

I threw my last apple core to the pigs and leaned into her side, solid as an oak, warm as sun on summer stone. Propped a knee up and let her steady me, calling a song from the harp, rippling, trilling, wind-dancing.

An old tune. "Pony Crossing the Mountains" was the name of it.

Finis

ACKNOWLEDGMENTS

I wrote this over a stressful winter, and kept myself going by sending each chapter to my friends as I finished it. Thanks are owed to Jessie McGowan and Tristanne Connolly for their enthusiasm for the adventures of Hedge and Pony, and to Tom Lloyd for coming up with a title that wasn't "The Adventures of Hedge and Pony." Cheers, guys.

www.ingramcontent.com/pod-product-compliance
Lightning Source LLC
LaVergne TN
LVHW010056110826
845155LV00028B/362

* 9 7 8 1 9 5 2 4 5 6 3 3 6 *